Healing Touch

Trish Copeland

Healing Touch is a work of fiction. Names, characters, places, and incidents are the product the author's imagination or used factiously. Any resemblance to actual persons, living or dead, events or locales is entirely coincidental.

Healing Touch

ISBN: 978-1-969292-03-3

Cover Design; Trish Copeland
Cover Picture: Laura Paraschivescu/Unsplash

Supervised by Scotchwood Hill Publishing Service

DEDICATION

To Mom and Dad. I finally did it, even if you two aren't here to see it completed.

ACKNOWLEDGMENTS

Thanks go to my editor Pat Blake, and Martha Rodriguez for all the help they gave me to get the manuscript ready to print. Both have been amazing help in getting my writing to a publishable stage from gibberish.

Special thanks to Carol Gunn, my sidekick and hero. Without her help I would never have been encouraged to continue writing and there would not have been any more stories in the series.

Thanks to my family, especially my sister Greta for being supportive in this new step in my life.

Chapter 1

The large sedan came out of nowhere. Its bright headlights reflected in the mirror, blinding Kat. Kat swerved around the bend, attempting to stay on the highway. No streetlamps or moon illuminated the curvy street. The car behind her tried to pull around on the double yellow line, pushing her onto the narrow shoulder. Her front wheel went off the road, hitting gravel. The steering wheel jerked in her hands. Kat yanked the wheel to the left, trying to control the car with great effort.

Kat's Lexus lurched forward when the car rammed into the back bumper. Her knuckles turned white from her death grip on the wheel. The sedan started around and slammed into the left back fender, causing the front wheels to hit the gravel. A car approached around a curve, and the lights blinded her. She lost control. Her car fishtailed off the edge of the road and flew down a grassy embankment, stopping with a resounding crash in a stand of trees.

Kat's hands clamped the wheel in a stranglehold. Her head smacked into the airbag, making her see stars. Dazed, she touched her forehead and drew back her blood-covered hand. She blinked as she saw a large male figure, coming down the hill. She moaned and blacked out as he yanked open the car door.

Beeping noises awoke Kat. The scent of antiseptic made her nauseous. She opened her eyes, only to shut them against the glaring lights. She opened her eyes again to look around the white-walled room filled with machines, the source of the beeps. She was in a hospital room. Kat fought back the need to be sick. Voices came from the unlatched door, and she recognized her father's voice.

Ambient light came from the crack in the doorway. From the dark window, she knew it was night. How long had she been out? Surely not long. Kat tried to move from the bed but found an IV connected to her hand. Her body ached even from that slight movement. She moaned. The door flew open shortly, and three men entered, her father, a police officer and another man wearing a white lab coat over scrubs.

"Kat! I was worried about you." With relief her father took her free hand, his eyes filled with concern.

"What happened?" Kat squeezed her father's hand. He still wore his work suit. She looked from one man to the other, wondering why a police officer accompanied the other two men.

"Ms. Anderson, I'm Officer Jordan. You hit your head when your car went off the road. A passerby said someone rammed into your car and knocked it down the embankment. What can you tell me about the incident?"

"Not much more. After I left the charity ball, a sedan turned from a side road and drove behind me—for a while. The car kept getting closer and closer, riding my bumper with its bright lights shining in my mirror. I hit the accelerator after the car rammed my rear bumper, but the car overtook me and hit my fender. I lost control and ended up at the bottom of an embankment against a tree. In the darkness, all I saw was a black silhouette in the other car. I have no clue who or why they did it." Kat bit her lip and shrugged.

"My daughter needs to rest." Her father stepped between her and the officer. "Maybe she can tell you more later."

"Can I go home?" Kat had a slight headache but otherwise felt fine.

The doctor stepped forward and said, "We want you to stay for the night. You have a slight concussion and bruises and abrasions. You were lucky."

"Dad, I'd rather go home."

"No, I've called Gerald to stand guard at your door and bring you home in the morning," her father said. Her father owned his own company. He always issued orders. "Gerald has his security team investigating what happened. Your mother and sister are concerned about you, too."

"Stepmother and stepsister," Kat mumbled under her breath. He had remarried after her mother died. In her stepmother Carolyn's eyes, Kat could never measure up to her stepsister Keisha.

A tall, blond, muscular male stalked into the room. He walked to Kat's father and glanced at her. Gerald held the position of bodyguard and chauffeur for her father and family. He once feigned interest in her until Keisha lured him away with her sex appeal. He wasn't the first boyfriend Keisha had taken from her. Her father acknowledged his presence with a nod. Dad was used to taking charge, and he abruptly dismissed the doctor and the police officer, closing the door behind them.

"Kat, the officer will be outside the door, but Gerald will stay to make sure you're safe." Her father motioned Gerald over and huddled with him in a whispered conversation. Kat tried to hear their exchange but only caught a few words: *attempted kidnapping* and *corporate* espionage. "Dad, why would someone run me off the road?"

"Kat, there's no need to worry. Gerald will keep you safe." Her father walked back to her side and kissed her cheek.

"Dad, please tell me. I'm an adult. I don't need Gerald's help if I know what's going on." Kat sat up in bed, wincing. Again, she fought back a wave of nausea. She exhaled and covered her eyes in exasperation. Gerald watched her through hooded eyes.

"Kat, let him stay tonight." Her dad's voice soothed her anxiety while he rubbed her shoulder.

"Gerald, leave. I want to talk to Dad alone." Gerald stood his ground with a glance at her father. Kat pleaded with her father. "Dad, please, let me talk to you alone before you go."

Her dad gave a put-upon sigh. "Gerald, give us a minute." Gerald gazed at Kat, gave a shrug, and stepped out of the door, closing it.

"Dad, tell me what's going on. Why are you insisting he stay when there's a police officer in the hall?" Kat hated being treated like a child.

"Kat, I want you to be safe." The older man sighed at his stubborn daughter. "Some of my corporate enemies are trying to push me out. They're not against using illegal tactics." He ran his fingers through his graying hair. His other hand rested on her arm.

"I'll go away where they can't find me. Gerald can guard Keisha."

Kat waited for his consent.

"Where would you go? There's no place that's safe. I don't want you to be in this mess. You don't have people around you all the time, like Keisha or Carolyn. They're harder to access. That's why they made you a target. You're my innocent baby girl." The older man sat on the edge of the bed and held her hand.

Kat gave him a sad smile and squeezed his hand. "I'm not a little girl anymore. I want my privacy. How about the cabin we used when I was a child?" she asked. "No one would know I'm there."

"It's run-down. You can't stay there." Her father frowned and shook his head. "There'd be no help if you needed it."

"Uncle Jeff still uses it, so it must not be in terrible shape. He had a phone put in. You can call to check on me, or I can check-in. Just you and I would know I'm there. Not Gerald or anyone you work with. Not even Carolyn nor Keisha. Please, Dad?" Kat stared into his eyes.

"I'll think about it, and let you know tomorrow. I'll call your uncle first. Get some rest." He kissed her on the forehead and left the room.

Gerald walked in, taking the chair by her bed. He leaned forward and said, "Kat, I..."

"I'm tired, Gerald." Kat sighed at the tightening of his jaw. She didn't have the stomach for more drama. Keisha had dropped Gerald, as soon as Kat found them kissing. Her stepsister let her know he showed interest because of her father's money. Keisha may even have set up the scene for her to witness. She ignored the man behind her, rolled over carefully because of the IV in her arm, and pulled the sheet up. She placed her fingertips on the knot on her forehead and concentrated until soft glowing energy surged through the connection. The warmth flowing into her head eased the headache, and she drifted to sleep.

Chapter 2

The cool dampness of autumn permeated the cabin, chilling the air. The fire sputtered, and sparks flew as a log shifted in the fireplace. Kat added another log and watched the flames dance around in a hypnotic multicolor flare. She jumped as a slash of lightning danced across the sky. *Were those headlights? Have they found me?* Her pulse raced at the thought that the attackers had found her. The rumble of thunder in the distance eased her mind. She took a deep breath to calm her thudding heart. *No. No one but her father knew about this isolated place.*

Kat returned to her chair, tugged down the bottom of her nightshirt and tucked her feet beneath her. She pulled a fleece blanket over her to lessen the chill created by three days of rain. She picked up her book but couldn't focus on the words. The soft, melodic sound of the rain pelting the tin roof lulled her into a drowsy haze.

Leaning her head back, her body relaxed into a twilight plane of consciousness. The book slipped from her grip and hit the wooden floor with a thud. Startled awake, she glanced around in fear. The electricity had gone off during her catnap, leaving the room pitch black. Her skin prickled with goosebumps. Something watched her. She glanced around and her gaze locked on silver eyes glowing in the glass panes of the patio French doors. She gasped and jumped up to grab a weapon. The blanket wrapped around her ankles, causing her to fall.

Kat struggled to free her legs from the cocoon of fleece. She glanced at the door, but the luminescent eyes were gone. She kicked off the blanket, grabbed the fireplace poker, and made her way to the door.

Cracking the door open, she peered into the foreboding darkness. Without thinking, she stepped out onto the wet boards. She caught sight of a shadow fleeing into the woods that surrounded the cabin. She stared at the darkened silhouette and shivered from the coolness of the dank boards and the drizzle of the rain.

Slipping back inside the cabin, Kat ran her fingers through her waist-length damp hair. She trembled, chilled to the bone as she locked the door and double-checked to see for herself the rest of the doors and windows were secured. Retrieving the throw from the floor, she tossed it back on the chair and headed to bed. She burrowed under a pile of blankets for warmth, and her mind drifted into a restless sleep, invaded by dreams of shadows, glowing eyes and being chased.

Morning arrived with the warmth of the sun on her face and no sign of rain. The glaring brightness reminded Kat that the shade hadn't been closed before bed. The heat of the sunbeams didn't lift the cool dampness that filled the room. She still felt numb from the cold and snuggled under the blankets for a few more minutes of warmth. The insistent shrill tweet of a bird pulled her from her half-sleep. Kat sighed when she realized the sound came from the ring of the cabin phone. She grumbled and crawled from under her warm nest of blankets. She slipped on her fuzzy house shoes to protect her feet as she shuffled to answer the phone.

"Hello," Kat mumbled sleepily into the receiver.

"Kat, is that you?" An annoying nasal tone came across the line.

"Who else would it be, Craig?" Kat groaned inwardly at the familiar condescending male voice.

"Kat, I wanted to hear your voice." The high-pitched male voice whined peevishly. "When are you coming back?"

"Craig, how did you get this number?" Kat's tone was harsher than warranted. No one knew about her trip to the cabin. Definitely not Craig. She had dated him twice because Keisha's date insisted, he wouldn't go out unless his friend Craig had a date. Now, the irritating man pictured himself in love with her. How did she always find such winners?

"Kat!" The impatient wail brought her out of her reverie.

"What, Craig?" Kat asked with irritation.

"You weren't listening to me. I said I miss you. I can't wait to see you again," Craig wheedled.

"Craig, I told you before that we are friends. There's nothing between us," Kat ran her hand through sleep-tousled hair as her frustration turned to annoyance.

"But Kat...," Craig's voice grated on her last nerve.

"No but to it, Craig. Find someone else. How did you get this number?" Exasperation tinged Kat's voice. She hated it when people ignored her.

"When I couldn't get your cell phone, Keisha gave me this number. She said you left it with your father for emergencies," Craig said.

Good old Keisha, her stepsister and her nemesis. Every day, Carolyn reminded Kat how much more beautiful, more graceful, more everything Keisha could be than Kat. She looked like the tall, thin supermodel figure men preferred.

Kat had other virtues. That didn't stop the men she liked from being attracted to Keisha. She had learned that each time she brought a boyfriend home, either they abandoned her for Keisha or were interested in Kat for her father's money. Kat decided that being alone was best for her.

It didn't surprise Kat that Keisha would give out a private number. "Yes, for emergencies. This isn't one. Goodbye, Craig. Don't call again." Kat hung up as he sputtered on the other end of the line.

The phone rang again. Heaving a sigh of discontent, Kat ignored the ring and felt a surge of pleasure as she pulled the landline plug from the wall. The cabin was located too far out in the wilderness to have cell phone reception. Besides, she didn't want to talk to Craig or anyone else from home. Hopefully, the thugs after her couldn't get the number.

Kat never felt comfortable around a lot of people. Keisha had taunted her about her special gift in front of others when they were younger. Most considered Kat strange and avoided her. After a while, she learned to use her ability in private that gift had aided speedy recovery that got her out of the hospital. A few times she used her ability to heal wounded animals she found. Carolyn, her stepmother, insisted Kat stop using the gift. When others found out, they ostracized her or drained her energy with their neediness.

Chapter 3

On edge from the phone call, Kat decided to walk in the woods. commune with nature always calmed her. Changing into a pair of comfortable jeans and a graphic T-shirt, she stepped from the bedroom into the main area of the cabin that contained both the kitchen and the living room. Her reading light had come back on in the night.

Dampness filled the air in the cabin. Kat added fresh wood and kindling to the large rock fireplace. She hoped a good fire would warm the room before her return. The kindling flared, and the fire sparked to life. Grabbing toast, she munched on a corner while she gazed out the French doors. She thought about the glowing eyes that had watched her the night before. Was it only her imagination or a wild animal curious about the light in the room. *Had the kidnappers found her?* Kat shivered at the thought. She wanted to be left alone. Only her father and uncle knew this location. Did her father give Keisha the emergency number? How many other people had her stepsister given it to besides Craig? Could someone trace her location through it? Heaving a sigh, she swallowed the last bit of sweet pulpy orange juice, pulled on a jacket, and headed out the door.

Kat stepped off the porch and tilted her head back to take a deep breath of the fresh, crisp morning air. She had not filled her lungs with such sweet air untouched by man-made pollution for a long time. Her blue eyes absorbed the surrounding beauty. The explosion of browns, oranges, yellows, and reds of the changing leaves surrounded the bright green of the majestic pine trees. The gorgeous scenery concealed the solitary cabin deep in the forest. Her fortress.

After Kat's late-night arrival, the rain kept her inside for several days. Today, she would explore the panoramic view since the rain had stopped. The scene filled her with a quiet peacefulness she hadn't felt since childhood. The dark side of life had filled her days in the city.

The solitude of wandering the trails around the cabin would recharge her inner batteries. After her close call with death, Kat recognized life as precious. She always felt safe here. Her parents came for family vacations until her fourteenth year, when her mother died. Her father remarried a year later to a woman whose biggest value was her position in society. They never returned. Her father's brother, Uncle Jeff, still used the cabin and kept it in decent condition.

Fond memories drew Kat to a spot covered in underbrush. Skirting the worst of the dense undergrowth, she spotted the huge flat rock where she used to play. Her hand rubbed the cold, damp surface as she gazed around. A break in the woods caught her eye. A smile played across her lips as she spotted the old path her family had strolled down to reach a stream. She had spent many hours frolicking in the water, followed by a picnic before they returned to the log house.

Kat pushed aside low-hanging, tangled branches that blocked the pathway she used to squeeze through on childhood adventures. She pulled a pair of gloves from her jacket pocket, slipped them on, and pushed branches aside to make her way through the lush foliage. The fallen leaves and brush, obscuring the overgrown trail.

Kat listened to the sounds of nature, as animals frolicked around her. A musty dampness filled the air after the rain. The distant gurgle of water and a chorus of frogs encouraged her to switch directions toward a babbling stream. She lost the path but continued toward the gurgling splash of the brook that beckoned her. Her pursuit drew her further into the tree-shrouded murkiness of the thicket. Breaking through a tangle of tree branches, she finally spotted the stream and approached for a closer look. A fine mist spattered against her cheeks. The plop of frogs hitting the water made her smile. She inhaled the fresh scent of nature and listened as animals rustled through the leaves of nearby trees and birds sang a cheerful song.

Kat leaned against a boulder, enthralled as the water splashed across flat rocks in a cascade of white spray against the dark green and brown of the creek. A prickly feeling on the back of her neck made her jerk upright, alert. Someone was watching her. She whirled around to scan the area. She spotted the dark shape of an enormous animal on all fours in the shadows of a nearby craggy bluff.

Kat shifted to get a better look. A large, muscular wolf stood deep in the shadows of the overhang. Unconsciously, she stepped forward, trying to see the wolf's features. The wolf watched her and slipped deeper into the shade of the trees, as she moved forward. All she saw was its silhouette and the glow of silver eyes.

Kat bit her lip. She stopped and the wolf stopped. Taking a step forward, she was disappointed when the wolf retreated deeper into the shadows. She stood still and coaxed the wolf, "Don't be afraid. I want to get a better look at you. I won't hurt you."

As if he understood, the wolf edged out of the shadow of the cliff into the sunlight. He raised his head and stood tall and unafraid. The wolf's silver eyes locked with hers. Invisible electrical sparks flowed through the air. Kat felt she couldn't breathe. She stared at the beauty of the huge muscular body, covered in a magnificent burnished bronze coat. The creature's glimmering eyes bored into her soul, filling her with a heated craving of desire unlike anything she had ever felt before. The powerful reaction confused her. She shivered and gasped.

"You're so beautiful." Kat hissed as she exhaled.

Entranced, she stared at the lupine figure and inched forward. Her foot slipped on a small clump of wet leaves, and she grabbed for a nearby branch. The branch broke in her hand, and her quick movement caused her to lose her balance. She twisted to avoid a pile of rocks and landed face-first on the muddy bank. Slimy mud, from the bank covered her cheek and forehead. The cold mud oozed between her fingers, covering her gloves. The wolf's intelligent eyes sparkled with mirth as he watched her plunge into the muck.

"Yuck. Oh, sure you think this is funny." Kat talked to herself and imagined amusement in the animal's silver orbs. He cocked his head at her words. The wolf gave a snort that suspiciously sounded like laughter and then spun away from her, disappearing into the trees.

Chapter 4

Retreating into the thick woods, Grigore Lupescu focused his attention on the human female. She intrigued him. Her citrus scent floated across the miles from her cabin to his house. Her fragrance pulled him like an addictive drug. The strange fragrance called to him. What was the source of the spicy, intoxicating aroma that filled the air? He had noticed the unusual essence a couple of days ago. The scent stirred a long-forgotten urge. Besides her scent, the woman appeared unusual. He shook his head. Her fragrance had bewitched him.

Grigore had observed Kat the night before. He had imagined how her long, wavy, brown hair would feel. The strands flowed like silk with her movements. He growled with the desire to bury his face in her thick mane and taste her lush lips. He must be insane. No stranger had ever affected him this way. Her gaze had locked with his before he ran off into the storm.

From his hidden vantage point, Grigore watched Kat as she shivered, removed the sodden gloves and dipped her hands into the cold spring to wash off the mud. She missed a blob on her forehead. He longed to run his hand across her soft skin to remove the offensive patch of dirt. She fascinated him. Most women would have felt scared if a wild wolf watched them. He could smell the sense of serenity flowing through her.

As the leader, he should be with his pack, helping to locate and stop Moog from gathering rogue werewolves and Alts into his fold. Moog wanted power over all the clans to defeat the Lupescu royal family,

Grigore's family. Grigore couldn't let that happen. Because he had a deep desire to thwart the impending battle, he had a spy reporting on Moog's movements. He hoped it wouldn't come to that. Right now, his sources reported relative calm. So, he spied on a human female.

Grigore withdrew deeper into the timberland. He took a shortcut across the woman's path back to the cabin, but the woman headed in the wrong direction. He skulked in the undergrowth near her, giving a menacing growl. He smiled to himself when she stopped and turned to head in the opposite direction and was shocked when she stooped to pick up two sticks for a weapon.

"Alright, you, whatever you are, I'm not a threat. Go back into the woods and leave me alone," Kat said. She pounded the sticks together to create a loud noise that punctuated her words. "It's not my wolf. He would've attacked me at the river."

Grigore's shock turned to bemusement at Kat's audacity. He decided on a different tactic. After all, he didn't want to scare her away from another trek in the woods. He wanted her to go in the right direction. He trotted closer and stepped out of the shadows for her to get a better look at him.

"There you are. Were you growling? I won't hurt you." Kat trembled, even with her show of bravado. She added with a humorless laugh, "I should've left breadcrumbs to get back to the cabin."

Grigore looked at her with his head cocked to one side, taken aback at her beautiful smile. His silver eyes twinkled at her next words. "You're wild and could kill me any minute. Somehow, I feel you won't." Grigore angled back toward the cabin. He looked over his shoulder, locked eyes with her, and led her home.

Kat followed him but had trouble keeping up on the slick and muddy trail. A couple of times he glanced back to see if she remained behind him. The rain drizzled again, surrounding her like a shroud. It made her brown hair glitter as if it were a dark halo. He saw rivulets of water slithering down the sides of her neck, accentuating the thrumming beat of her pulse. His preternatural hearing heard the loud, hypnotic thump of her pulse beckoned him to come closer. Grigore resisted the urge to approach the morsel in front of him. Once he knew that she could find her way, he vanished into the protective cover of the woods.

Chapter 5

Kat stepped into the clearing and turned in time to see the wolf pivot and disappear into the dense shadows of the trees. She felt grateful to the graceful creature. For a wild animal, he seemed tame. She had a funny feeling that he had deliberately led her safely back home. "Thank you, Mr. Wolf," she said under her breath, thinking he couldn't hear her in the distance.

Kat shivered, her clothes wet and muddy. The sprinkle became a downpour, and the temperature dropped. That was a good excuse for the goosebumps that covered her arms. She retreated into the cabin and added wood to the fire. Sighing, she peeled off the filthy wet clothes and climbed into the warm shower.

The day continued to be bleak with cloudbursts that alternated with relentless drizzle. At the start of her adventure, Kat had wanted to hide inside the log dwelling in the mountains. She had packed her car with supplies, which included a bag of books to keep her busy. Now, if the rain stopped long enough, she would explore the beautiful wilderness around the cabin. She wanted some pictures of the wolf. She would download the photos to examine them closer. Something about the creature called to her. Her photo programs on her laptop would provide an opportunity to view the animal from all angles.

Kat curled in a chair and threw the fleece blanket over her cold legs, while thoughts of the wolf's compelling eyes floated in her mind's eye. They brimmed with intense intelligence that seemed to study her as much as she examined him. His silver irises glittered with an evanescent brilliance. It was the same vivid glow she had remembered in the French door last night.

Restless, Kat paced the small distance of the room. She wandered over to gaze out the window into the gloomy afternoon, lost in her thoughts of the wolf. When the bright sun reflected off the rain-soaked ground, she realized the rain had ceased. Maybe this time the sun will stay long enough to dry the mud. People touted mud baths as good for a person's complexion, but Kat preferred not to wear mud every time she went outside.

Kat gathered her hair and pulled it back into a loose bun. Wandering onto the porch, she grabbed her clean jacket and surveyed the yard. The birds chirped. The squirrels and other rodents rustled around in the surrounding trees. Slipping her feet into the muddy hiking boots, she groaned as moisture from the wet footwear seeped into her fresh socks. She descended the stairs to wander around the yard to create a mental inventory of chores that needed done.

Overall, the yard was in good shape, but the building could use some work after years of neglect. Later in the week, Kat would go into town for supplies for the minor repairs. She'd also ask around for an experienced handyman she would need for the more extensive repairs.

Kat gathered more wood for the fire to stave off the dampness. She scrutinized the pile of wood. There would be plenty for a few more days. By then, hopefully, she would locate someone to deliver more. Her Uncle Jeff must have left the pile of wood. He considered the cabin one of his favorite hunting spots. Maybe he knew a handyman. She'd call him if there were none available in town. In the meantime, dead branches from the woods could be gathered if the pile ran low. It would be hard to burn wet wood, but if she became desperate, she would figure out something.

Kat walked around the building, bending to inspect the foundation. She stopped dead in her tracks at the sight of the toes of a strange pair of black boots on the edge of the step. Slowly, her gaze moved upward over a pair of faded blue jeans. Her gaze paused as she noticed the way the jeans hugged a pair of muscular thighs connected to narrow hips. Large masculine hands with a light dusting of amber-colored hair had thumbs looped over each pocket. She continued her visual journey and saw thick wrists that disappeared into the cuffs of a long-sleeved shirt. Muscular arms and the broad chest filled out the material of the light-colored plaid flannel shirt. Wisps of curly chest hair peeked over the collar.

Kat swallowed hard and debated whether she should run, but her eyes continued the expedition upward. Her gaze stopped at the most luscious lips she'd ever seen. The corners quirked upward. She took the plunge and made eye contact with a pair of gray eyes that twinkled in amusement. A lock of hair dangled across his brow. An almost overwhelming urge to reach up and brush the errant strand to the side flowed through her.

The handsome stranger stood silently on the edge of the stairs, observing the woman with the same scrutiny she'd given him. "Are you done with your inspection?"

"Who are you?" Kat gruffly responded to cover her embarrassment. She stepped back. Tension strummed through her body.

Chapter 6

This was the moment Grigore longed for. He yearned to see her up close with her long, wavy brown hair down around her shoulders. He couldn't see her front, but he bet her mane framed her face to highlight her natural beauty. He'd been correct. Some curls fell waywardly from the knot on the back of her head. Her blue eyes were the intensity of a cloudless sky, and her lips looked very kissable.

Grigore stepped off the stairs to stand beside her. The top of her head met his chin, making her the right height. For what he didn't know, but he wanted to find out. The curvature of her body would fit against him while he ravished those pert rosy lips. The pink color flushing her cheeks would deepen to red if she knew the direction of his thoughts. He found that this close to her, her pure citrus fragrance with a floral hint filled his mind with forbidden images.

"I'm Grigore. I live down the road. I thought I would drop by and introduce myself. Have you seen a brown wolf running around?" Grigore noted the suspicion in her eyes. He could smell the anxiety rising from her skin and hear her pulse race through her veins.

The woman hesitated before she answered, "Are you a hunter?"

"No, the wolf is mine," Grigore replied. "I didn't want you to get scared and shoot him. He's pretty tame. He's used to having the run of the land. He usually has a tendency to avoid strangers. There are poachers in the area, so I'm extra careful." He heard her heartbeat slow down.

Kat sighed with relief. The actions of the wolf had differed from a wild animal. "I've seen him. He's beautiful."

"I hope he didn't scare you, Miss...." Grigore fished for more information.

"No, he seemed more of a guardian. He helped me find my way back home after I got lost in the woods." She hesitated. "I'm Kat."

"Nice to meet you, Kat," Grigore said with a nod. Her unease was palpable in the air, and he turned to leave.

"Please wait," Kat said.

Grigore looked over his shoulder. "Yes, Kat?"

"Do you want some coffee or hot chocolate?" She bit her lip and waited for his reaction.

Grigore faced her and gave her a nonchalant shrug. "Sure, that'd be nice."

Kat walked around him to the stairs. Their hands brushed, making his hand tingle. He saw her stumble and grasp the handrail to keep her balance as she ascended the stairs.

Grigore followed her inside. He ambled to the large, overstuffed leather chair she had reclined in the night before.

"Would you prefer coffee or hot chocolate?" she asked. "I can make either." She glanced at him over the island that separated the kitchen and living room.

"Hot chocolate's fine. This is a pleasant cabin. Is Jeff your father? I didn't know he had children," Grigore said.

"No, Jeff's my uncle, my dad's brother. My father doesn't come here anymore."

He watched as Kat began to relax and focus on the task instead of on him. "I've lived in the area for a while and don't remember seeing you." Grigore gazed at her.

"Maybe you can help me." Kat faltered at his look of curiosity. She took a deep breath and rushed on. "I'm looking for a handyman, someone to do repairs, deliver wood and take care of chores to restore it. I can do some basics, but I plan to stay for a while. The place needs work." As if in confirmation, the wind picked up and whistled through the cracks around the windows. The floorboards creaked as she pulled the milk from the refrigerator. A log rolled over in the fireplace, sending a shower of sparks flying.

Kat gasped at the quick speed Grigore moved to stoke the fire and add wood. "I'll be glad to help," he said. "I have extra time right now. Make a list of things you need fixed. I'll start tomorrow if it's not raining."

"You will?" Kat responded. "That'd be great. I can get the supplies, and you can let me know how much I owe you." The scent of her excitement and apprehension filled the air, invading his nostrils.

"Not a problem. I'm sure we can work something out." Grigore grinned. He tilted his head as if studying her.

"Great." The beautiful woman smiled and handed him a steaming mug of hot chocolate. He took the offered mug and brushed his fingertips across her hand to see her reaction. His senses became inflamed with the same electric jolt as before. He hid a smile as she jerked her hand away, sloshing the hot chocolate over the rim and almost dumping the contents in his lap.

He eased into the large stuffed chair she had vacated the night before. He absorbed the leftover energy and inhaled her delectable scent as he glanced up to watch her move into the kitchen part of the room. When she asked where he lived, he pointed out the window in an obscure direction. The fact that he had lived here for several hundred years would frighten her.

With a quick grab of the cup, he saved the mug, the beverage, and his lap. His eyes glittered. He had seen her in action. This woman could be dangerous to herself.

Kat sputtered, "I'm sorry, I'm usually not clumsy." She searched for a kitchen towel to clean up her mess.

"No harm done," Grigore said. Grigore noticed Kat rubbed her hand and realized she felt the electric connection too. He could tell she wasn't immune to their attraction either.

Grigore sipped his chocolate and wryly watched her cheeks turn a delightful shade of pink. He felt tempted to take her then—to claim her and mark her as his and to see how dark that shade of red could get. The longer he stayed with her, the more his hunger for her grew. He couldn't understand it. He'd been with women in the past, but for this woman, he felt an aching hunger. Her chaste scent increased his appetite.

Grigore growled to himself. He abruptly set the mug down. "Thanks for the drink. I need to go. I'll be back tomorrow. The weather should be clear then."

Chapter 7

Kat started, "Thanks. I appreciate...," but Grigore was gone before she could finish. Unsure why his demeanor had changed, she walked toward the door but stopped when it clicked shut. It was best that he had left. Attractive guys made her feel uncomfortable. Boy, did she find this one attractive. She couldn't even touch him without reacting. He seemed unaffected, which made her reaction to the contact worse.

"Kat was glad he lived nearby and was willing to help around the place, but she hadn't thought before she asked. He might be one of the villains after her. Could he be stalking her? She had doubts since he knew the wolf. The criminals would be unfamiliar with the surroundings. She sighed and shook her head. A man this attractive never boded well for her.

Suddenly, Kat felt cold and moved closer to the fire, but the flame didn't abate the chill. It must be the wet boots she had forgotten to take off. Her trembling hands untied the laces. She kicked off the boots and set them in front of the fire to dry. She tossed her soaked socks to the side and pulled on a clean, dry pair, and then slipped her feet into the large, fuzzy pink rabbit slippers for added warmth.

The lowering sun threw shadows into the common area. The eventful day passed fast. Kat wanted to be alone in an isolated stretch of the country, but who knew there would be a handsome neighbor with a delightful wolf? She didn't have to worry about getting bored.

Although Kat had mixed emotions about her neighbor, she hoped to see the wolf again. The knowledge that the wolf wasn't wild filled her with happiness. Tomorrow, she would ask the wolf's name. She didn't plan on spending much time around her handyman. Experience told her to avoid him. While he made repairs, she would have a wonderful time exploring the area beyond the cabin and getting photographs for her collection. Maybe the wolf would be around to keep her company when the man came to work on the cabin.

A loud gurgle from Kat's stomach reminded her that toast and hot chocolate had been her only meal. She needed something more substantial. Rummaging through the refrigerator, she found hamburger meat and pulled out enough for herself. Then she reached back in and pulled out the rest of the pack for a treat for the wolf if it came tonight. She communicated better with animals than with people. The wolf seemed to be an ally that helped her stay on the trail. She laughed at herself for attributing human qualities to the beast and finished cooking the meat.

Because her car was still in the shop for repairs, she had borrowed her uncle's old pickup and packed it with the supplies for her time in seclusion. Tonight, she would indulge in a burger decadently made with the works. Ketchup and mayonnaise oozed from the side and dripped down between her fingers. She reached for a paper towel and wiped the goo from her hands. She glanced at the French door and spotted a flash of silver glitter in the half-light of the ending day.

Kat stumbled and almost fell over the huge slippers on her feet in her haste to open the door. This caused the wolf to bolt for the distant haven of trees. Leaving the door ajar, she retrieved the extra meat from the counter. She kneeled on the porch and scanned the distance for the lupine creature. Unable to spot him, she sighed and stood for a while until she glimpsed movement at the tree line.

Kneeling, she spoke in a soft tone to the muscular wolf. "It's alright. I won't hurt you. Grigore told me about you. Well, at least that you're his. I have a treat for you for helping me today. You helped me, didn't you?"

The wolf inched bit by bit out of the cover of the trees. His body crouched low to the ground. He slunk inch by inch closer to her. He paused, raising his snout to sniff the air. The wolf's stealthy movements mesmerized Kat as he approached. The beast came about halfway across the yard and froze in mid-stride. He cocked his head to the side as if listening to something in the distance. Kat heard nothing, but she knew the wolf's hearing was more sensitive.

Turning his attention to Kat, the wolf took another tentative step forward. Almost at the bottom of the stairs, he paused once again to listen. This time, the wolf whirled on his hocks and sped into the woods. Kat strained her senses, listening for any sound the wolf might have heard. A faint howl came from the distance. Did the wolf have a mate calling him? Disappointment filled her, and she returned to her cabin. After putting the food away, she settled in to read a book.

Kat laughed at herself. Perhaps her sanity had evaporated in the wreck. She felt frustrated because she couldn't coax an animal to come to her. Even worse, disappointment overcame her at the idea that the creature had a mate. She needed this self-imposed seclusion more than she realized. She flicked off the light and curled under the fleece blanket to watch the flickering flames. The changing colors lulled her to sleep.

Chapter 8

Kat twisted in the chair and opened her eyes to see the wolf standing just inside the door of the cabin. His amber fur shimmered in the firelight and enhanced the silver phosphorescence of his eyes, focused intensely on her. Through her cloudy thoughts, she wondered how he had gotten inside. He approached her with graceful and fluid movements, enthralling her.

As Kat watched, the hair on the wolf's body shortened and faded. His body appeared to mutate with every step he took. His front paws lengthened into long, elegant fingers and hands. He no longer advanced on four paws but on two feet. Except for his eyes, two glowing bright coals, his silhouette hid his features against the dying fire. A current of heat coursed through her veins when he touched her. She jumped when his fingertips caressed her jaw with a gentle touch. His hand slid upward to cup her velvety soft cheek. His thumb stroked her lower lip, causing her to moan. The scent of earthiness and musky masculinity filled her senses.

Kat's lips parted at the featherlike stroke of his thumb. The man dipped his thumb tip inside her mouth. Her eyes locked on the incandescent gray orbs that burned into her. She ran her moist tongue over the digit, tasting the salty warmth of his skin. She released a soft whimper when he pulled his thumb from her mouth.

The man gave a low, guttural growl at the sound of her whimper. He bent to brush his lips against hers. His tongue flicked out, teasing her lips, and slid in deeper in the exploration of her mouth. Kat tilted her head upward to meet his kisses. Her tongue slithered out to tangle with his, as if it had a life of its own. He thrust his hand into her silky hair and deepened the kiss.

Fire seared across Kat's skin from his caresses. He moved the fingertips of his free hand downward, teasing the flesh along her arm. His nails raked her arm in a light stroke, sending fire to her core. Her blood raced through her veins. His fingers moved downward, intertwined with hers as he raised her fingers to his mouth. He wrapped his lips around first one digit and then another, his tongue flicking out to tease each finger.

The man released Kat's hand. His mouth captured hers in another impassioned kiss. Kat's heart pounded. She momentarily felt deprived when he quit tantalizing her fingers with his tongue, but welcomed his embrace when his mouth returned to hers. He slid his free hand under her shirttail to tantalize her warm flesh beneath the waistband.

The man's fingertips scorched Kat's skin as they teased in a circular trail upward. She arched back, meeting his touch and moaned when she felt his finger torment her flesh in circles around the edge of her navel. He dipped the tip of his finger in to tickle the belly button opening. Her body trembled from the current blasting through her core. Gasping, she tilted her head as he nuzzled his mouth against her neck. She released a soft mew when his wet tongue traced along the hollow of her neck.

Instinct kicked in, and Kat spread her legs to offer herself to the stranger. Suddenly, her eyes snapped open when a shutter slammed against the wall. It was a dream that left her burning with a hunger for more. The fire flared into a cascade of sparks in its last dying embers. She heard the bang again, and a gust of cold air filled the room.

Kat realized she'd left the door ajar. Hopping up, she closed and locked it. Chilled, she added firewood. Lingering by the fire, she refused to look outside. She didn't want to know if the wolf came to the cottage tonight. She refused to think about the dream being real. After she checked the locks, she snatched her blanket from the chair and dashed into the bedroom to escape the erotic energy pulsating through her.

Kat lay in her bed, wide awake and staring at the ceiling. She was unable to shake the weird dream. She chided herself for being silly. The odd mixture of the day's events had created the dream. Wolves only turn into men in myth. There's no such thing as a werewolf she told herself, as she slipped into a dreamless sleep.

Chapter 9

Thunk... thunk... thunk... Kat jerked awake, disoriented by the sound. It took a few minutes for her brain fog to clear and for her to realize she was in a cabin, in the woods, alone. That knowledge didn't account for the sound she heard outside. Thunk... thunk... thunk... it reminded her of telling ghost stories around the campfire as a child. The light shining through the window blinds negated the ghost in the night theory.

Kat grabbed a T-shirt and sweatpants, slipped her feet into her bunny house shoes, and staggered across the room to the door. She looked out and saw Grigore in the distance chopping wood. His shirtless, sweat-covered body glistened in the sun. His muscles bulged and rippled each time he hit a log. The sun glinted off the blade he swung over his shoulder, and she could sense the weight of the iron blade as it came down to split the log. He worked with rhythm and precision. Swing, split, and position to strike the log in front of him.

Kat opened the door, and he seemed to hear her. Grigore dropped the ax against a tree, straightened, and walked toward the porch. "Did I wake you, sleepyhead?" he called.

"I need to be up anyway," Kat answered. Her cheeks flooded with warm color as he approached. She watched his gray eyes darken into the color of yesterday's storm clouds. Kat bristled in defense at the spark of amusement in the depths of his eyes, as he spotted her bunny slippers. "They're warm."

"I'm sure they are," Grigore said. Their eyes met. "They'd make a great chew toy for Lupescu."

"Who?" Kat asked in sleepy confusion.

"The wolf. You asked me about him yesterday." Kat squirmed at the intensity of his gray eyes as he watched her.

"What an interesting name for a wolf. Did you bring him today?" Kat looked around in anticipation. That name rang a bell. She had heard it somewhere before.

"The wolf comes and goes as he pleases. No telling when or where he might show up." Grigore hedged.

Kat's cheeks turned pink from thoughts of last night's dream. She said with a shrug, "Just curious. You said he belonged to you."

Grigore's eyes filled with mirth at her response. "The wolf is mine. He doesn't belong to anyone. He's wild and free-spirited."

"Of course, I didn't mean it as an insult." Kat shifted from foot to foot.

"I know you didn't," Grigore said with a smile, which made her feel better. The sun glinted off his sweat-covered sculpted arms, encouraging her wayward thoughts. She swallowed and changed the topic. "Want some coffee?"

"A break sounds good. Let me get my shirt, and I'll join you inside. I started early to take advantage of the beautiful day. I hope you don't mind." Grigore went back to the woodpile and pulled on a snug T-shirt.

Watching the handsome man's fluid movements, Kat admired how the T-shirt outlined every muscle. He might as well have left it off. No, he should put it on to hide the damp curly tufts of hair covering his chest that beckoned for her touch. Nope. Now it curled over the top of his collar to taunt her with what the shirt hid. So much better, she silently added, rolling her eyes. He put Chippendale strippers to shame with his lithe movements.

"Kat? Are you okay?" Grigore asked when she made a small choking sound.

"What? I'm sorry, did you say something?" Kat faltered and blinked, trying to focus on the conversation and clear her truant thoughts.

He gazed skyward. "The sun's out for the day."

Kat's eyes fluttered at his comment. She had watched him and hadn't noticed how the bright sun filled the sky and played across the ground. The sun took the chill out of the air, or maybe observing this half-naked stud before her made her hot. She realized the birds were singing. Even the fresh smell of earthiness that the sun drew out after rain made the day more pleasant.

"You're right, it's a beautiful day." Kat smiled. "I'll get coffee started." She slipped back into the cabin and left him alone on the porch.

Chapter 10

Kat's smile hit Grigore in the gut like a boxer's punch. Her smiling lips transformed her face, making her even more beautiful. When she walked outside, his body flooded with heat at the sight of her sleep-tousled hair and baggy clothes. He chuckled to himself when he spotted the fluffy pink shoes that dwarfed her feet. She didn't have a clue how enticing he found her. He didn't mention how alluring he found the thought of removing the fuzzy monstrosities to reveal the dainty feet inside. Her scent permeated the air. He knew she was to tense. He hoped to get her more comfortable around him in human form.

Grigore followed the tempting woman inside. His eyes went to the chair she had slept in the previous night. She would be horrified if she knew he had used his powers to shift with the shadows to enter the room. When she started to wake, he had little time to pull his hand from beneath her waistband. He felt deprived of the silky softness of her smooth skin. He shifted to blend into the shadows. The wind had caught a window shutter, slamming it against the side of the house. Last night, he used his ability to become one with the darkness of the shadows that flickered from the firelight as he approached her.

Grigore remembered how he had watched her from his hidden vantage point. He heard her heart pound in a loud staccato. Her scent was a pungent fragrance of arousal. Within the cover of the fluctuating shadows, his eyes followed her movements. Relief flooded through him as she locked all the doors and windows, although something so minimal wouldn't keep him away. In the shadows, he watched her for what seemed an eternity before her breaths became slow and even in the deep throes of sleep. He craved to touch her again. Stepping forward, his fingers reached out, but he asserted his willpower with reluctance and slipped out the door into the night. A solid click ensured it locked behind him.

Even now, Grigore wanted to approach her and finish what he had started last night. He stopped himself, not wanting to scare her. Kat already acted like a frightened kitten around him. He smiled sardonically at himself. She had a fitting nickname—Kat. She reminded him of a delightful kitten he could chase. He imagined this cat's claws could be quite sharp.

Kat's soft, melodic voice brought Grigore back to the present. Closing his eyes, he pictured the blissful look on her face and ran his fingertips across the back of the chair. His senses absorbed the remnants of her aura.

"How long have you been out there? Are you hungry?" Kat asked. "I have some bacon and eggs I can fix." Despite her attraction, she decided to play the friendly neighbor.

"I don't want to impose, but that sounds good," Grigore responded with ease. He leaned against the counter that separated the two main rooms.

"No trouble at all," Kat said. "I'm not a morning person. I don't eat this early, but the fresh air is invigorating. After we eat, I'll start getting the list together." The applewood smoked fragrance of the bacon filled the air. She turned back to the stove to flip the sizzling slices.

"It's been a while since your uncle visited. What brought you here?" Grigore watched her tense at his question. He heard her breath catch and her heartbeat speed up. The scent of anxiety oozed from her.

"I needed a change of scenery." She avoided his eyes.

Grigore shrugged with his usual careless ease and watched her through hooded eyes. "Few come out this far by themselves."

"My parents came for vacations when I was younger. Dad enjoyed getting away from the hustle and bustle of the city. We used to hike in the woods and go down to the river every day. We'd have picnics and play in the creek. I don't remember where, but there are some caves we explored." Grigore watched her face light up as she talked of her memories. "Dad would laugh and tell of a secret tunnel in one. It's supposed to lead to a fancy mansion in a magical kingdom where things weren't quite what they seemed. He told stories about the people there.

How they could change into other creatures with wondrous abilities. He insisted on never letting a creative mind go to waste. There are things in this world we need to explore. Never discount what we cannot understand. Being different doesn't make people bad." Kat sounded wistful as she talked of all the memories and the fantastic stories.

Grigore was shocked that anyone knew about the hidden tunnel that went into the alcove. Craggy bluffs and protective spells hid the tunnel from the valley. The protective wards and isolated location made the mansion inaccessible and kept anyone from stumbling onto the estate. The pack enjoyed the secluded nature of the domain. For generations, his family had bought all the land around. He remembered when they had homesteaded much of the area at a time when human civilization had not encroached on their privacy. Time and population expansion changed that.

A few years ago, Grigore had been away in the old country when a human got hurt in a hunting accident in the woods. One female in the pack brought him to the mansion and tended the man's wounds. The man and she-wolf had more than a platonic relationship during the man's convalescence. The human male didn't understand the seriousness of finding "the one," a true-mate.

The man insisted on returning to his human family. The female lycanthrope and the man met a few more times before he disappeared and never returned. Devastated, the female suffered from the separation of her true-mate, especially during the full moon. Grigore couldn't remember the rest of the story. He had thought the man had kept the existence of the manner secret. Grigore asked, "Why did your family stop coming here?"

"When I was twelve, my mother died," Kat said. "Dad changed. He became a workaholic, and a couple of years later he met Carolyn and remarried. After that, my stepmother and stepsister only wanted to attend posh events in the city." She shrugged and returned her attention to the bacon. Grease splattered, and she winced as it burned the back of her hand.

In one fluid motion, Grigore stood beside her and took the pan off the burner. He firmly took her hand in his and placed it under the cold water of the faucet. His thumb stroked the back of her wrist, and he spoke in a soothing voice. "I'm sorry to hear about your mother and your father's change of heart. There are magical things out here, not all of them bad."

Their eyes locked, transferring a wealth of emotion. Grigore's large hand held Kat's smaller one under the water. He felt her tug and let her hand go free, his body reacting to the current flowing between them.

Kat's mouth opened and closed a few times before she said, "I... I need to finish our breakfast." She looked away, as she dried the remnants of moisture from her hand. Grigore placidly leaned against the cabinet, as if the contact between them meant nothing. He heard her inhale and smelled the anxiety fade as her shoulders relaxed.

Kat scooped the food onto two plates, and they sat down to eat. "Yesterday, I noticed a trail on the other side of the river. Would that be a good place to take photos? I saw some animal tracks," she said.

"That's a scenic spot but be careful. You might run into something more vicious than deer or rabbits. Not all wolves are friendly. Some would love to eat a nice tender thing like you," Grigore said in a soft, deep voice. His eyes gleamed as he watched her shiver.

Kat coughed, choking on the last bite she took. She reached for her hot coffee, gulped, and spewed it out when it burned her tongue. Merriment flared in Grigore's eyes before he took a bite of his bacon, though he wore a mask of indifference. The sharp-smokey taste of the meat filled his mouth and remained on his tongue after he swallowed. "Are you alright? I can always kiss it and make it better. I hear that can help."

Kat finally stopped coughing. Blood filled her cheeks in mortification, giving them a rosy hue. "I'll keep that in mind," she said. "I mean about fierce wild animals being in the woods."

"There are other beautiful places with a lot of wildlife to photograph," Grigore said. "Be careful because there are some equally nasty things in the woods. You wouldn't want to get lost or stumble into something you weren't able to get out of. There are traps set by poachers or even worse horrors hidden in the brush." His brow furrowed with a frown. "Later, if you prefer, I'll take you around the area."

"Thanks for the warning, but I'm a big girl. I'll be careful," Kat said as she finished the last of her bacon.

Grigore watched her as she gave a stubborn lift of her chin. How she handled herself didn't impress him. Besides, he wanted to be along on her explorations. He couldn't get enough of her. If she wouldn't let him go as a guide, there were other ways. Keeping her safe was a better use of his time than working on the cabin. He said, "I can only stay part of the day. That's why I got such an early start."

Disappointment and apprehension flashed in her eyes. "I understand," Kat said. "You have other duties and didn't expect to be loaded with odd jobs."

"Tomorrow we'll start on your list. It'll give you time to make me a list of what needs done." Grigore smiled.

After he ate, Grigore chopped wood while Kat cleaned the kitchen. About midmorning, she grabbed her camera as she started on an adventurous trek into the woods, waving to Grigore as she left.

Nodding in acknowledgment, Grigore chopped wood until her scent faded in the distance. Then, he slipped into a dense thicket of trees, shed his clothes. He walked out of the underbrush, following her trail. His body shifted with each step. Hair grew to cover his body. His nose lengthened into a muzzle while his teeth changed into razor-sharp fangs. His bones realigned and shifted into the familiar wolf shape. As a shapeshifter, transmutation into a wolf became one of the first transitions he learned as a pup. Hunkered down on all fours, Grigore ran into the woods. He lifted his nose to sniff the air for the beguiling woman's distinct scent and headed in her direction. His sharp eyes spotted her in the distance, and he stooped down in the shadows to watch her.

Grigore slunk along the pathways near the trail Kat took and watched her movements. She stopped now and then to snap pictures of the stream, a jagged bluff in the distance, and wildlife she saw. She kept quiet and moved with care, not wanting to scare the creatures she wanted to photograph. Grigore was moved by her tenderness and respect for all wild creatures.

Chapter 11

As Kat wandered through the area, her fingertips brushed the tips of the flowers. She lifted her nose to sniff the sweet and musky variety of fragrances that floated up from the landscape. Now and then, she stopped to examine a crooked tree or a jagged bluff in the distance. Her fingers explored the various textures of things she hadn't seen before. So many beautiful and wondrous objects caught her attention, as she tried to memorize the landmarks for her return. She wandered along the bluff edge, oblivious to the trail's descent.

By mid-afternoon, Kat's explorations took her into a dip into a hollow with hills and bluffs surrounding her. She spun in a circle, enthralled by the dazzling panorama encompassing the glen. She took a deep breath of the crisp autumn air. There were several boulders and rocks, along with innumerous flowers in the valley. She took scores of photographs of the wildflowers, interesting trees, and odd clusters of rocks.

Finally, Kat stopped for a rest on a large flat boulder. She leaned back and closed her eyes. She laid her camera beside her on the boulder. She filled her lungs with the fresh, musty smell from the recent rains. A sudden sharp squawk jolted her from her meditation. A hawk plunged into the trees after prey. Kat heaved a contented sigh and surveyed the tree line around her. Smiling, she gave a muffled exclamation of excitement when she spotted the wolf watching her from under a tree. She'd half hoped she'd see him. She had figured he'd be with Grigore instead of in the woods. Kat bent forward and picked up her camera, her focus on the wolf. She cooed at the handsome lupine, "Hello again. I hoped I'd see you. Do you mind if I take your picture? You're such a majestic animal."

As if he understood, the wolf strutted a few paces closer and struck a pose. She snapped several pictures of him. The camera would never do justice to his magnificent beauty. The magnificent animal paced closer and stopped short of the boulder. She moved off the rock toward him, but he stayed out of her reach. Kat longed to stretch out her hand and touch him.

"It's okay, Lupescu," she said. "Grigore called you that. It's an interesting name. I've heard it before. It's a corporation, a competitor of my dad's." She laughed when the wolf cocked its head as if listening to her. "I'm more comfortable talking with animals than humans. I hope you and I can become friends. Maybe Grigore will introduce us sometime. Then you'll know I'm a friend. He makes me uncomfortable." She frowned for a second, and then babbled on trying to put the animal at ease.

The wolf sat out of reach as he gazed at her. His tongue lolled out as if laughing at her. Unexpectedly, the creature stood and glanced behind him before he trotted off into the distant underbrush.

"Never fails, every time I want to become better acquainted with someone, I scare them off or they scare me off." Kat gave a bitter laugh and watched the wolf vanish into the woods.

Lost in her enjoyment of the day, Kat realized the sun had disappeared behind the trees, immersing the valley in darkness. She tightened her jacket around her for protection against the sudden drop in temperature. Putting the camera strap around her neck, she shoved her hands into the jacket pockets and headed back.

Kat hiked back across the inclined terrain with a groan. She should've realized the further down, the steeper the trail would be on her return. Her legs ached and catching her breath was harder. She looked for a better trail around the cliff. Grigore's warning came to mind. The darkness increased on the moonless night, and trying an alternative path was not a good idea. Heaving a sigh, she continued upward.

She pulled her hands from the jacket pockets to keep her balance up the ledge's steep incline. With her heart racing, doubts filled her mind that this was the correct path. She stopped and looked for the earlier landmarks. She laughed at the sight of two intertwined trees bent in an arch beside the trail. From here, the stream wouldn't be far. She could find her way to the cabin.

The closer Kat got to the burbling sound of the stream, the thicker the darkness shrouded the trail. Cooler temperatures brought a misty haze that covered the path. The darkness kept her from seeing her feet or the trail through the encroaching fog. She took tentative steps and slid her toes out, tapping the ground before her. Nervously biting her lower lip, she became more confused in the unfamiliar surroundings. Gulping, she followed her instincts and lifted her foot to take a step toward the gurgle and splash of the small stream.

As Kat lowered her foot to find the path, she stopped as a growl scared her. A snarling bulk stood too close. Like a demon from Hell, a shape with glowing eyes hit her in the chest and knocked the breath from her. Her butt hit the ground. Her hands splayed behind her. Gravel gouged her palms as she scrambled backward, ignoring the pain. Whimpering, she threw her arms up to shield her face against an assault from the menacing wild beast. She cowered in the path and waited for the monster to rip her to pieces.

When nothing happened, Kat lowered her trembling arms and crab-walked backward until her back pressed against the side of the bluff. She shivered. Her teeth chattered from fear and the cold. She pulled her knees up, wrapped her arms around them and tried to regain her composure. A weak squeal escaped her when something wet pressed against her icy hand.

In her mind, Kat visualized blood dripping down her hand. The thought made her woozy. Something hairy nudged her hand, pushing against it. The beast pried an opening between her palms and knees. She jerked when something warm and moist dragged across the back of her hand. Her wolf licked her. The moist tongue flicked across the back of her hand again. She nuzzled the furry snout in a gesture of comfort.

"Lupescu, is that you?" Kat laughed nervously at her folly. "Even if it is, you can't answer me."

As if in answer, Kat felt the animal's nose nuzzle her hand to nudge his head under her palm. The creature scooted closer and pressed his large furry body against her for warmth. Relieved, she reached out, encircled the animal with her arms and nestled her face into his thick luxurious fur until her quivering stopped.

"I'm glad to see you. Thank you for rescuing me. I didn't mean to stay out this late. I lost track of time." Kat cuddled and drew comfort from the large muscular wolf. Tension faded, replaced by pain in aching muscles. She chuckled and teased him, even though he couldn't understand her words. "It's your fault. You distracted me, and I lost track of time."

Feeling a soft little nip from the wolf as if in response, Kat laughed and hugged him tighter. "Okay, I should've paid closer attention. I didn't realize it would get dark so fast."

Chapter 12

Relief flooded through Grigore. He'd been able to stop Kat from taking that last step and plunging off a cliff. With each encounter, he became more certain that she needed a keeper. How had the woman survived this long? He wouldn't always be there to save her. That thought made his heart ache. She could only be a short-term diversion for him, but what if he had found his true-mate? Ridiculous. She wasn't a wolf or a member of his pack. It would be irresponsible for him to get involved with her, a human. She was forbidden fruit for him in his position. The pack might accept an Alt, any alternate being with special gifts, but never a human.

Grigore, in wolf form, felt Kat's trembling abate. He tugged free from her arms, took the cuff of her coat between his teeth, and pulled until she stood. As a wolf, he pressed against her leg, slid his head under her hand, and encouraged her to move with him. Each time she hesitated, he ducked his head, grabbed the edge of her jeans in his jaws, and pulled.

The pair moved away from the cliff edge with measured movements. Grigore guided Kat around obstacles she would not have seen. He cautioned her to stop by blocking her body with his. He pushed his body against her leg to turn her at curves in the path. The bond grew between the woman and wolf with each step. Even when she spotted the cabin ahead, he was pleased that she continued to walk with him, seemingly happy to hold his scruff.

Reluctant to break the companionable connection, Lupescu continued to move as one with the woman across the yard and to the door. Her touch created an aching need deep inside him. He craved her company. Kat felt like his missing half. Until he met her, he didn't realize that part had been missing. Her fresh, pure scent made him drunk with an unquenchable thirst. Her touch made him quiver with anticipation. Even worse, the woman didn't trust him in his human form. He couldn't appease the inferno that burned inside him. How would the timid cat respond if she knew she had haunted his dreams? Tonight, he'd drop in to see how she fared on her daily outing.

They stopped on the porch. He sensed Kat's unwillingness to remove her hand from the soft fur on his broad head. Her fingers slid down his back, sending a chill of desire dancing across his nerves. Her fingers caressed his silky fur, creating sensations that resonated through his body.

Kat sat on the deck steps and faced him. She placed her hands on either side of his head. Her fingers gently massaged his satiny coat and moved across his torso. He rested his head on her knee and enjoyed the sensations that her stroking fingers sent through him. Heaving a quiet sigh as her fingers scratched behind his ears, he luxuriated in her touch. He yearned to feel her whole body rubbing against him. The pair lounged together as they soaked in the tranquil atmosphere of the night.

Lupescu reveled in Kat's attention until he noticed her shiver in the crisp coolness of the night air. The wolf withdrew. He looked at her with longing before he retreated into the ebony obscurity of the moonless night. His head hung low. His body ached with an unfulfilled need. He felt glad that his thick fur coat wouldn't allow her to see the arousal she had created in him.

Chapter 13

Kat subconsciously rubbed her hands together and patted her arms for warmth. "Good night, Lupescu. It's a shame you're not a man," she whispered with a sigh. Before he trotted off into the woods, the wolf looked back over his shoulder with his silver eyes glinting. Kat stood there long after her wolf disappeared into the gloom. Chilled to the bone, she finally retreated to the cabin.

Flipping on the lights, she took off her coat and slipped into her fuzzy house shoes before adding wood to the burned-out fire. She took out the first aid kit and attended to her scraped and bruised palms. A knock on the door sounded as she put on the last bandage. Who could it be this late? Opening the door, she saw Grigore casually leaning against the deck railing.

"What do you want?" Kat asked. Her voice was harsher than she intended. She gazed at him skeptically.

"I came to see if you enjoyed your walk," the enigmatic man replied. "It can be dangerous out there. Did you decide where to begin repairs tomorrow?" He cocked an eyebrow in amusement and ambled down the steps. "Maybe it's a bad time to ask."

"Wait. I'm sorry. It's been a trying evening." Kat continued, "Won't you come in? It's cold." Grigore wore a light jacket over his T-shirt. She wondered if he ever felt the cold.

He answered as if he had read Kat's mind. "The cold doesn't bother me. I'm used to it." He followed her inside, which caused goosebumps to cover her body as he watched her.

"I guess a body would adjust over time," Kat said. "I don't think mine ever will." She went to the counter to offer him some hot chocolate. Kat winced when she picked up the pan, shocked at how fast the man moved to stand beside her.

Grigore clasped her bandaged hand, and a jolt flowed through to her core. "What happened here?"

Kat yanked her hand from Grigore's grip when a warm tingle flowed through it. She hurried to the other side of the island, making it a barrier between them. "Nothing. I had a run-in with a cliff. Lupescu helped me get back to the cabin. Your wolf is amazing and intelligent. You trained him well."

"I can't take credit for his training, but thanks. I'm glad he could help. I'm happy you weren't hurt more. There is more to fear out here than the animals." Grigore shrugged. "I wish you'd let me show you around sometime. Thanks for the offer of the drink, but I'll head home. Let me know in the morning where you want me to start. Maybe I'll continue where I left off." Their eyes locked. Kat noticed his eyes burned, and a smile played across his lips.

Grigore's words brought her dream of his kiss to mind, and she flushed a shade of bright pink. She spun away in hope that he didn't see her embarrassment. "I'll have a list tomorrow."

"See you in the morning. Sweet dreams, Kat." Grigore's smooth, silky voice played on her nerves. He closed the door behind him.

Heat flowed through Kat's body. The man's comment brought the vivid dream back. She didn't usually have impassioned dreams. When she awakened in the chair, her skin burned as if his fingers had truly caressed her flesh. Her lips felt swollen from the scorching kiss. Kat shook her head and chastised herself. Had she become so desperate for a man that she imagined a wolf turning into a man to give her pleasure?

Kat tossed and turned again as dreams danced in her head, allowing her little sleep. The wolf stood out of reach in the distance, laughing at her. Grigore lounged nearby and watched her with flaming eyes that ignited a fire and a hunger that ached within her. He slipped away from her each time she got close. She longed to touch his auburn locks to see if they were as soft as the wolf's coat. Both creatures taunted her as they evaded her touch, yet lingered in her thoughts. Her legs felt as if they were bound preventing her from approaching either the wolf or the man. She lashed out at whatever held her captive as if some enemy had bound her and held her down.

A sudden strident sound reverberated in the distance. The wolf and man scattered into the shrouded mist on the edge of the dream. Kat lay helplessly confined.

The constant shrill sound grew louder and louder, demanding her attention. Kat rolled over and slapped at the offending noise to gain a moment of quiet. She slipped into the twilight phase between wakefulness and sleep. The obnoxious sound again shattered any reprieve she might have gained.

Kat's mind was foggy, and her mouth felt dry as if she had chewed cotton. Her legs couldn't move. The blankets had tangled around her legs during her dreams. All she could recall of the dream was that the man and wolf both mocked her. No other details came to mind except that her dreams had been as tangled as her bedcovers.

As Kat extracted herself from the enveloping layers of blankets, a frigid blast of air hit her. She grabbed clothes and went for a hot shower, and she took extra care with her hair. Grigore would arrive soon. She couldn't decide what to wear, but there were not a lot of choices. She had packed only the basics. She told herself Grigore had nothing to do with her anxiety over her appearance.

Finishing her chores, she set food out for breakfast in case Grigore joined her. Cooking for him was the least she could do to thank him for his help. What did he do for work? Did her repairs interrupt his schedule? She came here in search of privacy. In the process of meeting him, she had learned little about the man. What possessed her to invite him into her home and tell him she lived alone? For some reason, she trusted him, maybe because the wolf accepted him. Could he be the enemy she came to get away from? She needed to find out more about him.

Kat would ask Grigore how long he could help her. Grabbing a notebook, she compiled a list of needed repairs, both outside and inside that she had already observed. She knew there were things she hadn't noticed, like some painting and loose boards that needed to be fixed. He had already made headway in the supply of wood for the winter. That thought reminded her to double-check the cabin windows for winterization, otherwise, dampness would penetrate every crevice of the rustic old house. Where was Grigore? By this time yesterday, he'd already arrived. Maybe he decided not to return.

Pacing back and forth, Kat patted her forearms with her hands. She didn't even know the man. Kat heaved a sigh. She would fix what she could. During the rainy days, she cleaned every nook and cranny. The washer had a leak. It was a surprise that this rickety old place had a washer. It was an ancient one, but it still worked.

Kat jumped when a loud knock sounded on the solid wooden door frame. Taking a deep breath to shake off her jitters, she unlocked and opened the door to find Grigore on the other side.

"Shouldn't you ask for identification before opening the door?" Grigore frowned at her.

Kat saw infuriating glint of mirth in his eyes. "You said you'd be here this morning. I figured it might be you." Kat bit her lower lip between her teeth. A sense of relief flooded through her at his presence, which exasperated and infuriated her. She had a sudden urge to slam the door shut on his smug self-assurance.

As if the aggravating man could read Kat's mind, he reached his hand out to hold the door open. His eyes twinkled. "Are you going to ask me in or continue to let the cold air inside?"

"Sure, come in," Kat said. "I fixed breakfast. You can join me." She shrugged with feigned indifference. Then she whirled on her heels and rushed into the kitchen.

"Breakfast sounds great," Grigore replied. "But don't think you have to feed me." He moved up behind her without making a sound.

"I have to eat anyway," Kat said. "I might as well cook for two as one." Her heart pounded. She put water into a pot.

"What are we having?" Grigore's mouth was next to her ear, and his warm breath skimmed across her neck, like a fire across an oil spill. Kat jumped at his nearness and pressed too hard on the loose spigot. It snapped off, shocking her. Water shot out like a geyser. Blinking in surprise, Kat tried to replace it, but water sprayed into Grigore's face. His hand brushed against hers. She jerked her hand away as if electricity hit her. She dropped the knob and flung more water into his face.

Kat spun around and watched water drip from the unruly sprig of hair curled over his brow and down his aquiline nose to land on his kissable lower lip. She gazed at him and flicked her tongue out in an uncontrollable urge to lick the wayward drop off his luscious lips.

Her eyes latched onto Grigore, causing the lust to flow to her depths. She inched backward and reached for a towel while water continued to spray into the air and rain down on them.

Chapter 14

Tearing his gaze from hers, Grigore squatted down and opened the cabinet door to shut off the water valve. "I'll turn this off before we drown," he said. "Do you have any tools?"

"I saw some in the closet. I'll go check," Kat replied and scurried off toward her bedroom.

Grigore shook his head and walked over to peek into the bedroom. This woman with hair the color of milk chocolate was a menace, a walking disaster waiting to happen. She needed a caretaker. He examined her private lair while she dug in the closet for the tools. Scanning the room, he glimpsed the unmade bed with the blankets scattered every which way across the bed and hanging onto the floor. It looked as if she had had a fight with the bed.

He caught a hint of a fuzzy pink slipper with a long ear peeking out from under the edge of the bed, half hidden by an abandoned blanket. He smiled, thinking how alluring he found her when she wore them. He craved to see the enticing toes she hid.

Hearing Kat grumble inside the closet, Grigore walked over to see what had her attention. The sight of her round hips framed in the doorway sent a fresh wave of heat through him. His eyes glowed silver. Her heart-shaped backside wiggled as she dug through a box on the floor, spurring a long-buried craving. Grigore grew hard in his impudent thoughts. He hoped she wouldn't turn around, or he'd frighten the little kitten even more.

"I know I saw the tools here." Kat wiggled in frustration. Her behind swayed as she pushed one box away and dug through another.

Grigore groaned as unbidden primal thoughts of her rocking beneath him filled his mind. She exclaimed in triumph, crawled backward and bumped into his calves. "Aha! Here they are. There aren't many tools, but maybe you can fix the faucet with what's here."

Grigore started to squat to peer into the box. Kat's warmth against his legs made him change his mind. He stepped backward. The last time he touched her, the enticing woman gave him a cold shower when the handle broke off. No telling what would happen this time. Although perhaps a cold shower might be a good idea after he watched her behind bob in front of him.

Grigore didn't want to scare her. He had a feeling that this kitten had sharp claws. It would be interesting to find out sometime. For now, he'd settle for fixing the sink without another mishap. His stoic mask slipped into place. He reached for the box and hid his amusement when Kat stood and thrust it at him. He took the box, examined the contents, and pulled out the needed tools. Even as heir to the lycanthrope throne, living for hundreds of years, he had plenty of time to learn lots of useful skills. He could be a fair plumber. He headed into the kitchen. "This will work for now."

Grigore watched Kat grab an armful of towels from the bathroom. He followed her into the kitchen. She sopped up the water from the floor while he fixed the faucet.

The wet shirt and jeans molded to his body, outlining the muscles of Grigore's arms, legs, and torso. The wet denim, skintight against his slim hips, outlined each rippling bulge. Kat gawked as he shifted positions. Her eyes wandered to the bulge in his crotch. He accommodated her and shifted his position, parting his legs a bit more.

Kat's eyes jumped to his face. She felt mortified at being caught examining his hard, wet body. His eyes danced with mirth as he returned her gaze. Grigore stretched his arm toward her, and she flinched as he tugged at a towel to retrieve it from her immobile hands. She held a death grip on the towel. He jerked again, harder this time. She released the piece of terry cloth and bit her lower lip.

Grigore lifted an eyebrow inquisitively. He wiped the moisture from his hair and noticed her shiver. "Why don't you get out of those clothes?"

"What?" Kat took a step back until her body pressed against the cabinet. She stared at him with wide blue eyes.

"You're shivering in those wet clothes," Grigore said. "Go change into something dry. I'll add wood to the fire." He took a step toward her.

"A good idea. You're probably cold too." The blaze reflected in his eyes for an instant, as she walked into her bedroom.

"Maybe my uncle left some clothes that will fit you." Hearing a deep, throaty chuckle from behind her, she closed the door with a slam.

Chapter 15

The slammed door brought another chuckle from Grigore. He glanced toward her chair and spotted her fleece blanket. Walking to the fireplace, he stripped off his shirt to reveal tanned skin and wisps of hair covering his body. The sheen of moisture caused his muscles to glisten in the firelight.

Grigore's muscles flexed with his movements. He unbuttoned his pants, working the heavy, wet material down over his hips. When he had the denim waistband halfway down his hips, the bedroom door creaked open, and a strangled noise came from behind him. With slow, deliberate movements, he pulled the jeans back up, slid the zipper halfway, and leisurely faced the naïve woman.

Kat gaped at Grigore, snapping her mouth shut when he cocked one eyebrow up. Hesitantly stepping forward, she held out a wad of clothes with a shaking hand. "I found these things. Uncle Jeff is a little shorter than you, but maybe these will help until yours dry. I couldn't find any underwear though."

"I don't wear any," Grigore brushed his fingers against hers as he took the clothing. The woman's cheeks flamed as she yanked her hand back.

Kat's eyes were wide as she scanned his well-defined torso, visually tracing the hair scattered across the chest that tapered down to the half-opened zipper. She licked her dry lips at the sight of the curly wisps of hair that disappeared below the waist of his jeans. Emitting another strangled groan, she backed against the wall. Reluctant to pull her eyes from him, she croaked, "I'll give you a chance to change while I get into dry clothes." She hurried into her bedroom.

Kat leaned against the closed door. Her heart pounded. She felt she would self-combust. The sight of the gorgeous man had awakened long-buried feelings. Tilting her head against the door, she took a deep breath, trying to calm the fire ablaze inside her.

She didn't want to be attracted to him. Men like Grigore had always spelled trouble for her. The cabin was a hideout from the criminals and a place to get away for peace and quiet. A change. The man in her living room represented a change, but not the kind she needed. He represented the opposite of peace and quiet. She shook her head.

Pushing herself away from the door, she stripped off her wet clothes. Her damp skin emphasized the cold temperature. Cool air hit the damp flesh, and her nipples grew hard. She shivered and quickly dressed in dry jeans, a baggy sweater, and warm socks before slipping her feet into her fuzzy rabbit slippers. As she ran a brush through her damp locks, she closed her eyes and took another deep breath to calm her nerves before opening the door.

A laugh almost choked her at the sight of the man in the other room. Grigore stood in front of the fireplace with his back to her. The jeans hem hit just below his knees, and the shirt swallowed him in girth. The sleeves stopped in the middle of his forearms. Hearing her giggle, Grigore turned around, and she burst into laughter. He wadded the waistband in his fist to keep the slacks from falling around his ankles.

"I think I'm better off wrapped in the fleece blanket." Grigore pointed toward the throw on her chair. His eyes twinkled, and the corners of his mouth quirked upward in a wry grin.

"Those pants are awkward, for lack of a better word," Kat said. "Sorry I don't have anything that fits better. If you feel more comfortable, you can wear the blanket instead." Her voice purred, and her eyes gleamed in mirth.

Grigore stepped closer and brushed his fingertips across Kat's cheek. The familiar fire flowed between them. With a knuckle under her chin, he tilted her head up, gazing into wide blue eyes. His voice soft and sensual. "Only if you're sure. I make you uncomfortable. I don't want to make things more awkward."

Grigore's tender tone lulled Kat into a sense of security. She leaned into his touch until the memory of another sweet talker flashed through her mind. She pulled away, her voice filled with laughter. "We could both fit in those clothes."

"True. We could fit under the blanket much better." Grigore wiggled his eyebrows in jest.

"That's not what I meant, and you know it." Kat gave a burst of nervous laughter at his lascivious leer. She stood in front of the fireplace, holding her hands out to warm them. She thought that would serve better than the urge to caress his rugged jaw with them.

"I made some hot chocolate to warm us while the clothes dry. I thought that would make you feel more comfortable. I'll be right back." He glided through the bedroom door.

Kat placed two steaming mugs in the living room and settled in the plush chair that had become her favorite place to relax. Grigore walked back into the main room with a blanket tied around his hips and his upper body bare. He sat in a chair opposite hers. Kat's mouth went dry at the sight of his rolling muscles. The solid lines of his body flexed as he picked up the mug in front of him. His shielded eyes watched her but gave nothing away. Kat felt drawn to him like a bee to a budding flower. She enjoyed his company. His presence comforted her enough to relax and drop her defenses. Each moment spent in his company awakened a hunger to be touched by him and to curl up in his muscular arms. The wayward curl on his forehead taunted her. When he stood near her, she caught his unique, earthy, masculine scent. She longed to know if his kiss was as sweet as it had been in her dream.

Clearing her throat, Kat rambled on. "Have you always lived here?" She blew into the hot liquid in her mug.

Kat could get lost in Grigore's gray eyes, the color of liquid mercury. Desire flowed through her as he flicked his tongue out to lick away some melted marshmallow from his upper lip. "No," Grigore explained. "My family stays here part of the time. Business would draw my parents back to another house they have in Europe."

"That must have been hard for schooling," Kat said. She shifted, leaned back in the chair, stretched out her feet on the worn leather footstool, and wiggled her toes, making the bunny ears flop back and forth.

Grigore licked his lips and cleared his throat. Kat noticed he had a touch of huskiness in his voice. "Our family homeschools,' he explained.

"We are all trained to follow in the family business. My siblings, cousins, everyone in my family all go pretty much through the same schooling."

"You must have a big family then. I'm an only child. Well, I was until my father remarried. My stepsister and I aren't close, though. I always wondered how it would feel being part of a big, close family." A smile played at the corners of her lips as she leaned back in the chair, curling her feet beneath her. Dipping her tongue in the mug, she scooped out a bit of marshmallow and drew the confection into her mouth.

Entranced, Grigore watched the woman as the pink bunny slipper ears twitched and waved at him as if baiting him to see what lay beneath the fuzzy pink exterior. She had been oblivious to his body's reaction to those wiggling toes. Now, she tormented him by scooping marshmallows onto her tongue. His imagination ran wild with possibilities.

Grigore groaned inwardly with the desire to catch and explore Kat's feet, not just her feet but her entire body. To kiss and capture her delectable tongue between his teeth. He swallowed and took a sip of his drink. Tamping down his desire, he gave a sardonic grin. "I often wondered about being an only child. My family is very close, though. Sometimes, it is too close. They're always in my business."

"At least you have someone who cares what you're up to," Kat said. "What kind of business does your family do?"

Grigore took a sip of his cocoa while he debated what to say. He'd omit that his parents were reigning monarchs of the Versipellis lycanthrope pack, and he was the heir to the throne. Swirling the contents around in his cup, he decided he would tell the truth to a point. "It's an old business. It's been in the family for generations. There are corporate offices all over the world. You may have heard of Lupescu Industries."

Kat started. "I've heard of them." Her eyes brightened as she stared at him. "You're Grigore Lupescu? *The* Grigore Lupescu? The notorious playboy who's always in the tabloids with different beautiful women all the time?"

"I suppose I'm that Grigore," he admitted. "Although that's not how I'd describe myself. The tabloids sensationalize stories." His expression became guarded. Tension filled his body. She didn't seem to be a gold-digger. Had he misread her? Had he told her too much?

"I didn't mean to sound that way," Kat said. "You surprised me.

You look different in the pictures. It must be hard to conduct business out here. Aren't you more comfortable in the city? There are no beautiful women out here. None of… this is coming out as I wanted it to." Kat stopped and took a deep breath before she put her foot deeper into her mouth. "You must think I'm an idiot."

Grigore sat in silence for a moment to evaluate the direction of the conversation. He could smell the sharp scent of her anxiety increasing. He delayed his response as he studied her. Kat pulled her feet off the footstool, curled them under her, and fidgeted. Her actions deprived him of the pleasure of seeing the bunny ears wiggle.

Grigore gazed deep into her eyes and finally responded, "I'd never think of you as an idiot. I must be in the city for business from time to time, but I prefer the solitude of the wide-open spaces. The city noise can be overwhelming. I love the serenity and freedom of the countryside. Technology allows me to work long distances. I'm on vacation right now, but accessible if I'm needed." Pausing, he systematically scrutinized her entire body, from head to fuzzy pink-clad toes. Then his eyes returned to hers, his voice soft. "There is a beautiful woman here. Why did you decide to return after all these years?"

Kat stared at Grigore with her mouth agape after his last comment. It was obvious she didn't consider herself beautiful. He examined her with a guarded expression. Her long brown hair curled around her heart-shaped face, which highlighted her innocent blue eyes. She had curves in the right places and would fit against him perfectly. Her unique natural fragrance captivated him and pulled at him like an aphrodisiac. He longed to touch her creamy, delicate skin. The way she blushed so easily titillated him. When she bit her lower lip, her pout stirred his blood. He wanted to kiss her, to feel her against him, and to taste her sweetness. The next time he kissed her, his desire wouldn't be a secret.

How could she not see her beauty? Both outside and inside. Kat showed kindness to his wolf-self when others would have been terrified of the creature. Grigore had watched her interact with nature. She was gentle and caring. Even the trees and flowers responded. She moved with ease. Well, at least she did when being a hazard to herself or to him. Someone must have destroyed her image of herself at some time.

Chapter 16

The stunning man had called her beautiful. Kat didn't consider beauty one of her assets. People called her stepsister the gorgeous one. Regaining her senses, the blood flowed up her neck and heated her cheeks. *I must teach myself to stop blushing every time he is around.* She placed the mug on the table, stared into space and came to a conclusion.

Kat felt comfortable enough to tell Grigore most of the story. "I haven't been here since I was a child and needed to get away. Someone tried to run me off the road and kidnap me. They wanted to use me as leverage to force my dad, Carter Anderson, to sell his company. One of his competitors attempted to kidnap me. I needed time away from what people call civilization. I've found I prefer the wilderness to a city full of people."

"I know Carter. Does the kidnapper know where you went? A competitor kidnapping his daughter could give him leverage in the buyout. I had heard another group attempted a hostile takeover of Carter's company, but he stood in the way." Concern filled his eyes, and he leaned toward Kat.

"Not as far as I know," Kat said. "My stepsister gave out the phone number. No telling what she has spread. Keisha delights in making my life miserable, especially where men are concerned. If I show interest in a man, she turns on the charm, snaring him like a snake swallowing a rabbit. After they lose interest in me, she dumps them." Kat glanced down, absently wiggling the slipper bunny's ear back and forth with her finger.

Intrigued, Grigore watched her play with the oblong, pink, fuzzy ear. A warm tingle flowed through him at the sight. Such a simple gesture aroused him. The movement filled his mind with errant thoughts of what he wanted to do with the dainty feet inside those oversized house shoes. Grigore moved his eyes from the shoes to her lips. A flame sparked in his eyes at the thought of those teeth nibbling on him. His hunger for the woman grew. It churned inside him like a cauldron ready to boil. He had to get a grip on his desires. She'd run even in those silly pink rabbits on her feet if she knew his thoughts.

Grigore focused on the light scraping of even white teeth against soft pliant lips as Kat nibbled slowly and rhythmically on her lower lip. He said, "Those other men must have been buffoons. It's obvious they missed the true jewel."

"No, they couldn't deal with my stepsister's snake-charmer charisma." Kat shrugged as she met his eyes. She released a soft hiss when she gazed into intense gray eyes. He shielded the powerful hunger on his face.

"What about now? Some man must have been lucky enough to catch you. Is your stepsister stealing him away?" Grigore asked as he watched emotions cross Kat's face. She wouldn't be a good poker player.

"I had a fiancé once, but we broke it off. I don't date." Kat shrugged her shoulder in feigned indifference.

Sadness showed in her eyes. Grigore moved beside her in a protective gesture. "What happened?"

"Keisha, my stepsister, has stolen my boyfriends in the past. I found my fiancé in my bed with her the night before our wedding. He told me he wanted me pure until after the marriage. Later, he said that my looks revolted him. He wanted a vice-presidency at my father's business, but he didn't think that if he married Keisha, it would ensure him the position. She has someone else now," Kat sighed.

Grigore brushed the hair from her cheek with his fingertips, making her jump. He felt her shudder when he spoke. "The man was blind to what mattered. You'll find someone who will treat you like the prize you are."

He bent down and brushed his lips lightly against hers. His tongue traced along the gentle bow of Kat's lower lip. He could sense her body's reaction. Her pulse quickened in his ears. The scent of blood flowed like lava toward him. Her rhythmic heartbeat sped into a staccato beat and the sharp, pungent smell of fear mixed with the spicy scent of her arousal.

Asserting every ounce of his willpower, Grigore pulled away from her inviting lips. His resolve to walk away was about destroyed when Kat emitted a soft whimper. If he allowed himself to sample this tasty morsel, he wouldn't be able to stop until he devoured her. She deserved to be savored and enjoyed in a slow, gentle manner, like any delicacy.

Grigore walked to the hearth, checking his clothes. He felt the intensity of her gaze as she watched the muscles of his half-naked body flex with his smooth, liquid gait. The sensation of her eyes, boring into his back, aroused him. Feeling himself harden, he lingered until he regained control. He didn't want to frighten the little kitten away by letting her know how she affected him. Scaring her was the last thing on his mind. His clothes were still damp, but he thought it best to get dressed. He pulled on his shirt and left it hanging unbuttoned, grabbed his jeans, and headed to the bedroom. "We'll go over the list when I come out."

Kat finished the to-do list and showed it to him when he stepped back into the room. Grigore said they would start with minor repairs. First, he would install sturdier locks on the doors and windows for her safety. He'd have his security team check out her past. He would ensure that no kidnapper or anyone else would hurt her. She showed him the location of the winterization items for the windows and doors. Together, they compiled a list of supplies. Kat spent her time washing the drenched towels from the mornings fiasco before preparing lunch for them.

Grigore felt bemused that for the rest of the morning, Kat would pick a job in another area of the cabin to avoid him. Some interaction would be inevitable, but he noted her determined attempt to avoid physical contact.

They worked through the day. Late in the afternoon Grigore stood in the doorway and watched Kat. He sensed the change in her body and inhaled her pungent scent. He felt the primal urge surface again. His keen eyesight noticed hardened nipples, pushing at her shirt. He heard her heart racing, causing his body to tighten in response. She avoided him while he wanted to sweep her into his arms and claim her. He'd never had such a powerful reaction to any woman. He had been with plenty.

Unlike other lycanthropes, his position demanded his true-mate be a lycan or Alt.

Grigore cleared his throat, startling Kat, and watched in amusement as she whirled around, a look of horror on her face at being caught. "I didn't know you were there," she said.

"I just walked up," Grigore said. "It's getting dark, a good time for us to quit." He needed to check in with the pack to ensure their enemies were not creating problems.

Shadows danced through the windows as the sun descended behind the trees. "I didn't realize how late it was. Will you be able to get home before the sun sets?" Kat asked.

"Probably not, but I love being out in the woods late at night. The stars light the darkened sky like sparkling diamonds. The air is crisp and clean." Grigore thought of running through the forest in wolf form, dodging trees as he felt the damp air move across his muzzle. He could feel the effortless strength in his legs.

"You make it sound enticing. Perhaps I'll take a walk tonight out in the moonlight," Kat said.

"I'd be more than glad to go with you. There are dangerous animals and pitfalls you might find here." Grigore knew the woods inside and out. He could sense danger long before encountering the source.

"That's okay, I'll stay close to the cabin," Kat said. "I'll enjoy the fresh air and gazing at the stars." Caution filled her eyes. He could tell she didn't want to be around him after dark.

"The woods are hazardous in the day but dangerous at night, unless you're familiar with the terrain. The best time to go is during the full moon since it lights the sky. Right now, it's too dark," Grigore said. The woman would end up in trouble if she went out after dark. She was a magnet for disaster, but he couldn't order her to stay inside.

"Perhaps you're right. Another night would be better," Kat said. Grigore cocked his head and frowned. Her quick concession made him suspicious.

Walking to the window, Grigore looked up at the sky. "The clouds are thick tonight. It'll make things even darker outside. It looks like we may get more storms."

"Surely not tonight." Kat hedged as she moved across the cabin and stoked the fire.

"The rains could come before morning." Grigore sniffed the acidic odor of the impending rain. It mingled with her distinguishable citrus musk. "It's in the air." *Along with another familiar scent.* He headed out the door.

"You can tell by smelling?" Kat stood beside him on the porch. She sniffed the air, stared at the sky, and then looked at his silhouette framed in the doorway.

"There are a lot of signs to help predict the weather, if you know them," Grigore said. "Another reason I should get on my way. I wouldn't want to get caught in the deluge. I nearly drowned once today already." He laughed.

"It was your fault, you know," Kat teased.

"My fault? How do you figure that?" Grigore looked at her in surprise and smiled at her teasing tone.

"If you hadn't surprised me from behind, I wouldn't have broken off that weak faucet. You deserved that bath." Kat chuckled and punched his solid arm.

Emitting a soft growl, Grigore pulled Kat against him and gazed into her eyes. "Watch out playing with fire. You might get burned." When her eyes widened, he winked and squeezed her arms as he released her.

"Good night, Kat. I'll see you tomorrow." Grigore sniffed the air. His supersensitive sense of smell caught a trace of a familiar aroma lingering in the distance. The smell agitated him. He gave a wicked grin. "If it rains, I'm sure we'll find something to do."

"Good night, Grigore," Kat said.

Grigore inhaled her mix of confusion and arousal as he slipped out the door.

Chapter 17

Grigore jogged in human form to the edge of the clearing and transformed in the security of the trees. He shed his clothes, leaving them strewn along the trail as his body shifted into the shape of a wolf. He felt the shift as it edged throughout his body. The momentary tingle in the tips of phantom fingers as they shortened, into paws as his claws grew long and sharp, the prickle of tendons and bones as they realigned. His body mutated into the form of a large, muscular wolf. Hair covered his torso. Exhilaration caused his heart to pound when the wind hit his face, accentuating his feeling of freedom. Pushing his limits, he raced across the rocky terrain, through the trees, and bursting into an open meadow. He became a blur moving across the field.

It had been too long since Grigore had let himself race with such invigorating abandon. His muscles twitched with exertion. He kept going, speeding faster. A blur to the naked eye. He ran farther and farther away from the woman, trying to shake the overwhelming need to watch her. To guard her. To claim her. His lungs ached with the need for oxygen. He slowed to a trot and gulped air into his aching lungs. Her powerful, intoxicating scent remained with him, even at this distance from her cabin.

Grigore changed directions and sprinted toward a rock overhang deep in a copse of trees. Slowing to a walk, he slid under the huge chunk of rock that jutted out from the bluff. Moving into the depths of the hollow in the stone, he slipped through a shallow tunnel, and then out into a large hidden garden near his home. A trail from the garden led him into a large grassy lawn. Increasing his speed once more, he raced through the grounds until a monolithic structure loomed over him. His home.

He stopped to admire the majestic beauty of the massive mansion before him. This had been one of his childhood homes and held many memories for him. The estate had been in this family for centuries. The house had originally been a small cabin and transformed over the centuries into a large Queen Anne-style mansion, furnished with antiques, most bought when they were new. Their property included several thousand acres for the pack to run on and for privacy. Their land connected to the outside world through a national forest, adding another several thousand acres that his family used and roamed. The sanctuary of the home and lands were protected.

The family built the mansion on an isolated hillside that overlooked the valley. Trees surrounded it. A variety of gardens encircled the perimeter of the house. A maze on the outermost edge of the front garden became an added safeguard from intruders. Once through the maze, the tunnel opened into a rock and water garden that used the resources nature provided. Over the years, there were more gardens created. His mother's rose garden remained one of Grigore's favorites.

The main entrance to the mansion faced off a dirt road that turned onto a small country path. Further down the cattle trail, the road turned onto an asphalt drive blocked by a huge double-wide wrought-iron gate, decorated with a large L entwined with a wolf standing guard. An electronic surveillance camera and intercom would be activated by anyone or anything that approached the gate. Once through, they would drive down a highway-width asphalt driveway to the entrance of the mansion. The property had a self-contained airstrip and helicopter pad. A protective force field, a creation of Lupescu Industries, protected the entire perimeter of the estate. Several spells and wards created by powerful wizards and witches provided an extra layer of security.

Lupescu Industries researched, created and manufactured a multitude of technological devices far more advanced than human technology. Some of their mechanisms were mass-produced and sold to the public. Many apparatus were designed for the Alt communities. Humans didn't know, but many Alts lived and intermingled with humans. Individuals in the Alt community had special abilities and were called mythical creatures or legends by the human population. Unknown to the human world, the Versipellis ruled their own domains under the guidance of their father, Cristofer. The Alts had their own clans and groups but came to the lycanthrope Alphas with any major problems. Ancient, deposed deities of many cultures also lived among the humans with a ruling system separate from the Alts. The deities preferred their own classification, living alongside the Alts, sometimes in peace and sometimes not.

Grigore slowed his pace as he approached the back garden closest to the Château. Sniffing the air, he caught the scent from the cabin. He trotted up and glowered at an old friend, reclining on the balustrade of the porch. "What were you doing there?"

"Hello to you, too." A large, black-haired man leaned back in a chair, his feet propped up on the railing. With his ice-blue eyes he watched Grigore approach with feigned disinterest.

Grigore transformed into human form, ignoring his nakedness. He snarled softly. "I don't like to repeat myself, Kane. What were you doing at the cabin?" he demanded.

"Sure, pull the Alpha male card on me." The dark-haired man started and then saw the steel glint of determination in his friend's eyes. He lifted one shoulder in a shrug. "You haven't been around much. I became curious. Besides, you have company. I didn't want to deal with her alone."

"Company? A female? Who is it?" Grigore glanced around. He sniffed the air and groaned at a familiar fragrance.

Before Kane could respond, a female with strawberry blonde hair bounded out of the double doors onto the back porch. She ran up and gave Grigore a bear hug and shrieked, "There you are. No one would tell me where you were. Just that you were out in the woods. What's so important out there you couldn't come see your sister?"

The woman sniffed her brother's hair and smiled. "Do I smell a female on you?" She sniffed again. "A human female? Leave it to you, brother dear, to be out dallying around when there is important business to discuss."

Grigore dodged the topic of the female, reading the underlying message. "What business? Has Moog done something?"

"Yes, he has, and we can discuss that in a pack meeting. Right now, tell me about the woman."

"A good idea, Grigore. Tell us about the woman." Kane faced his friend. The corners of his lips quivered to fight a grin.

"She's none of your business, Elena, or yours either, Kane. I've been helping her repair her cabin." Grigore growled, stalked toward the house.

"There has to be more," Elena insisted. "You're preoccupied with the woman. Her scent is all over you. She's human. Since when have you volunteered to help repair cabins?" Elena never left her brother in peace. She looked at him closely and gave him a tight hug.

Elena inhaled the scent that clung to her brother, familiarizing herself with the foreign smell. A flowery yet citrusy fragrance with an underlying hint of sexual arousal made her eyes grow wide.

"Yes, she's human," Grigore pulled himself from his sister's embrace. He retreated into the house, aware that his friend and sister stared at his back. He paused and barked over his shoulder. "We'll meet in thirty minutes in my office to discuss the urgent business that interrupted my introspection in the woods."

Grigore walked into the house and closed the door behind him. Three wolf cubs of various sizes pounced on him, knocking him backward into the door. Wrestling with the cubs, he grinned and ruffled the fur on the head of the biggest. He gave an endearing chuckle. "What are you furballs up to?"

"We've been waiting for you. We want to play. Come on, Uncle Grigore. Play with us." The largest of the three cubs yapped, and the others scrambled for his attention.

"Daniel, I'll play later. I must meet on pack business." Grigore scooped the other two cubs into his bare arms and snuggled them against his chin. He placed a kiss on each bobbing nose. "How are you two beautiful ladies?"

The girls giggled and lapped his cheeks in excitement. They squirmed in his arms and yapped simultaneously at the man. "We wanna play, too. Do you gotta go to the meeting? Can't the others go?"

"I wish," Grigore said. "I'd rather spend time with you. The welfare of the pack takes precedence. Off with the lot of you. Go find something to get into." Setting the two girls down, he swatted their behinds playfully. They gave energetic yips and wagged their tails as they ran toward the back of the house.

Grigore smiled and shook his head. He dressed in something more formal for the meeting. To the pack, human nudity felt as normal as fur was to the wolf form. Most of the time, clothes were worn when conducting pack business.

Chapter 18

On the way to his suite, Grigore glanced out of a large bay window. He contemplated what Kane, his friend and pack member, considered so crucial that he searched for him and risked his wrath. Kane had taken the role of a self-appointed bodyguard for Grigore.

Grigore dressed in a pair of khaki pants and a lightweight button-front shirt. In the office, he opened a fireproof file cabinet, pulled out folders, and placed them on the desk. He settled into a comfortable leather chair behind an ancient mahogany desk. He fingered the edge of one folder, opened it, and re-read the contents while he waited for the others.

Moog, his cousin and onetime friend, had lived with Grigore's family after his own father, Dronel, was exiled and removed from the throne. Dronel was the half-brother of Cristofer, Grigore's father. Being older, Dronel had inherited the throne, but he had abused his power. Grigore had been a cub at the time and didn't remember the events. Moog had been older and held bitter memories that festered into hatred over time. When they grew into whelps, Moog chose his father's path. He craved power and control of the pack. He claimed his destiny was stolen. However, his father's abuse of power had altered his fate.

Grigore, the eldest son of Cristofer, had been raised and primed for the leadership of the pack since birth. His father was the ruler, *Regele Alfa*, of his pack and all Versipellis packs around the world. A motto of honor and integrity governed the pack ruled by his father. His father ruled with a firm but kind hand, unlike Dronel. Grigore's innate leadership had infuriated Moog to the point where he tried to take Grigore's life.

The vivid memory of the fight remained in Grigore's mind. Kane was almost killed when he jumped in to save his life. Moog and Grigore had been playing in the woods. When Moog attacked Grigore from behind, sinking his sharp wolf's teeth into his victim's neck. His forelegs gripped Grigore's upper body like a vice.

Grigore struggled to shake the sharp lupine teeth that ripped through his flesh. Moog had aimed for the jugular vein. Grigore couldn't shake off the bigger wolf, his strength ebbed away with his life's blood. Grigore staggered beneath the weight of his friend-turned-enemy. Growing weak, he could gain no advantage against his opponent.

As he fainted from the loss of blood, Grigore heard a furious bellow from behind. Moog was knocked off his back. Grigore staggered and whirled around to see a huge black wolf fighting with Moog. White flames flickered in the wolf's ice-blue eyes. The two circled each other, snarling and growling. The black wolf blasted Moog with a guttural growl, warning him to leave.

Moog laughed. He advanced on the new opponent and launched himself with a snarl and a roar. "This is none of your business. Leave before you meet the same fate he's destined for."

Rolling defensively to the side, the large muscular black wolf regained his footing. Gnashing his teeth at Moog, the black wolf lunged forward, ripping a gash in Moog's shoulder. Grigore found reserved strength and launched himself at Moog's back, knocking him into a boulder. His champion closed in on Moog's flank. Moog threw the pair off with a snarl and bared razor-sharp teeth. He backed away until he found a niche between two trees on a bluff. Then he whirled and escaped.

Grigore's father banished Moog from the pack. He never returned. However, he didn't give up his dreams of power. The exiled wolf formed his own deadly pack. After the black wolf helped the wounded victim return home. Grigore learned his name was Kane. He revealed nothing else about himself but had earned Grigore's trust. Grigore's natural healing process during a regenerative sleep obliterated any signs of the wounds on the outside. Inside, he ached for the friendship he had lost and the pain of being used by his cousin.

From that time, Kane and Grigore were connected. Kane had been a lone wolf, interacting with few. In saving Grigore's life, the black wolf had become part of the family. They were inseparable. Kane appointed himself as Grigore's bodyguard and became a valuable member of his staff and pack. He developed unique skills, becoming the pack's greatest tracker and fighter.

Chapter 19

Grigore looked up from the file, when Elena, his favorite sister, opened the door. She was a trusted advisor She crossed the room and settled into a chair. Shaking his head, Grigore teased, "You still haven't learned to knock."

"Only when it's you, big brother." The gregarious woman grinned and tucked her feet beneath her. "Tell me about the woman. Kane says you're spending a lot of time with her."

Grigore opened his mouth to speak. A sharp rap on the door saved him. "Come in."

An impeccably dressed brown-haired man with the bearing of a warrior entered and took the chair to the left of the desk. He placed his briefcase at his feet, crossed his legs and straightened his tie. His British accent was evident when he spoke. "Where is everyone? We must get business underway in case briefs need to be prepared."

"Patient as always, Marcus." Grigore grinned and shook his head. Marcus was another valued member of the pack and a close friend.

"I want to ensure things are legal. It's already late. If need be, I want things ready for court first thing in the morning." The man nodded and glanced at his unneeded, ever-present watch. Lycans had an impeccable sense of time with bodies attuned to the moon. The attorney lifted his hand to squeeze the bridge of his nose.

"Marcus, you do a great job. You need a woman to loosen you up. Seems even the best fall under the charms of the right one," Elena said. She chuckled and looked at her brother. "Now, while we wait for the others, tell me about her."

"Elena, this isn't the time or the place," Grigore answered. His sister could be like a cat drawn to catnip. She wouldn't let the topic fade until she got her answers.

"Grigore...," she started but another knock on the heavy oak door interrupted her.

A tall, elegant, dark-haired man entered, walked over to Elena and kissed her on the cheek. "*Mon trésor*, my treasure, your brother's right. Now is the time to discuss business. Later, you can interrogate him."

"Harrumph, Andre, you shouldn't listen in on our conversation." His wife pursed her lips. She leaned her head back against her husband's chest.

"You should be more concerned that your brother hasn't initiated the sound barrier alarm for the meeting instead of nagging him about his new true-mate, *Mon Amour*," Andre said. "Werewolves with acute hearing are all over the house."

"She's not my mate," Grigore growled.

"We believe you. That's why you spend all your time there, instead of being concerned with what's going on here," Elena grinned at Andre. They had fought the natural attraction when they first met. Once the mutual chemistry of a true-mate became apparent, destiny doomed the pair to follow it.

"Enough! Other things need to be discussed." Grigore snarled and bared his teeth. "Where's Kane?"

As if on cue, Kane sauntered into the room and clicked the door behind him. He typed the encryption code into the keypad to engage the soundproof device designed specifically for the acute hearing of his kind. Ambling to the right of the desk, he dropped into a chair and slid down with his jeans-clad legs stretched out in front of him and crossed his ankles. His placid face exhibited his usual look of indifference. "You bellowed?"

Taking a deep breath, Grigore shook his head to clear it and began the meeting. "Each of you can inform the others later. What's there to report? Kane?"

"Moog has been at a club in the city. His gang has grown in number. He uses the club as a base for recruitment of any disgruntled outcasts he can find. He isn't picky, and his growing flock includes more than werewolves. I'm unsure how many there are. I think they're more afraid of Moog than loyal to his cause. Once we conquer Moog, his renegades will disband. Word is, his plans include going after you and the wolf that helped you escape him years ago."

"Moog still hasn't figured out it was you who defeated him?" Grigore felt shocked that the secret had lasted this many centuries.

"No, he never got a good look at me. There were too many other scents and sounds in the air for him to recognize me. I can slip in and out of the club without notice." Kane nonchalantly shrugged his shoulder.

"Are you sure it's safe to infiltrate Moog's pack?" Elena asked. "You're too valuable to lose. You're a wonderful friend and part of our family."

"I'm sure. I've been right under his nose a time or two with nothing more than a dismissal," Kane said. His friend could be observant and shrewd, fooling others with his façade of disinterest. Over the centuries, Grigore had become one of the few able to read his subtle body language.

"Can you go undercover and become more established in his pack?" Andre asked. Elena glared at her husband.

"I can. They're used to seeing me in the shadows. It won't take much to move up in the inner circle." Kane's lips twitched when Elena switched her glare to him.

"Grigore, don't let him," Elena pleaded. "The danger is explicit. It's one thing, taking on Moog with backup. It's another to be surrounded by his thugs without help."

"That's the best option, Elena. I don't like it either, but Moog must be stopped. Others will be on alert in case he needs help. Kane is the most qualified for this job. You know he prefers to go undercover alone," Grigore reasoned with his sister.

"Marcus, talk some sense into them," Elena stressed vehemently.

Clearing his throat, Marcus agreed with the men. "Elena, Kane has the training. It will be more beneficial for him to work from the inside. I'll get him the documentation he needs with a believable identity. I'll need a few hours to get the information into the right computer databases. Then he can go undercover."

"You're all impossible. Kane's unparalleled at what he does as you are, Marcus. Who would have thought a computer nerd would come in handy for a lycanthropic pack?" She threw her hands up in the air, glaring from one male to the next. Marcus appeared to be a computer nerd but had also been a knight of King Arthur's Round Table. He used his tenacious demeanor to become an expert in all forms of technology.

"It's decided," Grigore said. "Once we get the documentation, Kane will embed himself within Moog's pack. Kane, don't take any unnecessary risks. If at any time you sense danger, bail out at once. Is that understood?" Grigore stared at his friend, knowing his words were falling on deaf ears.

"Sure, boss, have I ever done otherwise?" Kane gave his friend a cocky grin, his ice-blue eyes twinkling. The others in the room appeared to have sudden coughing fits.

A discussion of other concerns and everyday business for the pack followed. Once finished, Andre wandered off to check on the children. Marcus headed to his office to start the paper trail of Kane's temporary identity. Grigore knew his sister wouldn't be dismissed as easily. Kane enjoyed the entertainment value of the arguments between Grigore and his sister.

"Elena, don't you need to check on your cubs?" Grigore asked. "The last time I saw them, they were in search of mischief." He hoped to sidetrack his sister but knew it wouldn't work.

"Andre's checking on them," Elena answered. She leaned closer. "Spill the beans. Tell me about this human woman."

Grigore turned to his friend. "Kane, don't you have something to do?"

"Nope." The large man studied his fingernails and smothered a grin at the resulting growl. He picked at nonexistent dirt under one of his nails.

"You two are insufferable," Grigore said. "There've been plenty of women in the past and you've shown no interest in them. There's nothing there." He said adamantly, adding in a soft, forlorn tone. "There can be nothing there."

"Aha! You wouldn't keep disappearing and staying away for a flirtation." Elena said, "Kane said she's not your usual type. When the chemistry flares, there is no usual type. I found that with Andre."

Elena's comment earned Kane another glare. Grigore grumbled, "Kane needs to mind his own business."

"Hey, I followed orders," Kane held his hands up, as if defending himself.

"You've never followed orders in your life," scoffed Grigore. "Besides, what orders?"

"Elena ordered me to find you, or she'd kill me." Kane feigning seriousness.

"We all know how scary she can be, so you caved under the pressure," Grigore rolled his eyes at his muscular, six-foot-five friend. "The top of her head barely reaches your shoulders."

"Very funny, you two. Now, get back on track. Tell me about her." Elena planted her hands on her hips and looked at both men.

Grigore knew her cross-examination would continue until he responded. With a sigh, he said, "Elena she's human, and I'm a shapeshifter, a Versipellis. One day I will lead our pack. No matter what kind of chemistry there is, it's not destined to happen. There can't be anything between us. Our people would never accept her. They expect me to take a member of the pack as my true-mate."

"Grigore, we only find our true-mates once in a lifetime, if then. You can't ignore your destiny," Elena responded with sad eyes.

"Which destiny should I pursue, Elena? Either way, I have to give up something. Do you want to be the leader or allow Moog to get what he wants?"

"There has to be some way," Elena said.

"I'll continue visiting her, but I'll return to my true nature, my destiny. She has no clue about the truth. This is for the best. Leave it alone." Grigore stood and walked from the room.

As Grigore left, he noticed Kane and Elena looking at each other. They knew he told the truth. Any special quality to make her an Alt would be more acceptable than being a mere human.

Kane shrugged. His face showed no emotion. "I'll do what I can to keep him safe on his trips to visit her. At least until I leave for the assignment."

"I can always count on you, Kane. In the meantime, I may try to meet this woman myself. Grigore is my favorite brother. He deserves the best. There must be some way he could have both." She had always been the optimist.

The soundproofing alarm for the room had been disengaged earlier. Grigore frowned and shook his head at the conversation he overheard.

Chapter 20

Grigore located Andre and the cubs in the library. They were in human form, looking like any father with his three young children. The cubs in their pajamas picked out a bedtime story. Seeing Grigore, the children forgot the book and clamored to surround him. In human years, they resembled any three, five- and seven-year-old. Grigore loved his nieces and nephew, but they were a handful. His nephew had the strong will of his sister. He always managed to get into trouble.

"Unca Grigore, will ya wead us a stowy? Pwease?" Ana, the youngest, gazed up at him with big brown puppy dog eyes that he couldn't resist. Daniel and Lucia joined in the chorus for a story.

"Grigore has other things to do, children," piped in Andre.

Smiling, Grigore glanced over at his brother-in-law. He hoped that one day, as head of the pack, to be lucky enough to have children. "Andre, it's okay. I don't mind reading a story. I told them earlier I'd play with them for a little while. Do you mind?" The thought popped into his head that Kat would make a wonderful mother. He mentally kicked himself. No, that would never happen. Their lives had different destinies.

The children chimed in again, begging in unison. "Please, Daddy, can we? We'll go to bed when Uncle Grigore says it's time."

Chuckling, Andre gave affectionate consent. "They can stay up an extra hour. Keep in mind that the little hooligans will coerce you into letting them stay up later."

"Yippee!" they cried and the three pounced on Grigore, knocking him backward onto the couch.

The foursome scuffled until the imposed deadline. The requisite begging to stay up ensued. Finally, getting them all tucked into bed, Grigore read the bedtime story they chose, an old version of "Little Red Riding Hood" his family had rewritten, making the wolf the good guy and victor. One by one, the children fell asleep in the large bedroom that was part of the nursery. Tucking the blankets around them, he kissed their foreheads and slipped downstairs and out into the cool night air.

Chapter 21

Grigore glared at the enormous figure reclining in the shadowed breezeway. "Don't follow me."

"I wouldn't dream of it." An aloof reply came from the shadows.

"I mean it, Kane. I'll know you're there. Don't follow me." Grigore growled. Leaping from the top step, he changed into wolf form before landing on all fours and sprinting at full speed into the garden. He headed into the darkness of the forest. He stopped at the hidden cavity in the rock wall, and cocked his head to the side, listening and sniffing for any sign of Kane. He heard only the sounds of the night but detected Kane's aroma in the far distance. He dived through the opening and raced over the miles back to the cabin.

Grigore stopped at the edge of the cottage's clearing. He inhaled Kat's delectable spicy aroma. Each time he drew in the distinctive smell, his addiction grew. He had to quit torturing himself and leave her alone. Each visit prolonged the inevitable, and his attachment to the forbidden fruit tightened like a noose. Tonight, he'd go as the wolf and enjoy her company. He assured himself that only her love of nature caused the chemical reaction, nothing more.

As the wolf, Grigore trotted to the porch. He gazed through the glass pane of the door and saw Kat stretched out on the rug in front of the fire. Her legs were propped up on the hearthstone as she warmed her pink toes. Her feet were delectable. He visually explored the exquisite lines of the small feet and slim toes. He smiled at himself. His imagination went wild as he pictured all kinds of things to do with the delicate, wiggling digits. He pressed his nose against the glass, and his warm breath steamed the window. Stretching his paw out, he scratched the outside of the door frame to get her attention.

Kat rolled over to see what had caused the noise. Pleasantly surprised, she hopped up, slipped on the fuzzy pink bunnies, and cracked open the door. "Lupescu! I'd given up hope of seeing you tonight. I figured you'd be curled up in front of Grigore's fire." Standing in the door with her hand hanging loosely at her side, she stared at the wolf.

He nuzzled her hand out of the way, slipped his nose between her arm and the crack of the door, leaned his shoulder against the solid object, and pushed his head inside.

Kat laughed, opened the door wider, and waved her arm in a flourishing motion. "I'm being rude. Please come in, Your Highness."

Grigore gazed up at her, thinking if she only knew. He trotted to the rug in front of the fire, circled twice and lay down. Her bubbly laughter played on his nerves. His body quivered. Sitting up, his eyes followed her into the kitchen where she retrieved a bag of marshmallows.

She grabbed a long wooden stick and carried it toward the fireplace. "I found these sticks on one of my explorations in the woods and saved them for a special time," Kat said. Grigore ducked his head, his ears alert as he watched her approach. Her eyes glittered. She reached out and scratched him behind the ears. "I thought it an excellent limb to roast things in the fire. Don't worry, I won't hit you. These sticks are for toasting a few marshmallows to eat."

Kat tossed the wolf a marshmallow from the bag. He snatched the sweet treat in his jaws and swallowed it. His silver eyes watched her spear another marshmallow on a stick and place it over the flame to warm. He'd never been a great one for sweets, but he'd make an exception tonight.

Grigore watched Kat pull the treat from the stick, hold it up and blow on it with pursed lips. Sticking her tongue out, she licked the soft edge of the concoction. The melted gooiness stuck to her lips. Unable to resist the temptation, he licked the sweetness of the treat off her lips and snatched the treat away.

"Hey! That's mine." Kat laughed and pushed him away.

Grigore blinked and gave an unrepentant look, waiting for a chance to do it again. They lost time as they snacked and played keep-away with the marshmallows. He took every chance to lick her or touch her with his paws.

Kat laughed, running her fingers through his glossy hair, never guessing what her touch did to him. The wolf rolled over on his back, exposing his belly as he enjoyed the woman's fingers rubbing and teasing his stomach. He felt his manhood respond and rolled over to hide his reaction to her attention.

Grigore caught sight of the pink rabbit ears flopping as she wiggled her toes. He lunged for the peculiar foot coverings. Tugging with his teeth, he pulled one off, playfully running with it in his mouth. He dodged this way and that, as Kat grabbed for the slipper. He paused when he caught a whiff of that tantalizing fresh citrus scent so close that it intoxicated him. Kat tackled him and got the shoe away from him and sat down to put it on. He snatched the shoe off her other foot.

"Give me back my shoe. You already have this one covered in slobber." Kat laughed as she snatched at the furry footwear.

The wolf flipped the house shoe into the air over her head. He panted happily with his mouth open, a smile on his lupine face. Kat sat cross-legged on the rug with him curled up and pressed against her side, watching her. She reached down and scratched him behind his ears. He tilted his head against her hand, lost in her tender touch. She leaned back against a chair, unfolded her legs and slipped her bare toes under his belly. Kat had a dreamy look on her face, as she absentmindedly wiggled them against his underside.

"Who needs house shoes with you around? Your fur's warm and soft. It would be great to keep me warm while sleeping." Grigore turned his head and licked her hand. His gray eyes locked on her blue ones. A hungry need flashed deep in his eyes. Each moment he spent in her company made him ache at the thought of never seeing her again.

Kat stretched out on the rug, wrapped her arm around him, and ran her fingers through his hair until she dozed off. He slipped from beneath her arm, cautious not to wake her. Tugging the fleece blanket from the chair, he covered her and tucked it around her with his nose.

Grigore watched the beautiful woman for a few minutes with longing in his eyes. He retreated to the door and glanced over his shoulder once more before he locked the door behind him. He slipped into the night lost in his thoughts. He walked for a while. *How could he fool himself into thinking that being the wolf would make things less complicated? It made him crave her more. If he could have fun with her in wolf form, how explosive would a connection in human form be? Why did human men scare her? He renewed his determination to make her more comfortable with him as a man.*

He knew these thoughts were dangerous for both of them. He inhaled the cool night air in hopes it would clear his mind, but it didn't help. Deciding to do the only other thing that helped him think straight, he ran.

Faster and faster, he ran, covering miles of land. He ran until his lungs felt they would erupt. Then he ran harder and faster. Distracted by introspection, he slammed into an unseen obstacle. He groaned at the solid brick wall that knocked the breath out of him.

"What are you doing here? I told you not to follow me." Grigore panted. He glared at the brick wall he had rammed into. Kane didn't flinch.

"I didn't. When you didn't return, I wanted to ensure your safety. Moog is a threat. Go home and get some sleep. Everyone will wonder where you've been." Kane's kept his usual cool composure.

"Who are you to tell me what to do?" Grigore snarled. His hair bristled on the back of his neck at his friend's calm self-possession while he felt only confusion. He glared at his friend and bared his fangs as he took an offensive stance.

"Is that what you want, my friend?" the black wolf asked. "Do you need to fight? Will that help you blow off some steam?" Kane spread his legs, ready to reciprocate.

Sighing, Grigore lowered his head and tucked his tail. He gloomily headed toward the estate. "No, I don't want to fight, at least not you. Let's go back home. You're right, I need some sleep."

"Grigore, it seems dark now, but things will work out," Kane bumped his snout against Grigore's side in reassurance.

"Let's hope." Grigore heaved a sigh.

Chapter 22

Kat woke from her slumber, stretched, and arched her back before glancing at the clock. She felt wide awake at six in the morning. After she met the man and the wolf, she'd had many restless nights, filled with wild dreams. This morning, she felt refreshed and energetic. Maybe going for a hike before Grigore arrived would warm her up. The fire had died in the night, allowing the frigid dampness to collect inside the cabin.

Kat threw the blankets back and slapped her arms for warmth against the chill. She yanked on jeans, a heavy sweatshirt, and slipped on the slobber-covered bunny shoes. Memories of the previous night made her smile. The wolf made a game of tugging her shoes and licking her toes. She wished she could feel comfortable with the man. Wouldn't it be interesting if they were interchangeable? Like in her dream. Laughing at the fantasy, she lifted the shade and gazed out the window.

Grigore said it would rain. The heat of the bright sun evaporated the gloom, which bloomed into a beautiful day. A strong wind blew the white clouds across the sky and pushed storm clouds closer. Kat thought there would be time to go for a walk before the rain started. She built a fire, pulled on shoes, fastened her jacket, and shut the door behind her.

Grigore had the list of items to complete if he arrived before her return. Kat deviated from the usual path to explore a new direction. The way she felt this morning, she needed some new diversions. She'd rely on her memory to find the way back home, as if that had helped in the past. Maybe it would be a good idea to find a map of the area if she planned to stay.

Kat focused on the surrounding trees to use as landmarks. She tripped over something hidden in the undergrowth. Looking down, she spotted the gnarled end of a stick. She reached down with care and pulled the branch from its hiding spot beneath the grass. She smiled. It was the right length for a walking stick. One end of the small branch had twisted, as if carved into a fancy knob for a cane. The other end tapered to a point. Nature's artistic designs were amazing.

Kat tapped her new treasure on the ground as an aid to avoid any obstacles on the path. She'd curve along the path attempting to stay close to the clearing and cabin. The bird's tweets and chitters occupied her mind. She wandered along until she encountered a fork in the footpath. One side appeared to be an obvious pathway. The other walkway, which barely seemed a discernable trail. It was covered with sporadic underbrush and vines. The scene brought to mind the poem "The Road Not Taken" by Robert Frost.

Kat knew Frost said, "Taking the road less traveled made all the difference." She stayed on the more prominent path. Glancing over her shoulder at the smaller trail, something shiny buried in the underbrush caught her eye. The silver object glinted in the sun's rays. She retraced her steps with care, making her way through the underbrush, and stretched to see the hidden treasure.

When she reached for the silver object, a missile knocked her down. She landed on a rock, and pain exploded in her side. Sprawled on her back, she opened her eyes, gazing at a massive black wolf, the color of a moonless night. The animal had his front paws on her shoulders, holding her down. Fear swept through her at his glare and snarl. Sharp teeth bared. His ice-blue eyes flashed with fire. She shivered in fear and groped around for the rock that she had landed on to use as a weapon.

Without warning, Kat heard a snarl approach from a new unseen adversary. The new arrival caused her to freeze with terror. She might stun one wolf with the rock, but there was no chance of escape from two wolves. A sense of doom filled her. She wished Lupescu was here. No, it was best that he stayed away. She doubted even he could fight off two opponents. She wouldn't want him hurt.

Kat swallowed hard and closed her eyes in silent prayer. She felt the pressure on her shoulders lessen. The ebony-colored wolf eased his weight off, inching backward in retreat. The new unseen wolf growled and snapped at her attacker.

The black wolf emitted a soft rumbling growl, communicating with the new wolf as it continued to back away. It circled Kat. She gasped in amazement. Lupescu had saved her. His amber fur bristled around his neck and down his spine.

Lupescu pranced between the prone woman and the inky black wolf on guard as he nuzzled and pushed her shoulder as a signal to get up. The pitch-black wolf snarled louder. It took a step forward only to be met with a resonating growl. Lupescu lunged and snapped at the larger wolf's throat.

The massive black wolf could have made mincemeat out of Lupescu. Instead, he lowered his head in submission. The creature sidestepped toward Kat's staff. He grabbed it between his teeth and jammed it into the silver object Kat had reached for. The rod triggered a mechanism that slammed the steel-tooth bear trap shut. Kat gasped in horror, watching the staff snap in two. Her hand might have been in that trap.

Kat got up and brushed the dirt and grass off her clothes as she guardedly watched the two wolves. She winced in pain and grabbed her aching side before she took a tentative step toward the trap. Both wolves growled in unison. Lupescu stepped between her and the offending object.

Kat talked to the wolf with a tremble in her voice. "It's okay, boy. I want to get rid of this horrible thing before that monster, the poacher, can reset it. I wouldn't want any animal stumbling onto it by mistake."

Lupescu hesitated. His eyes narrowed in suspicion. He stepped aside, watching her, just in case something went wrong. The black wolf tried to intervene. A glance from Lupescu stopped him. They both scrutinized her movements. Kat used another branch as a lever. She wedged the branch into the metal frame of the trap, prying it loose from the ground. She took a step toward the black wolf, stopping at his low growl. Lupescu maneuvered between them.

Kat squatted down, keeping her eyes averted in submission. Her heart still raced from being knocked down in the ebony wolf's attempt to save her. She gave a tentative smile. "Thank you for helping me. You don't seem as tame as Lupescu, but you know him. I'll do my best to get rid of any traps, so you and no other animals get hurt."

Kat grasped the trap and held it by the chain as if she were holding a dead rat by the tail. "I'll get rid of this, so it won't be used again. Maybe Grigore will know what to do with it. Lupescu, are you coming?"

Chapter 23

Grigore nudged her hand with his nose and gently pushed her with his side, guiding her in the right direction. Turning back to face his large black friend, he growled at the merriment in Kane's glacial eyes. "What are you laughing at, Kane?" Grigore spoke in the pack's Versipellian language.

"Nothing. I never thought anyone would turn the great Grigore Lupescu into a lapdog." Kane grinned and answered in the special way the pack communicated. In this form it made communication easier when humans were around.

Snarling, Grigore chased Kane deeper into the forest to avoid being seen. He jumped into the middle of the larger wolf. The pair tumbled on the ground in a mock fight, and then they ran and jumped with bursts of speed. Grigore bumped Kane with his shoulder to veer him away from the cabin. He watched Kat, hoping she wouldn't get lost again. The two paused on a bluff that overlooked the river. They spotted a deer in the distance, tempted to chase it across the expanse ahead. Looking at each other, they let the moment pass.

"Kane, thanks for saving her. What were you doing out there?" Grigore's brows drew together in contemplation.

"I thought I'd watch your true-mate when you weren't around. Trouble seems to follow her," Kane said.

"She has a knack for needing to be rescued." Grigore grinned and watched her from a distance. Kane's comment sank in. He frowned and snapped at Kane. "She's not my true-mate."

"If you say so." Kane shrugged.

"We had this discussion. It can never happen." Grigore shook his head. Sadness filled his gray eyes. The attraction was inevitable, no matter how much he fought the pull. His destiny as Alpha decreed that he marry an Alt or a werewolf.

"You can pass the responsibility to your brother, Geofri. You'd be free to have her as your mate." Kane pointed out, knowing Grigore took his responsibility seriously.

"That isn't a possibility. He's too pretentious. Can you imagine him in charge?" Grigore gave a scornful laugh. "The last time I saw him, he remained obsessed with his royal position. He likes to impress the females."

"Like another wolf, I know." Kane responded, his eyes sparkling. "You're right. He isn't ready to lead the pack."

A sudden noise brought their attention back to the river below them. Kat stepped onto the riverbank. Her heel slid into the mud, and her arms swung wildly as she lost her balance. She took a step forward with her other foot, trying to regain her equilibrium. That made things worse. Both her feet slipped out from under her. She threw the steel-tooth trap up in the air, and bounced down the slippery slope on her backside. She landed with a loud slurping splash in the wet muck at the edge of the river. She looked up at the steel trap falling straight for her head.

Grigore shook his head as he watched Kat heave herself up and dive to the side. The trap barely missed her as it landed with a splatting thud on the waterlogged ground. She lay face down in the slick slime of the boggy riverbank. She groaned and pushed up with her hands. The cold mire oozed between her fingers.

Rising to her knees, she pulled free from the mud. She groaned, covered in mud from head to toe. She tugged the trap until it was free from the thick sludge and then rinsed her hands in the river. Exhausted, she lifted the metal contraption and started toward home.

"It appears your true-mate needs your help again," Kane stated the obvious and tried not to laugh. "Maybe you should mark all the trails with a ribbon, so she won't get lost. No, I know a better way. Put a leash on her to keep her within easy reach."

Grigore growled and snapped good-naturedly at Kane, "Very funny. She's not my true-mate. You might be right about confining her though." He ran down to the bank and sat on the edge watching Kat. He glanced at Kane on the bluff and gave a slight nod before he returned his attention to the bedraggled woman.

"Lupescu, it seems I wanted another mud bath. Want to come join me?" Kat laughed when he took a step back. "Yeah, I know that's a dumb question. I need to figure out how to keep my balance while I'm getting up the slippery bank." She lamented and shook the grime from her free hand. The pungent smell of the mud clung to her flesh.

Grigore glanced around and spotted a stick that would aid Kat in gaining the needed balance to get out of the situation. He retrieved it between his teeth, dragged it to the edge and pushed it toward her with his nose. She grasped it with one hand, still holding the trap in the other.

"You're so well-trained," Kat beamed, "Watch out. I'm throwing the trap up to the top of the bank. I need both hands to get out."

Kat dug the end of the branch into the sticky wet earth for support on her trip across the river. With effort, she made her way up the slick slope. Hauling herself over the edge, she flopped down to catch her breath. Lupescu sidled out of her reach and watched her.

Kat chuckled. "I don't blame you. I wouldn't want to touch me either." Drained of energy, she boosted herself upright with the aid of the stick. She said, "It's time I head back. I bet Grigore is already fast at work and wondering where I am."

Kat started in the wrong direction, which would take her deeper into the woods. Lupescu shook his head and nudged her with his nose until she took the right path. Kat stroked his head and grinned at the wolf. "I bet you'd never guess that I have a horrible sense of direction."

Grigore gave a mirthful yap, seeming to agree with her.

With Lupescu's guidance, the rest of the return journey remained a peaceful and uneventful walk. Kat didn't see Grigore anywhere when she walked into the yard. Lupescu disappeared into the trees. She stumbled up the stairs onto the porch. With his hypersensitive hearing, he heard her mutter, "Good to see you, Lupescu. I wish you'd stay, but I know you enjoy roaming the woods."

Grigore transformed into human form as he ran deep into the woods. He located the clothes hidden earlier, dressed, and ran to the cabin clearing. His eyes flared when he spotted Kat on the deck. Heat flowed through his veins as she wiggled those curvy hips, peeling down the wet denim bit by bit to expose her lower body. The moisture on her naked skin gleamed in the sunlight. He licked his lips. Her muscles flexed attractively with each move she made.

Grigore's breath caught in his chest as she pulled off her shirt, unveiling the hidden treasures beneath. Her baggy clothes usually concealed her curves. This view of her stimulated parts of his body he didn't want to think about right now.

Chapter 24

Cold and tired, Kat dropped the trap on the ground and surveyed the area to ensure no one was around. She unlaced and kicked off the wet, mud-covered boots. Her white socks, now dull brown, clung to her feet like a wet second skin. She scraped them off. With a wiggle of her hips, she peeled down her soggy, grimy jeans. She slipped out of the jacket and tossed it on the pile of dirty clothes. Her shirt and underwear remained. She grabbed the waistband of the sweatshirt, lifted it upward, tugged it over her head, and threw it on the pile in one motion. The cold air hit her wet flesh, and she shivered. Her nipples hardened and pressed against the lace of her bra. The dank, musty smell of the river clung to her body. Reaching for the door handle, she heard a familiar voice call out her name.

"Kat, isn't it a little cold to be outside with so few clothes?" Grigore's amused voice came from behind her.

Squawking like a strangled chicken, Kat ran into the house and slammed the door. She leaned against the rough wood. Her head tilted back against the hardwood as her heart raced. She panted in distress and bolted away at a light tap on the other side. She scrambled to the far side of the room near her favorite chair, where she snatched the fleece throw off the chair and wrapped it around her torso. The sandalwood scent of the man clung to the fabric after he had wrapped it around himself in the faucet fiasco.

"Kat? I didn't mean to startle you. I arrived at the wrong time. I'll go chop more wood while you get dressed." She caught a hint of humor in Grigore's tone.

"It... it's okay." Kat stammered, heading to the door that divided the main room from her bedroom. "Come on in. I'll go into the bedroom and dress."

Kat closed the bedroom door when she heard the back door open and shut. She grabbed the first outfit she saw and slipped into the bathroom for a quick shower. She closed her eyes, relishing the sensation of the hot water sluicing over her ice-cold skin, massaging away the aches and pains. Instead of just a shower, she would have loved to soak in a tubful of hot water. She imagined Grigore's fingers caressing her flesh with soap lather.

No other man made her feel the way he did. His slightest touch could ignite. The overwrought woman climbed out of the shower and grabbed a towel. She moaned as the rough texture grazed her sensitive nerve endings, assailing already fraught emotions. Kat dressed, slipped on the pink bunny slippers and wandered back into the living room. She blinked at the flash of heat in the handsome man's eyes when he spotted the slippers.

"Sorry, I'm late. I had to take care of a little repetitive problem this morning." Grigore's lips quirked at the corners.

"I hope it isn't too much of a problem. If you need to go, I understand." Concern filled her eyes.

"It's contained right now," Grigore said. Mischief danced in his eyes.

"What's on the agenda for today?" Kat hoped to continue the pattern of being in a different room while he worked on repairs.

"I thought we'd go to town for supplies. We need them before we continue. We can have lunch in town." Grigore leaned against the counter with an air of nonchalance.

"Can't you go without me?" Frantic, Kat looked around the room for an excuse to stay.

"I thought you might need some personal supplies. Besides, the ride goes faster with someone to talk to," Grigore responded.

At Grigore's comment, Kat nibbled her lip in panic, trying to come up with an excuse. Reluctantly, she agreed when she couldn't find any. "You're right, I do need things."

Chapter 25

Lists in hand, the twosome climbed into Kat's borrowed pickup as they chatted. Grigore shook his head as he watched Kat press against the truck door to avoid touching him as he drove. Her tension felt palpable. He could taste the bitterness of anxiety. It filled the truck. He could hear the erratic beating of her heart and smell the scent of her disquiet.

Grigore turned a corner sharper than necessary to throw her against his side, even with her seat belt fastened. He reached down, touching her arm with his fingertips, feeling a shock as if lightning flowed between them. He heard her pulse race through her veins. The acrid scent of her fragrance mixed with sweet arousal floated across the cab to fill his nostrils.

"Are you alright?" Grigore said in a soft, soothing baritone. His thumb caressed her forearm. He smelled the subtle decrease in her anxiety.

"I'm fine," Kat answered curtly and swallowed hard.

"Why are you uncomfortable with me? Have I done something?" Grigore's thumb brushed against her soft skin in a hypnotic, calming gesture.

Tension flowed from Kat's body. She gazed at him for a moment before she answered. "You didn't do anything. I run from anyone I'm attracted to. It's a holdover from my stepsister stealing all the guys I dated. You've always been helpful and sweet."

"Sweet? What every guy wants to hear," Grigore teased. He grinned at her, and his eyes twinkled. Kat returned his grin. "I could say you're comfortable, like Kim Darby told John Wayne's character in True Grit."

"Would that mean I'd sleep with you like she did?" Grigore laughed. His body tightened at the thought. He wanted to pull her into his arms, to press her delectable body against him. He feared she'd demand he stop so she could get out of the truck. There was no way he'd leave her alone to get into trouble again. At least for a short time, he contained his "little repetitive problem" with him on this trip to town.

"You know that's not what I meant." Kat's cheeks tinged light pink. "Keisha used beauty and a wiggle of her hips to get what she wanted."

"You're pretty when your cheeks turn pink." Grigore smiled, and heat flared in his eyes.

His words caused more blood to flood her cheeks, changing them from light pink to bright rose. Kat said, "You make me blush more than any time I can remember in a long time. Most guys prefer someone with experience."

"Kat, I only say things I mean. You're beautiful," Grigore said. "Your ability to blush shows you have an air of innocence a lot of women don't have anymore. It's refreshing." He slid his hand up her forearm, entwining his fingers with hers. He drew her hand to his mouth and kissed the back of it, lowering her hand still clasped in his.

Kat didn't pull free. Grigore saw a smile play on her lips. Her fragrance shifted as calm flooded through her. "Is your house in this direction?"

"No, it's the other way. Some time, I'll take you there." *When you're ready for the shock*, he added silently. "This is the way to the town, Wolf's Haven. It is a small town about thirty minutes away. We can get what we need there," he said.

Grigore mused about how she would react to the knowledge that the occupants of the town were actual wolves—werewolves. People established the town decades ago, before automobiles made travel to the city more convenient. The town lycanthropes were all part of the Versipellis pack under his protection. Some grew up there running businesses, and others retired in the area after years of service. Wards guarded the entrance to the town to keep people from stumbling into it.

"When I came to my family's cabin, I drove straight from the city. I thought we'd drive back there for what we needed. I'm glad a small town is this close," Kat said. Grigore watched, pleased as she seemed to admire the beautiful scenery of the area.

"Good thing this is close. The rain will be here soon." His thumb brushed back and forth across the back of her hand.

Kat gazed out the window to scrutinize the ominous black clouds. "I can drop you off at your house on our way back," she said. "I bet your place is pretty."

"Some think so." Grigore chuckled, thinking fondly of the mausoleum-like monstrosity. "It's larger than your cabin."

"I bet your family enjoys spending time throughout the year. How big is your family?" Kat asked and glanced at him.

Grigore gave a wry chuckle. "Too big to count. It's a large, extended family. They're all over the place. I have several brothers and a sister I'm close to. My brothers are scattered all over, and a little brother, much younger than I am, is still with my parents. He's a whelp." A loving smile crept across his face. He loved his family, no matter how aggravating they could be. His family accepted many people including a lot of wayward Alts, as part of the extended pack.

"Whelp? What an interesting thing to call your brother." Kat glanced at him with a quizzical tilt of her head.

"You'd have to know him. The term fits because he's always on the prowl and thinks he's quite the ladies' man." He said, doing a quick save for the slip of his tongue. Humans called their offspring children and teenagers. The pack called theirs cubs and whelps.

"I suppose most teenagers are on the prowl for something." Kat laughed. A cheerful sound that sent heat through him.

"True, but annoying to an older brother." Grigore chuckled. "The last time I saw Anton, he copied Kane with his leather jacket and sunglasses. Anton drove Kane up the wall, mimicking his movements." He gave an affectionate grin at the memory. He'd forgotten his friend couldn't turn a corner without his little brother right on his heels. Better Kane than him this time. Anton had emulated both on more than one occasion.

"Kane?" Kat blinked, puzzled.

"A friend of mine. Maybe you'll meet him sometime." Grigore responded. *In human form.* A smile played on his face at the thought of this little kitten meeting the formidable big bad wolf.

"I want to meet some other people. I plan on living here for a while." Kat nibbled on her lower lip and stared at the buildings in the small town.

Groaning inwardly, Grigore watched her lip wiggle in a sensuous dance against her upper teeth. The main road contained the bank, grocery store, hardware store and a few other scattered between them. When he parked near the hardware store, Kat jumped out of the passenger side before he could move around and open her door.

Chapter 26

Kat stood beside the truck and gawked at a large two-story building with a brick front. The architectural style was at least two hundred years old. Large windows were across the front, and a short corridor led to the door. The windows had displays of various types of machinery and household appliances. There were no bars or other protective devices over the windows. In the city, someone would have destroyed the windows long ago.

Kat scanned the surroundings as Grigore walked up beside her, placed his hand against her lower back, and guided her inside. His light touch elicited a familiar warm tingle.

"We'll get the house supplies first, and then go to the grocery store. There's a great little diner where we can eat lunch," Grigore said in her ear. His warm breath brushed her neck, setting her skin on fire.

"Lead the way." Kat noticed they were the center of attention. The clerks inside were solicitous and dropped what they were doing. Everyone followed Grigore's movements and saw to his needs. She looked at him with a question in her eyes. He shrugged in response. Kat felt like a specimen under a microscope because of the attention of people examining her. She moved closer to Grigore.

Sensing Kat's unease, Grigore moved along the aisles, grabbing tools and supplies. He could smell the curiosity of the townspeople. Word spread that he had been spending time with the strange human woman. One thing about small towns, everyone knew everything about everyone and what they were doing. The news spread faster than a forest fire in California. He could have ordered the supplies to be delivered, but she'd be suspicious. The woman insisted on asserting her independence and paying for anything he bought.

Grigore slid his hand from Kat's waist and touched her hand in reassurance. He couldn't reprimand or command the others in the store without increasing her disquiet. When they finished their business under the watchful eyes of the clerks and customers, the pair approached the counter. Placing their purchases on the counter, Grigore gave a snarl only the lycans could detect, "Do you always stare at new customers?"

The others in the store dispersed through the building and turned their backs on the duo. Some customers disappeared through the door, escaping outside so they could spread the word of Grigore and the human's arrival.

"No, sir, they're a little curious, is all. We don't have many strangers in town." The clerk answered as he rang up the purchases and bagged the items. "Do you want this on your bill?"

"No, I'm paying." Kat jumped in before he could say anything. She pulled out her wallet, frustrated when she noticed Grigore's covert nod of assent to the aged man waiting to be paid.

"Walter, this is Kat. Kat this is Walter, a longtime friend of the family." The older Versipellis lycanthrope maintained a covert position of guard with his role as store proprietor. The lycans in the town helped monitor any strangers in the area. They reported any irregularities to the main estate. Many appreciated living near the Alpha knowing that he would keep them safe. All lycanthropes in the store and outside would overhear the conversation and pass on the information.

The gray-haired man looked at the younger man with wide eyes at the mention of her name. Grigore smiled, and his eyes filled with humor from the man's response. Walter knew the family's true nature and caught the irony of the match between a wolf and a cat.

Walter's eyes filled with kindness. He bobbed his head at Kat and said with a hint of a southern drawl, "Nice to meet you, ma'am. I hope you'll come back again. I promise no one will be rude next time. We don't get many visitors here."

"Nice to meet you, Walter. They're curious," Kat said with a warm smile, hoping to make him feel more at ease.

Lifting his head, Walter returned her smile, little dimples showing in his round cheeks. "Thank you for your business, ma'am."

"I plan to live here for a while. It's good there are friendly people around," Kat bantered with him and glanced around the store. Walter's eyes twinkled with merriment.

"I've known him for a long time." Grigore exchanged another covert but meaningful look with the older man. "Walter is a good friend. He'll be glad to help."

"Yes, ma'am. Ask if you need anything." Walter nodded.

"I will." She gave him a kind smile. "You can call me Kat."

Grigore again placed his hand on the small of her back to guide her out the door. This time, people filled the street, gazing furtively their way, instead of gawking at her.

Chapter 27

The rest of the shopping adventure followed the same course. Kat felt the hair on the back of her neck prickle from staring eyes. When she glanced back, no one appeared to be looking. It unsettled her. As they wandered down the street window shopping in the pleasant atmosphere, Kat's stomach rumbled loud enough for Grigore to hear.

"Let's go to the diner," he said. The corners of his mouth quivered upward. He clasped Kat's smaller hand and tugged her across the street. Kat enjoyed this excursion, amazed at how fun being with Grigore could be. She found herself relaxed and enjoying his company. She felt safe. He appeared to have fun with no ulterior motives.

The pair walked hand in hand toward the small country cafe. They came to an abrupt stop when a woman with glistening black hair and flashing brown eyes flowed toward them with rehearsed seductive ease. Kat blinked and watched in fascination as the woman approached, her hips swaying rhythmically from side to side. The ba-pa-boom, ba-pa-boom of drums seemed to sound in the background with each flowing step the woman took. She walked like a street walker was the only way Kat could think to describe her movements.

Kat had never seen such long, sleek legs as the ones that extended from the woman's short leather skirt. Her hips swayed with a smooth, silky grace without missing a step in black high-heeled boots. Short black hair framed an angular face, which emphasized her classic beauty. The woman knew how to apply makeup to highlight her features. Kat observed that the woman's red-painted fingernails matched her lipstick.

Approaching Grigore, the svelte woman stood eye to eye with him and slid her hands upward across his chest in a seductive caress. She draped stylish wrists across his shoulders. A gold charm bracelet jingled as she moved. The long, slim fingers of one hand ran through his thick brown hair. A manicured nail flipped a curly lock from his forehead. Her lips pressed against his clamped lips in a devouring kiss. She leaned against his chest and tilted her head, deepening the kiss, oblivious to the fact Grigore stood stiffly, an inactive participant.

Kat felt Grigore tighten his hold on her hand and used his free hand to push the woman away from him. He pulled Kat closer against his side and introduced the two women. "Roxie, this is Kat. Kat, this is Roxanne."

"My friends call me Roxie," the woman said with disdain as she dismissed Kat without a glance. "Grigore, I heard you've chosen a true-mate at last. I'm so excited about the news. I've been waiting for a long time. I thought you'd never pick and now we can..."

Grigore cut her off with a growl. "We can do nothing. I don't know where you heard the news, but I haven't chosen a true-mate. I've told you before, we aren't true-mates, Roxie. The necessary chemistry isn't there. Get it out of your mind."

"But Grigore..." Roxie's lips quivered to a pout. She tilted her head down and gazed at him through her fake lashes.

Kat watched and wondered how often she practiced that move to get the right seductive, little girl look. The memory of seeing her stepsister Keisha in front of a mirror practicing such a move flashed in her mind. Keisha told her once that the gesture had to be right to keep the guys under her control. Countless times, Kat watched that polished gesture thrown out like a fishing lure each time her stepsister reeled in an unsuspecting male.

"Grigore, chemistry isn't necessary. A mate can be chosen for other reasons, too. Being an ordinary human isn't one of them." Condescension filled her voice. Kat shrank back when Roxie turned her full attention on her. She could feel the venom in the woman's gaze.

"Roxie, there's nothing ordinary about Kat. She's extraordinary and beautiful. Something you need to work on," Grigore snarled. The gorgeous woman gaped at Grigore, and her arms dropped limply to her sides. He placed his arm around Kat, stepped around Roxie, and continued their journey to the diner. Kat ignored the stares from the crowd that Roxie's commotion created in the street.

Shocked satisfaction filled Kat. She was awed that Grigore, or any man, would turn down what a woman like Roxie offered. None of the men she knew would reject such a beautiful woman. They'd be giddy and panting from the passionate kiss. Kat smiled with self-satisfaction and realized Grigore differed from the other men in her life. He wasn't just being kind. This encounter moved him a notch higher in her book. She cared for him. She feared admitting how much she liked him. No, her feelings went deeper than like. She had fallen in love.

"What?" Grigore watched the feelings flit across her face.

"What, what?" Kat blinked and smiled at him.

"What are you thinking?" Grigore asked. "You seem lost in a dream." He gazed down into her face, and his hand caressed her arm.

Chapter 28

Grigore's attraction to Kat grew every time they were together. She didn't know how beautiful and charming he found her, which made her more enticing. Kat was a human, a forbidden fruit for him. She made him feel alive. Other women meant nothing to him and gave him no gratification. He felt selfish, enjoying her company for now. It would make it harder for them when the time came to let her go.

Kat gave a broad smile, which took his breath away. Grigore had seen her smile before, but not a full headlight on high beam radiant smile. Seeing Kat so happy warmed him deep inside. He brushed the hair off her cheek with his knuckle, surprised when her head tilted into his touch. His body tightened in reaction to her sudden openness and acceptance. They had to get past the major obstacle of him being a werewolf and, as Roxie indelicately put it, she was "an ordinary human." He found her anything but ordinary.

Laughing, the two slipped into the cafe, taking a secluded corner booth in hopes of some privacy. After the server took their order, Grigore saw emotion flit across Kat's face as if she were debating internally. She played with her straw, and swallowed asked. "What did she mean your true-mate has been chosen?"

Grigore cringed while keeping a placid mask. "Just a term. Roxie wants to be my wife. I don't love her. We grew up together. She has the idea that we're destined to be married. She can't accept that I'm not interested in her."

"But she's gorgeous," Kat blurted out.

Grigore hesitated, deciding to use wife instead of true-mate.

"There's more to consider in a wife."

"What did she mean by an ordinary human?" Kat glanced at him with a faraway look in her eyes. "Is there anything but human?"

"Roxie has this idea in her head that all people are not equal," he answered. "It's one reason she and I are not as compatible as she wishes." Even though Alts lived among the humans, they were not ordinary. Each had a uniqueness, whether it be a body feature or ability, which made them stand out from humans. Now was not the time to tell Kat. Too many other things needed explaining first.

Kat frowned. Grigore sensed the wheels turning in her head. He changed the topic. "I hope you don't mind, but I gave the grocery list to a friend. He will fill it and see that the items are loaded into the truck. The storm is getting close. I didn't know how much time we had to finish."

Lost in her thoughts, Kat blinked at the change of topic. "What? No, that's fine. Let me know how much I owe you for the bill. A good thing we made the lists out before we left." She touched his hand and smiled.

They continued talking and became lost in the camaraderie of each other's company. They didn't notice the dark clouds filling the sky until a blast of lightning flashed in the background. Thunder reverberated and rattled the windows. Grigore gazed outside to see another streak of lightning zigzag across the sky. Thunderhead clouds filled the darkened horizon, ready to burst any minute.

"We better head back before the downpour," Grigore said and tossed some bills on the table. He grabbed her hand and rushed out the door.

"You think we can beat the storm?" Kat stared at the ominous, dark sky. She stepped out the door, caught unaware by the force of the wind, which knocked her sideways into Grigore. He put his arm around her to help her regain her footing and pulled her tight against his side.

"We can try." Grigore hit the unlock button, helped her inside and settled into the driver's seat as sprinkles began splashing on the windshield. "Hang on, love. We might be in for a slow, bumpy ride."

Chapter 29

Grigore felt the wind pummel against the pickup as he pulled onto the road. The truck veered to the side, but he expertly maintained control. About halfway back to Kat's cabin, the heavens opened, unleashing a torrent of rain. The water fell with such intensity that it made an impenetrable visual barricade. Grigore fought the steering against the strength of the wind.

Unwilling to risk Kat's safety, Grigore found an open spot along the road and pulled over to wait out the worst of the storm. The rain pelted down onto the truck with a deafening barrage. The fierce wind rocked the truck with its intensity, while lightning periodically pierced the darkened sky, followed by a clamorous boom of thunder resonating through the air.

Unfastening their seat belts, Grigore moved sideways from behind the steering wheel. He wrapped his arms around Kat and pulled her back to rest against his chest. She shivered, and he slid his hands down her arms.

"Are you alright?" Grigore's mouth brushed against Kat's ear. His warm breath caressed her neck. Her heart sped up at his touch.

"A little cold. I should've brought a jacket." Kat leaned back against his warm, hard chest and leaned her head against his shoulder, closing her eyes.

"Here, put this on." With reluctance, Grigore released his hold to slip off his jacket and place it over her chest. She slipped her arms into the sleeves and rested against his chest again. He nuzzled his face against her hair in the crook of her neck and inhaled the unique, delectable scent of arousal mixed with a delicate, chaste citrus fragrance.

"Thanks." Kat squirmed, trying to get comfortable, unaware of how her movement affected the large man.

"Do you mind sitting still?" Grigore's voice was soft and husky.

"There's a lump pressing against me. I can't get comfortable," Kat said as she wiggled her behind against him again.

"If you keep squirming, the lump will get worse instead of going away," Grigore croaked, feeling his arousal press against his pants.

Hearing the change in Grigore's voice, Kat looked at him. She felt his hardness press against her thigh. Realization dawned, causing her cheeks to flame and her eyes to grow wide. She twisted around and sat stone still. "Oh!"

"Oh, is right." Grigore's voice filled with strained amusement. He enfolded Kat in his arms and pulled her tight against him to prevent any more movement. He nestled his head against her hair. With regret, he watched the meteorological storm die. But the storm of emotions continued to rage inside him.

Both were reluctant to break the serene connection. They lingered a little longer and snuggled together. Knowing the storm could unleash its fury once more, Grigore gave her hand a gentle squeeze and slid back behind the steering wheel. "Let's get you home before this thing returns with a vengeance."

"You don't think it's over?" Kat looked out the window at the clouds. They were still threateningly dark with little light between black masses.

"For the moment, but there'll be more."

He inched along the road to dodge branches and debris blown into the truck's path. When he arrived at the cabin, he parked the truck on the driveway. They surveyed the yard after the storm damage. Many fallen limbs would have to be picked up. Another trip to town for replacement shingles would be necessary. All-in-all, minor damage had been done to the sturdy little cabin.

The rain drummed down again as they climbed from the vehicle. They dashed for the cottage, reaching the steps as a deluge of rain began again. Kat fumbled with the keys, which prolonged their stay on the porch. Finding the right key, they burst inside, out of the wet. The cabin was still warm from the embers of the fire.

Standing inside the door, the pair made puddles on the floor. Kat shivered, her teeth chattered, and she pulled Grigore's coat tighter around her. This galvanized Grigore into action. He added new logs to the fire, which soon began to snap and burn.

"Seems when we're together I always get wet," Kat shook out Grigore's jacket. She whirled around at the sound of a loud thud behind her. "Are you alright?"

"Sure, a log slipped from my hands," Grigore said. He squatted, picked up the wayward log, and swiveled on the balls of his feet to hide his lower body's reaction to her words.

"I'll get some towels." Kat disappeared into the bedroom.

Chapter 30

Kat slipped off her shoes and changed into dry clothes. Heat flowed through her at the memory of Grigore in nothing but a blanket last time. She remembered how his skin glistened in the firelight. His muscles flowed in fluid motion with each movement. Her juices stirred at the remembered peek of his tight muscular buttocks and chiseled abdomen. Had that been only a couple of days ago? Now, instead of being afraid of him, she wished she'd taken advantage of the situation.

Tonight, Kat decided she would make up for lost time. Her feelings toward Grigore had made a drastic turn. She wanted him. She was falling in love with this gentle, caring man. He didn't take advantage of her or use her for his own pleasure. After all, he could have Roxie, but he chose her. He wasn't after her money. The billionaire didn't want her father's money. Lupescu Industries' net worth far exceeded her father's company's value.

Kat smiled, grabbed some towels and returned to the other room. She moved behind Grigore as quiet as a cloud in her fluffy slippers. She dropped his towel on the settee, drew back and lightly popped him with the towel in her hand. He growled and swung around, grabbing for the towel she held. Kat squealed, jumped back, tangled her oversized slippers in the throw rug and fell backward in front of the hearth.

"You little devil. You're going to get it," Grigore growled as he grabbed the abandoned towel off the stool. He spun the towel and popped it at her, missing on purpose. The air swooshed against her as the towel flew by her side.

"Oh yeah? You couldn't hit a fly." Kat giggled, rolled over, and crawled out of reach. She snatched a pillow from the couch and threw it, hitting him in the chest.

"We'll see, said the wolf to the kitten." With a silver glint in his gray eyes, Grigore stalked over, pinned her to the floor and bopped her with the fluffy green pillow. Tossing it to the side, he positioned his hands and knees on either side of her. With a wicked grin, he grasped both her small, delicate hands in one of his enormous paws. He stretched them above her head and tickled her with his free hand.

"No! No fair," Kat cried out as she squirmed and rolled to get away. He held her hands fast and left her with nothing but the fuzzy rabbit slippers to defend herself. She pushed at him with her covered feet.

"It's an attack of the killer rabbits." Grigore laughed as he shifted positions to hold Kat down with his torso. His free hand tugged at one of the offending slippers and pulled it off her foot. She stared at him as he lifted the house shoe to inhale the heady aroma. He slid the soft, fluffy obstacle along her pink cheek. The luscious man gave a low rumble at her gasp. Her pulse raced against his hand as her mood changed from playful to aroused.

Grigore emitted another soft growl, tossed the shoe over his shoulder and tickled her foot. "I always thought your bunnies would be your downfall."

Kat's foot tingled from Grigore's touch. The warmth flowed upward into her leg like a snake slithering into the heat of the sun. She convulsed and hissed when he touched a sensitive spot on her toes. The titillated woman renewed her struggle to get away from him.

Transferring Kat's wrists into his other hand, Grigore reached for the other rabbit with his freed hand. Despite her wriggling beneath him, he removed the offending object. Her eyes grew wide when the bulge in his tight pants pressed against her inner thigh.

Kat shifted positions and hooked her bare feet together around Grigore's waist, out of his reach. Realization struck at how bad an idea this was when he rocked against her and pressed his hardness between her legs. She looked into Grigore's eyes and saw a hungry fire burning within their depths. One of his hands still held her wrists. The fingertips of his other hand stroked her cheek. His thumb feathered across her rosy lips. His eyes appeared to glow with silvery phosphorescence as his head descended, and his lips met hers in an airy kiss.

Grigore pulled back from the kiss. Kat lifted her head and flicked her tongue out to trace his lips. With a rumble, he deepened the kiss. His lips parted and she tasted the potent mix of saltiness and fresh anise. Kat parted her sensitive lips and felt his tongue slip deep in her mouth, exploring. Her hips gyrated against him, lost in the kiss. An aching desire to run her hands through his thick curly hair filled her. She craved to find out if his chest hair felt as soft as it appeared, to feel the warmth of his flesh against hers.

Grigore groaned. His mouth left a trail of kisses along Kat's chin, across her jawline and down her neck. The sound of her blood roaring through her veins filled his senses. The pungent scent of her body inflamed him. He wanted to devour her. Ardor filled the air, causing his nostrils to flare.

Grigore's mouth continued its downward journey, stopping at the soft flesh of her throat above her artery. The coppery scent of blood raced through Kat's veins. Her pulse was an erratic throb against his lips. Her blood-filled nipples pressed into his chest. She arched her back as he licked and nibbled on the inviting neck. His teeth lengthened and grew sharper. His beast wanted to claim her. The animal instincts of his wolf side vied for control. His primal animal urged him to take her. Claim her as his mate.

Now.

His.

The woman belonged to him. A low guttural rumble escaped from deep within him. Grigore fought the primal impulse growing inside. He fought a rampant internal battle. This wasn't the time. Too many things were in the way. Decisions had to be made. Kat needed the truth of his true nature so she could decide on her own. He moved his mouth back to her lips, gave her another hard kiss and ground his hips against her. He was on fire from the electrical current that flowed between them. Groaning and asserting his willpower, he released her hands. With a low howl, he pushed away from the beautiful woman.

Grigore leaned back and gazed down at Kat when she gave a soft whimper. He untangled her legs from his waist. He found first one, then the other discarded slipper and slid them back on small, attractive feet.

"I didn't mean for things to get out of hand. I need to go. I'll see you tomorrow." Grigore helped Kat off the floor and disappeared out the door.

Kat stared in a confused daze at the closed door. Her mouth gaped open as she wondered what had happened. Through a foggy consciousness, she spotted his coat by the fire, grabbed the denim garb, rushed onto the porch, but didn't see him anywhere. She sighed. The gloomy day reflected her mood. At least the rain had stopped. The sogginess of the porch boards soaked through the furry slippers, and she went back inside.

Next time, Kat would ask the bewildering man what had happened. Maybe Grigore was dating someone else. He didn't go for Roxie, but the woman said he had a mate now. He probably already had a girlfriend and had gotten lost in the heat of the moment.

Kat heaved a sigh of discontent and went through the evening's routine in a mechanical haze. She wished Lupescu would show up. Craving the company of a wolf was ridiculous. She shook her head and decided it would be a good idea to get a pet for company.

Chapter 31

Grigore transformed into wolf form as he ran into the woods. He gave a burst of speed, pushing himself to the edge. What was he thinking? He hadn't been. The closer the full moon got, the harder it became to control his need to claim his true-mate. He'd have someone lock him up in one of the dungeon cells at the estate unless another solution arose, he couldn't claim Kat as his true-mate. He didn't feel the exertion in his muscles from the adrenaline flowing through his body.

He stopped and pivoted at a familiar scent behind him. He snarled, "What are you doing here?"

"What? I can't go for a jog in the woods? When did you make that rule as Alpha?" Kane jogged in front of him, looking casual and blasé.

"Jogs are allowed if you're not playing watchdog." Grigore exhaled loudly. He appreciated his friend watching over him most of the time. His mood darkened. He wanted solitude to work out the turmoil of his thoughts and emotions.

"Nope, as a wolf, I don't play dog." The large black wolf sniffed the air and smirked. Grigore knew he could smell the human woman's arousal on him. The wolf continued, "Unlike some who are lapdogs these days."

Grigore snarled, trotted off, and stopped when he heard Kane's next comment. "I thought you should know Elena is looking for you."

"What does she want?" Grigore sighed and looked at his friend.

"I'm not sure. Maybe it's because your parents are arriving from Romania in a couple of days." Kane shrugged his shoulder and trotted off in a different direction. He knew he had Grigore's full attention, "Oh, and Roxie came by to see you, too."

Whirling, Grigore ran in front of Kane, glaring at him. His tone was a low snarl. "What?"

"Roxie came by. She left excited when Elena told her you found your true-mate." Kane stopped and licked an imaginary speck of dirt on his leg.

Baring his long, sharp canine incisors, Grigore snapped at Kane. He knocked him down with his front paws. "Why are my parents arriving? I know about Roxie."

"You're up to date then. I thought you were lost in your own world with your lady love, and not getting any information. I'm impressed. Of course, I heard about a minor scene in town that involved all of you today." Kane said. His eyes sparkled with mischief. He dodged sideways to avoid Grigore's snapping teeth.

"Kane, I'm not in the mood." Grigore snarled. He hung his head and walked off into the woods.

Kane looked at his friend and acknowledged that something was wrong. Sniffing the air, he caught the scent of confusion and sadness. "Elena sent for your parents with the news that you had found your true-mate."

"When are they arriving? Maybe I can stop them." Not waiting for an answer, Grigore growled an obscenity and bolted for the estate, unaware Kane was on his heels.

Grigore reached the house with his sides heaving. He didn't bother to change into human form. He lunged through an open window and ran up the stairs to his sister's room. "Elena!" Grigore's bellow reverberated through the hallways as he approached her room.

Elena heard him and peeked out the door, whispering, "Do you mind? Lower your tone. The cubs are trying to sleep. At least they were until you came in yelling loud enough to wake the undead."

Grigore slanted his gaze at his sister and stalked toward her. He snarled under his breath. "What's the idea of sending for our parents with the news I have a true-mate?"

"Is that what this is about? I was a dutiful daughter. They'd never forgive us if you go through the mating ritual without letting them know. They wanted to come and meet her first." The shorter woman stretched and yawned as if the topic bored her.

"She's not my true-mate. How many times do I have to tell all of you?" Grigore's voice grated. He transformed into human form, throwing his hands up in the air.

"Until you believe it yourself, brother dear. Maybe you should open your eyes and quit lying to yourself," Elena said. She stood with her hands on her hips and watched her beloved brother pace.

"It won't work. She's human. She doesn't know what I am." Grigore had too many responsibilities to let his infatuation go any further. He'd find someone to do the work at the cabin and let Kat know he could not come anymore. The thought of not seeing her again tore at his heart.

"Then tell her," Elena said. "It can work out if you want it badly enough. It's obvious that the chemistry is there." She sniffed the air and gave a knowing smile. She patted his shoulder for reassurance. "When are you bringing her over to meet us?"

"I must tell her about the family first. Our family isn't one you pop in on without prior notice." Grigore ran his fingers through his hair as he imagined Kat's reaction to seeing the family in lupine form or lying around nude, both forms natural to them.

"Things will work out. It did for Andre and me. Go to bed. You'll be up early going back to her cabin." Elena went into her room, quietly closing the door behind her. Grigore stood alone in the hallway, deep in thought.

Chapter 32

The gray haze of daybreak slanted through the cracks around the window shades, waking Kat. She snuggled under the piles of blankets, resisting the call of nature, and stayed in bed longer. She had no reason to begin the day. Yesterday started with a bang and then fizzled. She couldn't face that again today. She closed her eyes, determined to sleep in. Why get up early? Grigore wouldn't return after her forwardness last night. She didn't have the skill to seduce men like Keisha did.

Kat heard a persistent banging as she drifted in the hazy twilight zone between sleep and wakefulness. First, she heard a light tap but it became a loud thump with intermittent pauses. Now it had progressed to a loud, thunderous bang.

Fuzzy-headed, Kat dragged herself back into the land of the conscious. The fog in her brain cleared, and she realized someone was pounding on the door. A high nasal voice shouted from outside. "Katarina, I know you're in there. Katarina, open the door."

Kat groaned in recognition of the thin nasal voice. She rolled onto her side and pulled a pillow over her ear. The relentless banging continued. Sighing in resignation, she kicked the covers off, slipped on sweatpants and a t-shirt, and slid her feet into the house shoes.

Kat staggered to the door in a groggy stupor, opened it and stared at the mousy man at the threshold. A short, thin man stood there shivering, bundled in a parka and dingy gray pants. His greasy topknot of hair peeked out of his hood. She said wearily, "What are you doing here, Craig?"

"Is that a way to greet your boyfriend? I drove a long way to see you. Aren't you going to invite me in?" Craig's petulant voice clawed at her nerves.

"Craig, you're not my boyfriend," Kat said. *And never will be.* "You need to leave. I dated you so Keisha's date would go out with her. There's nothing between us." She pushed the door shut, but he shoved it open. The move surprised her and revealed he had hidden strength.

"You're not dismissing me. We had a fun time. We can be more," Craig groused and reached for her. He puckered and tried to wrap her in his arms for a kiss.

"Let go, Craig." Kat struggled and pushed his chest. Relief washed through her at the sight of Grigore walking around the corner of the house.

"I believe the lady said leave," Grigore clenched Craig's parka hood in his fist. The larger man yanked the bully backward off his feet and easily flung him off the porch.

"Lady? Kat's no lady. I had her, and it's apparent she's putting out for you. She's desperate and has sex with whoever shows her attention. She even had her bodyguard. Are you in it for the money, too?" Craig shouted. He staggered as he tried to keep his balance before he fell and landed at the edge of the stairs.

"Apologize to the lady." Grigore snarled and snatched another fistful of parka. He pulled Craig close, almost touching his nose with the smaller mans. Grigore glared into his seedy eyes. Craig stumbled backward when Grigore released his hold on the parka. The momentum caused the lean man to stumble backward on the stairs. He landed prone at the bottom.

"I won't apologize for the truth," Craig whined as he pushed himself to his feet.

Grigore started down the stairs. Kat touched his arm to get his attention. Hesitating, he looked over his shoulder, gazed into Kat's eyes and acknowledged the unspoken message. She watched him take a deep breath to calm himself. Craig scrambled backward in a crab walk toward his car. "Don't touch me, or you'll hear from my attorney. I'll sue you."

"If you don't leave now, you won't be able to contact your attorney. Get in your car and go. I wouldn't recommend that you stop in town either. They don't care about strangers who molest women. Never come around Kat again, or you'll deal with me." Even though his voice grated, its softness surprised her. Kat saw silver flare in his eyes as he glared at the groveling man. She knew these were the same silver eyes she had seen gazing through her patio door. "Isn't there something you want to tell the lady before you leave?" Grigore turned his back to Kat. She heard him growl, and a terrified look came across Craig's features.

"I'm sorry, Katarina," Craig spit out the words as if it left a foul taste in his mouth. He climbed into his car and sped away, tires spitting gravel behind him.

"Thank you, Grigore. I'm glad you showed up today." Kat said. Relief flooded through her as she took a deep breath and blew it out slowly. The thudding of her heart slowed back down to a normal beat. She couldn't look him in the eyes, fearful of what she'd see there. She turned her back on him and started back into the house. Fighting back tears, her voice quivered. "He's right. Guys date me for my money or to get in good with my father." She hung her head and ran up the stairs.

"I told you I'd be back today." Grigore placed a hand on her shoulder, turning her to face him. He cupped his hand under her chin, tilted her face and gazed into sad, sky-blue eyes, seeing the shimmer of tears in their depths. "Kat, anyone who doesn't see your true beauty is shallow and not worthy of your time."

"Then why did you run when I showed interest in you?" Kat sniffled, trying to turn her head away. A single tear escaped from the corner of her eye.

Grigore brushed the tear away with the pad of his thumb. "I didn't run away. I left before more happened. You felt my body's reaction to your touch. I left before I lost control. I didn't want you to think sex is why I'm interested in you. There are too many things we need to talk about first."

When a man told her that he needed to talk, the situation never boded well. Last night, their petting on the couch got heated. Kat never got that carried away or felt such hunger for a man. She'd never done more than kiss. None of the kisses affected her the way his did. They started an inferno burning inside her. Compared with Grigore, she felt nothing for the others. Grigore's slightest touch set her blood on fire. Like now. Kat leaned her cheek into his hand and felt warmth flow through her body, like a wildfire out of control.

"We can talk over breakfast, if you prefer." Kat noted his distracted gaze straying toward the woods. Following the line of his vision, she saw the large black wolf in the shadows at the edge of the forest.

"I would, but I can't. Something unexpected has come up that I have to deal with. I'll return tonight if I get this resolved. Please stay close to the cabin today." He brushed his lips against hers in a feather-light kiss. His hands dropped to his sides, and he headed off toward the tree line.

"Is the hunter out today?" Kat called after him, but he'd already vanished into the trees.

Chapter 33

What is it? I told you I'd be back for the meeting." Grigore growled at the waiting black wolf. He glanced up to see two other wolves behind him. When he acknowledged them, he became aware there was a problem. "Marcus, Andre. What's wrong?"

"An attack occurred last night. We think Moog's pack was involved. We were going to wait until the meeting, but Andre had concerns about Elena hearing that the danger is this close." Marcus glanced around at the group.

"Let's find a more secluded spot." The wolves went deeper into the forest, into a thicket of trees, guarded with a wild growth of tangled briars.

Inside the hidden alcove, Marcus spoke, "The attack happened at the headquarters in Paladin's Portal. A hodgepodge of misfit Alts went in and attacked Artie, the Keeper. Luckily, the Portal has a protective spell that prevented them from creating much damage. It's neutral ground. Artie banned the group from returning. They demanded information about the location of Kuspe's Key. Artie sent an emissary to our pack and the other heads of the various Alt groups as an alert."

"What about the keys?" Grigore knew the keys were powerful talismans. The group that attacked must not have realized Kuspe's Keys are comprised of seven different keys, not a single key. Each key gave the holder different powers. Together, the keys wielded extreme power for the bearer. The ancient Alts and deities battled for the keys. Deities sought the power to create a world where they were once again worshipped as they were in the past. Wise ancient Alts gained control of the keys, dispersed them and hid them with safeguards so the keys would never come together in one place. The knowledge of the locations remained a well-kept secret. The ancients all hid one, telling no one the locations. If all parts of the key were found, Moog would have unlimited power.

"They got nothing. No information and none of the keys." Andre shifted on his feet and glanced around the area. He sensed something had to be wrong. He tilted his head and listened.

Chapter 34

Kat took the laundry outside to hang on the line while she enjoyed the sunshine after yesterday's torrential downpour. A distant noise caught her attention as she reached to clip a sheet to the thin wire. She dropped the sheet back into the makeshift clothes basket and headed toward the edge of the clearing, where the noise had come from. The noise sounded like a cry of pain. She closed her eyes and concentrated. Her eyes popped open in recognition of a wolf's howl of pain. Was it Lupescu? She hadn't seen him for a couple of days. Was he hurt? Did a poacher get him?

Filled with apprehension, Kat disregarded Grigore's warning to stay near the house and tore into the woods toward the sound of pain. She thrashed through the undergrowth in a direct path toward the pitiful wail. She ignored the scratches from low-hanging tree limbs. The coppery scent of her blood floated on the wind and mixed with the dank smell of the dead leaves along the path.

The sound of the howl grew louder, and she sped forward even faster. She slowed her approach as the sound grew louder. She needed something to defend herself in case a poacher was there, so she picked up a short, thick branch to use as a club. Using her free hand to part the leaves in front of her, she glanced through the natural camouflage.

At first, Kat didn't see anyone or anything, but a movement near the base of a tree caught her eye. A wolf had been captured in a steel trap. Not just a wolf. A cub, its leg ensnared in the teeth of the contraption. It was a miracle that the appendage hadn't snapped in half from the force of the trap clamping shut. She sidled from behind the tree and murmured to the helpless cub. "I'll free you from the trap."

She realized that the wolf cub panicked from her human scent causing it to be unable to focus on her soothing words. She watched his renewed struggle against the trap. The spiked teeth cut deeper into his tender leg, and blood dripped from the wound. Then she heard a faint howl in the distance. Dubiously watching her, the cub gathered courage and strength, calling back with a weak howl.

Chapter 35

Grigore raced over the terrain and howled in reply. He heard the familiar voice respond and changed directions. Cresting a hill, his preternatural vision focused on the wolf cub imprisoned in the steel snare. He ran at full speed with the others on his heels. The big brown wolf lunged over the edge of a cliff and transformed into human form as he hit the ground near the trap. The steel teeth bit into the cub's tender flesh. Strong human hands gripped the cold, cruel steel trap and snapped it open. The metallic scent of blood assailed his nostrils, and he could taste the cub's bitter fear. He eased the damaged paw free from the steel jaws and cursed under his breath at the familiar female gasp behind him.

Grigore cradled the cub in his arms and pivoted to face Kat, watching emotions play across her face. She looked back and forth between him and the wolves that flanked him. Man and wolves all froze, staring at the woman. Her blue eyes scanned over him, growing wide at his nudity. Amusement flashed in his eyes for a second when her gaze stopped at his naked manhood. "I see you heard the distress call, too," he said.

"You... you're nude," Kat stammered in shock, mouth open. She remembered the poor cub in Grigore's tender grip and tore her gaze away to stare at the cub cradled in his brawny arms. The cub's mangled leg bled from the ruthless teeth of the trap. She spoke through gasping breaths, "I tried to free him. He feared me and fought the trap. I thought a hunter had gotten Lupescu. I came to find him."

The wolves glanced at each other at the mention of Lupescu. Their attention focused on her. Kat looked back and forth between the man and wolves, blinking in recognition of the big black wolf. She hadn't seen the other two before. She took a step towards Grigore and the cub but froze when a big brown wolf closed in. With sharp teeth bared, the big brown wolf advanced. Kat looked up at Grigore. "I can help. I'm afraid he could lose his leg."

"I'll take him back and bandage it. It'll take time to heal." Grigore watched the woman. He knew she hadn't seen his transformation from his wolf form.

"Please, Grigore. Let me see what I can do. I feel responsible for part of the damage. I... I have a bit of a healing touch. Trust me, please, Grigore." Taking another step forward, Kat stopped at another snarl from the brown wolf.

Grigore felt torn but relented. "All right." Andre would do anything to protect his son, and Grigore wanted the best for his nephew. Furthermore, Kat needed to know he trusted her. He would give her a brief chance. "For a moment." The brown wolf shot Grigore a pointed look and stepped closer as the human approached the cub.

Kat inched toward Grigore and placed her fingertips on the cub's injured limb. He whined at her touch. She cupped the fingers of both hands around the gaping bloody wound, careful not to touch it. The injury exposed the bone. She closed her eyes, concentrated, and prayed her special gift wouldn't fail her. It had been years since she'd tried anything this complicated.

Kat pushed the doubts from her mind and focused on the wound between her hands. A tingling warmth flowed from her body, down her arms and into her hands. The air jumped with static electricity as the area around the wound heated. Again the cub whined. The same brown wolf took a step closer but stopped when the others stepped toward him.

An incandescent force field formed around the wound, glittering and shimmering through Kat's hands. The woman took a deep breath and focused her energy on the affected area. Her hands functioned as a conduit that healed the wound. She sensed the wound closing. Starting at the bone, the tissue grew and reformed as it knitted together to repair itself. The tendons, blood vessels and muscles reconnected, forming new tissue. The scent of blood faded as flesh covered the veins and arteries. Kat smiled at the sensation of the reformation of the animal's leg in her cupped hands. She slowly stopped the flow of energy between her and the wound. The wound was not completely healed, but nature could take over. The radiant light dimmed as she closed the mental connection, and she swayed under the unusual strain.

"I think it worked." Kat smiled at Grigore before she crumpled to the ground.

Chapter 36

Andre sniffed the area where fresh flesh covered the old wound. He examined the new tissue. "There is barely a wound. Grigore, you didn't say she was an empathic healer."

Grigore gently laid the cub on the ground and knelt by Kat. He lifted her head to rest on his bent knee, cupping the back of her head in his hand. He caressed her cheek. "Kat, are you alright?"

Opening her eyes, Kat glanced into Grigore's worried gray eyes. She smiled. "It worked. I thought I had lost the ability. I'm glad I haven't."

"Yes, it worked. Why didn't you tell me you had healing powers?" Grigore brushed her hair from her face with his fingertips.

"It's not something that comes up in conversation. I can stand up." Kat inhaled and swayed but stood upright. She focused her attention on the cub and the other wolves. She noted one less wolf and another naked man on his knees beside the wolf cub. "Where did that man come from?"

Embracing the cub in his arms, the second nude man faced Kat and spoke with a French accent, "Thank you for healing my son's wound. I'm not sure the wound would've healed correctly on its own."

As he finished speaking, the cub's body transformed. The limbs lengthened into a new angle, and hair receded from his body within seconds the wounded cub transformed into a naked little boy. Kat gaped at the scene and she backed toward the trees. She whirled and ran in fear and confusion. Kane, still in his wolf form, intercepted her. Grigore walked over and placed his hand on her shoulder. Kat's attention was drawn back to the brown-haired man and the child. She became transfixed by the interplay between the pair.

"What are you doing out here?" Andre gave a menacing growl to the young cub-turned-boy.

The boy said petulantly, gazing up at his father. "I wanted to see Uncle Grigore. I didn't see him yesterday. I tracked his scent."

"How many times have you been told to stay with the pack? This could have been worse. The hunter could have found you and made your hide into a fur coat. At least, you didn't attempt a transformation. The damage could have been irreparable." Andre gave another ominous snarl, with his brow furrowed in fear.

"Are you mad at me, Papa?" The cub looked at him with big puppy eyes.

Melting, Andre shook his head. "*Non*, I'm not mad. You're lucky you didn't lose your leg or have that hunter find you. Rules must be followed. Number one is to stay with the pack."

"Yes, sir, I will. I wanted to explore the woods, like you and Uncle Grigore." The boy reached for his father's hand and glanced over at his uncle.

"We'll explore another time. For now, we go back home." Andre held his son in his arms as the pair walked off into the woods. Grigore and the black wolf stayed behind with Kat.

Seeing the end of the absurdly unbelievable scene, Kat bolted into the woods. Unprepared for her movements, Grigore hesitated for a split second before chasing after her. Kat ran. She tripped over a log buried in the underbrush and fell. She scrambled on all fours before she regained her footing and took off again. The tears that filled her eyes didn't help her escape. A branch caught in her hair as she dived sideways to dodge a sound in the rustling underbrush.

"Kat, stop, so we can talk. You're going to hurt yourself. You're already bleeding," Grigore pleaded.

"Go away. I never want to see you or any of your wolves again." The fleeing woman freed her hair from the branch. She darted under the tree, her retreat thwarted by the black wolf's unexpected appearance in front of her.

Grigore came up beside her and held his hands out toward her, palms upward. "At least let me get you back to the cabin safely. You could get hurt in your state of mind."

"He can take me," Kat stabbed a finger at Kane, "but I never want to see you again."

Feeling helpless, Grigore glanced at Kane, receiving a nod in response. "As you wish. He'll guide you safely back. I hope you reconsider and let me explain."

"What's to explain?" Kat shook her head, refusing to think of the irrational things she had seen today. "No, it's best if we end it. All right, doggy, let's go."

Snarling at the term, Kane pushed her hand with his snout, trotting in front of her. Kat sniffled and traipsed down the path behind him, trying to make sense of what she'd seen. She mumbled, "Men and kids who turn from wolves into boys. Fresh air isn't as good for me as I thought. That's it, I'll leave. Once I get back to the cabin, I'll pack and go. Find somewhere sane. Yeah, right, there is no such place." Lost in her thoughts, she didn't realize they were back at the cabin until she stepped into the clearing. The black wolf disappeared into the trees without notice.

Chapter 37

Kat sighed and went inside, the basket of clothes forgotten under the line. She sat in front of the fire's remnants, motionless and numb as she debated what she should do. She had opened herself up to him. He acted as if he cared about her. She fell in love. Blinking at the revelation, she acknowledged the truth. She loved him. Her head dropped as a feeling of defeat deflated her energy. It was time to leave. Dazed, she got up and went through the motions of packing. Locking the door, Kat blindly drove her truck toward the city.

She looked for the turn into Wolf's Haven but didn't see it. She sped down the road in a stupor, jerking her attention to the rearview mirror at the sound of a siren behind her. Cursing, she glanced at the speedometer. She hadn't been speeding. She grumbled and pulled over. "Yes, officer?"

"Ma'am, I need you to come with me." He stared down at her with eyes hidden behind his dark sunglasses.

"What did I do?" Kat felt as if she'd been hit in the gut. *What else would go wrong.*

"Sorry, ma'am, you can come peacefully or..." He reached for his cuffs, his hand on the butt of his gun.

Kat argued. Muddled thoughts raced through her head. Could she get away? She glanced at the man's hand on his gun and realized she couldn't outrun a bullet. "No, I'll go with you. I'm sure this is a misunderstanding." Kat swiped the back of her hand over her wet eyes, locked her truck, and climbed into the back of the police cruiser.

"I'll have someone pick your truck up later." He drove off with her in the back seat.

Making a u-turn, the officer headed back toward Wolf's Haven but passed the turn. Halfway back to her cabin, he took another road and followed it for an indeterminable amount of time. She didn't remember seeing this road before. He drove down another narrow dirt road, increasing Kat's apprehension. Had the kidnappers found her? Anyone could get an elaborate disguise.

"Tell me what you want. Where are you taking me? We passed the town a long time ago. This isn't even a road." Kat glanced at the door and saw no lock or window control on her side.

"We're almost there." Ignoring her questions, he pulled onto a well-maintained double-wide asphalt drive. The ride seemed to take forever until he stopped at a huge wrought-iron gate with a golden wolf looping around a calligraphic L. The cop spoke into an intercom at the side of the road. The gates opened.

"No! I demand you let me out. You can't keep me prisoner here." Fear filled Kat. The car doors didn't have any handles. She pounded her fists on the window in frustration.

Stopping the police cruiser in front of an immense mansion, two men dressed in jeans and black T-shirts came out to meet them. One of them was a huge dark-haired man with glacier-blue eyes, like the black wolf. He had to be at least six and a half feet tall and all muscle. The other one was a shorter, blocky man with red hair and a beard. His muscles bulged beneath his tight T-shirt. Kat spotted several wolves standing in the distance. She checked all directions and noted that Grigore wasn't anywhere in sight.

A blonde woman stood on the front porch beside the brown-haired man that had been with the child from the woods. This time, they wore clothing. As the sheriff opened the back car door, she debated whether to balk at getting out or make a run for it. Kat looked around at all the people present. They were all bigger and probably faster than she was. Fighting or running would be futile. Taking a deep breath, she resolved to make the best of the situation. She would memorize things and escape later, as if her memory had worked great for her so far.

Kat climbed out of the car with her head held high, pushed her shoulders back and walked between the two guards onto the porch. She opened her mouth to accuse them of kidnapping her but snapped it shut as the woman approached excitedly. The brown-haired man was on her heels.

"Andre, she's even prettier than you described her. I didn't think my brother had such good taste." The gregarious woman bounced across the porch where she stood. Kat felt fear and anger surge through her.

Chapter 38

Kane told Elena that the woman planned to leave, but instead of bothering Grigore, Elena called the sheriff to detain her. After all, the town residents were werewolves and knew this woman was Grigore's true-mate. Keeping the woman off guard, she gave her a bright smile. "My name's Elena. You've already met my true-mate, Andre. He told me what you did for our son, Daniel. Thank you so much. I wanted you here to show my gratitude."

"Your son?" Kat's anger became confusion. She looked from the man to the woman and back.

"The cub you helped save from the trap. He's our oldest child and impulsive, but he worships my brother, Grigore. Yesterday, he didn't see him. He hoped he could track Grigore's scent. He's doing well for such a young age, too." Elena slipped her arm from Andre's and moved to stand by Kat.

"How old is he?" Kat felt dumbfounded and continued the charade of the conversation.

"He's seven. I told him you were coming. He wants to thank you too. I made him lie down and rest. His leg looks great. I insisted he regenerate the remaining tissue on his own." A worried frown creased her brow.

Kat blinked and bit her lip as her mind tried to digest the woman's casual comments. She answered as if this were a normal conversation. "The rest will do him good."

"Now, let me show you to your room. My parents will be here before long to meet you." The bouncy woman slipped her arm around

Kat's and started into the house.

"Hold it. Hold it right there. What do you mean by my room? I'm not staying here. If I stay, I will go back to the cabin where I've been living. Are you holding me captive after you kidnapped me?" Kat broke free from the woman's grasp, facing her with hands on her hips. Her sky-blue eyes grew as dark as a storm cloud.

"Kidnapped? Where did you get that silly notion?" Elena gave Kat a mortified look and congratulated herself on her acting ability. Then she smiled. "I wanted to show my thanks. I thought you'd rather stay here. It's much more comfortable. Let's talk. I want to learn more about you. The sheriff left, but someone can give you a ride if you prefer that drafty cabin." She motioned toward one man at the bottom of the stairs.

"No, I'm sorry. I didn't mean to offend you. It's been a taxing day. Please show me the room. I'll stay one night." Exhaustion overwhelmed Kat. When would the nightmare end? Heading into the house, the woman slipped her arm back into Kat's.

"You'll be a delight to have around. How long have you been an empath?" Elena resumed her natural bubbly demeanor as she led the stunned woman into the house.

"A what?" Kat blinked in confusion.

"An empath. You know, a healer." Elena felt shocked that the woman didn't know the term. Grigore said Kat had repressed her ability.

"I've always had it. After my mom's death, my stepmother forbade me to use it. People considered me strange and avoided me. My special ability hampered my stepmother's interaction with the upper social class. I still practiced healing animals when there was no chance people would see me." Realizing the irony of her statement, Kat flinched, glancing at the woman.

"You'll be able to perform your skill here anytime. We welcome anyone who has a special gift. How can we refuse other Alts when we are Alts?" Elena looked at her.

"Alts? What's an Alt?" Kat again nibbled her lip.

"Alternates. People who differ from the mainstream. There are more Alts in this world than people admit. We're the ones that people have designated as myth and legend. Some call us monsters. A lot of humans can't tolerate anyone different. If they knew we existed, they'd hunt us down and kill us. As a myth, they can enjoy the idea of imitating us. Ironic, isn't it?" Elena gave an effervescent, contagious laugh that filled the room.

Kat gave a weak smile and shook her head. "But you... you can turn into a wolf."

"And you can heal people with the touch of your hands. Does that make us different in the eyes of ordinary superstitious humans? At one point in history, you would have been considered a witch and burned at the stake," Elena shrugged and walked through a doorway. She motioned toward the contents of the room. "This will be your bedroom, if it's acceptable."

The elegant furnishings astonished Kat. The cabin would fit inside this artistically decorated room filled with antique furniture and a massive ornate European-style bed. Gold leaf highlighted the wood carvings on the bedstead, and an impressive marble mantel surrounded the fireplace. Her stepmother would be envious. "This is way too much. This must be for royalty. It isn't for me."

Elena smiled, knowing the woman would become royalty when she married her brother. She paused in closing the door to inform Kat of the evening's events. "I'll see you at dinner in the dining room. Tonight is a special evening. We have a surprise guest."

Holding her hand up before Kat could interrupt, she pointed at the large armoire in the corner. "I'm sure you can find something to wear in there. We can chat more later. I must check on my cubs." Giving Kat another of her radiant smiles, she closed the door.

The conversation preoccupied Kat's thoughts as she wandered around the room to examine the contents. How could such a beautiful woman be a wolf? Is the other beauty, Roxie, a wolf? This day had been confusing. It had to be a dream—no, a nightmare, and she'd wake up soon. She needed to sort out and muddle through her confusion.

Walking across the large room, she fell backward onto the bed, sinking into the soft feather comforter. The adrenaline rush from this morning had faded and drained her energy. She couldn't believe what the day had entailed, and it wasn't over yet. She closed her eyes and found herself adrift in the soft cloud of a dreamless sleep.

Chapter 39

Andre hugged his wife. "Does Grigore know she's here?"

"Does it matter? He'll be glad to see her. The poor girl must have been shocked to find out about our true nature the way she did. The dunce should have told her long ago. There isn't much time for her to adjust before she meets the family at dinner. Our parents should arrive by then. Meeting her will be the first thing they'll want to do." Elena straightened her husband's tie and ran her fingers through his hair. "We'll find out if he knows the woman is here when we walk into his office for the meeting."

Sauntering arm in arm into the office, Andre escorted his wife to a plush chair in front of the desk. He acknowledged the others gathered in the room as he sat beside his wife. He observed Grigore through hooded eyes.

"Thanks to you, Elena, our parents are arriving this evening," Grigore said with resignation and nodded toward his sister. He caught a whiff of Kat's scent in the house. It must be his overactive imagination and his desire for her to be with him. Kane had told Grigore that Kat planned to leave. Her decision was best for her. Alts treasured her healing abilities, but their interest in the ability did not guarantee her safety in the impending conflict. Grigore rubbed a hand over his tired eyes and returned his focus to the group in front of him. "Marcus, do you have the documents and new identity in place for Kane?"

"Yes, things are all set. He leaves tonight to start his infiltration into the enemy pack." Shuffling through his briefcase, Marcus placed a folder in front of Grigore. "This is the driver's license, passport and dossier about his new identity. Cyber-databases were correlated to confirm this information, if anyone searches. Kane has been briefed."

"Kane, are you sure you want this? You know how dangerous it will be." Grigore worried about his friend, but Kane was the best operative they had. Sometimes the large man didn't always take his safety into account.

"It's for the good of the pack and the other Alts. The key must remain secure. I'm packed. I'll leave after the meeting." Kane appeared at ease, his legs stretched out, crossed at the ankles. The stillness of his body belied the tension inside.

"Don't you want to stay for dinner?" Grigore extended upraised palms and raised his eyebrows at his friend.

"No, I'll head out. I can get there and scope out the bar before midnight when the patrons become active." He brushed an imaginary piece of lint from his black T-shirt.

"Marcus, what about you?" Grigore looked over at the brown-haired man.

"I'll head to the city in a couple of days. Paladin's Portal will be my temporary headquarters. The delay in my departure will allow Kane to establish himself without drawing the suspicion of too many lycanthropes arriving at the same time. I'll relay information and be a liaison for Kane. While doing his dossier, I created a new identity for myself as well." Marcus, an Arthurian knight turned technical wizard, placed the items back into his briefcase. He had planned every minute detail.

"Good plan. Neither of you should put yourselves in danger." Grigore knew that telling Kane to be careful was useless. He jumped headlong into danger. He could blend in most situations for someone large and intimidating.

Hearing a knock on the door, Grigore checked the identities of the newcomers on the security camera before disengaging the security system. Moving away from the desk, he opened the door. "*Tata*, Mama, welcome. Please join us. Did you have a pleasant trip?"

"Grigore, my *prețioase fiul*, precious son, the long trip is worth it to meet your *colega,* your mate. Where is this delightful woman your *soră*, sister, has told us of?" Sweeping into the room in a black cape, the tall, elegant woman hugged Grigore before she took his arm and dragged him to Elena's chair. "My *prețioase fiica*, my precious daughter, I'm glad you called us about your *frate's colega*. He would not have allowed us the privilege of coming to his *împerechere*, mating ritual."

The white-haired man towered over his wife. He took her hand in his and led her back to the door. "My *dragă*, dear, we have interrupted something important. Perhaps Elena will take you to see the cubs before we discuss this."

"As you wish, my *inimă*, heart." Affection shone in their eyes as they gazed at each other.

Elena hesitated and gazed over her shoulder before she departed with her mother. "Yes, Mama, there is much to tell you." The two women disappeared through the door, lost in conversation.

The elegant patriarch glided with confidence to the chair behind the desk that Grigore had vacated. The regal man leaned back in the leather chair, glancing at each man in the room. "Give me details of what has occurred."

Closing the door, Grigore typed in the security code. He and the others told his father, the *Regele Alfa*, high alpha, about Moog, the attack and the plans. Grigore left out any details about his interactions with Kat, other than the incident with Daniel and the trap.

Chapter 40

A knock on the door woke Kat. Brushing her hair from her groggy eyes, she glanced around the darkened room. The shadows of dusk filled the recesses of the room, and Kat realized she had been asleep for a while. She shook the cobwebs from her head at the sound of another knock and focused her attention. "Come in."

The door creaked open a crack, and a gray-haired woman peeked around the edge of the door. "Miss, dinner will be served soon in the dining room. Do you need any assistance?"

"Sorry, I fell asleep. I can dress myself. Elena said there were things in the wardrobe." Kat waved toward the corner.

Opening the door wider, the elderly woman shuffled over to the wardrobe and opened the door wide. "Yes, Miss. She didn't know what you'd want, so she placed several items in the wardrobe."

Kat gasped at the wide array of dresses and other clothing stuffed inside the armoire. She walked over and examined the variety of attire. There were formal evening gowns and some casual pantsuits, all designer brands. Her stepsister and stepmother had clothes from these designers. "This must be a mistake."

"Oh no, Miss. Mrs. Elena chose these specifically for you. Don't you like them?" The woman gave her a suspicious look as she held the door open. "Miss, they will be waiting."

In other words, hurry. Don't be late, Kat read between the lines. She wondered how Elena had a chance to gather such an extravagant collection of clothing for her. Running her fingers over the textures of the various garments, Kat settled on a simple, sleek black dress hanging in the back. When she moved the dress she was amazed to see her fuzzy, pink slippers.

"I'll take a few minutes to change, but I don't know my way to the dining room." Kat stared at the multitude of clothes.

"I'll show you, Miss." The droll woman disappeared out the door, closing it behind her.

Kat placed a dress on the bed, stripped, and tossed her rumpled clothes to the side. Slipping the black knit dress over her head, the swing-style skirt floated down to hang at an angle mid-calf. She clasped the halter-type top around her neck. The neckline had a slight dip in the front and the back zipped closed just above her waistline. The dress suited any occasion, casual or formal. The material clung in the right places, accentuating her curves. Kat cringed when she picked out a pair of low black pumps from the bottom of the wardrobe. She almost broke her neck walking across the room the last time she wore high heels. She hoped to be more graceful this time.

Kat moved to the dressing table and peered in the mirror as she ran a brush through her thick locks, wondering what to do with her hair. She spotted a pearl-encrusted comb and piled her hair on top of her head. She placed the comb in her hair to hold it in place. A light knock sounded on the door as she finished with a touch of blush and lipstick from her bag.

"Miss, are you ready? We must not be late." The older woman's voice came from the other side of the door.

Kat glanced one last time in the mirror, patted an errant curl back into place and headed out the door. She didn't want to be late and become the center of attention. She would rather blend into the background once she was in the dining room. "I'm coming."

The talking stopped when Kat stepped through the large ornate double oak doors into the dining room. Everyone's attention focused on her. Kat's first inclination was to turn and run. She would embarrass herself or worse in the heels. Glancing around, she noted that there were several people in the room. Elena, the woman she had talked with earlier, was on one side of the table beside her husband, Andre. At the end of the table sat a man with a regal air. His long white hair hung down around the shoulders of his exquisite black evening jacket. A beautiful older woman with auburn hair streaked with white sat in the chair beside him. The woman's classical features lit up when she gave Kat a radiant smile. One glance at the pair and Kat knew from their distinct features that they were related to Grigore.

He, along with the other men, stood as she walked through the door, gave her the once-over, and nodded. Several other men and women sat along the humongous table. Across from Elena stood a teenage boy introduced as Anton, Grigore's youngest brother. His brown hair was spiked, and he had a look of curiosity on his face.

Another man came around the table. He held out his arm and gave her a curt nod. "May I show you to your chair?"

With a tentative smile, Kat linked her arm in his and followed him to her chair across from Elena. He pulled the chair out and pushed it into place. Beside her sat an empty chair. The rare gentlemanly manners of showing respect to women seemed abundant in this room.

Elena smiled at Kat. "I'm glad you are joining us for dinner. Let me introduce you to everyone. You met my husband, Andre, earlier. This is Marcus, our friend and attorney," Elena said. She nodded to the man who seated her. "At the end are my mama and *tata*, my mother and father, Cristofer and Maricara Lupescu." Elena's introductions were interrupted when the door opened, and Grigore rushed into the room. Elena's face lit up. "Grigore, there you are. I wondered if you would join us. I introduced the others to our guest."

Grigore moved to the table and sat down before he glanced at Kat. His mouth gapped open, and his eyes widened.

"Grigore don't be rude. Come greet your Mama and me. Then have a seat." The tall, elegant man admonished his eldest son.

Reluctant to turn away from Kat for fear of discovering her to be a hallucination, Grigore faced his parents. He couldn't get her out of his thoughts. Hunger for her drove logic from his mind. He thought he had imagined her faint scent this morning while talking with Anton. Each member of the family had a distinct odor, all similar through their relationship with the same parents. He often caught a hint of a difference in Anton's fragrance, chalking it up to him being young.

Grigore walked to the end of the table, kissed his mother on the cheek and hugged his father. He stiffly took his place beside Kat, at the opposite end of his father. "*Tata,* Mama, are you refreshed from your journey?"

"We had a little nap that helped offset the jet lag. The full moon will be here soon. We're looking forward to the ceremony. Where will it be?" Maricara responded in her soft lilting voice, a smile playing across her lips.

Taking a sip of wine from his crystal goblet, Grigore choked at his mother's words. Kat looked at him with curiosity. His sister chimed in before he could regain his composure. "It hasn't been decided yet. Won't it be fun to help plan the details, Mama? It'll give us all a chance to know each other better."

Cristofer glanced at Grigore, sensing things weren't quite right. With a smile, he changed the topic. He would find out the truth from his son later. "Did Kane leave already?"

"Yes, I saw him off before dinner. He should be settled in tonight." Grigore could feel Kat's eyes on him.

"Good. Marcus, when do you leave?" Cristofer asked.

"In a couple of days. We didn't want our arrivals too close together in case it raises suspicion." The man who guided Kat to her chair spoke. He changed the tone of the conversation for the rest of the meal, saving Grigore from any more questions he may have no answers for.

Chapter 41

The dinner dragged on forever with intermittent comments between the couple. The others there hindered Grigore's ability to talk with Kat. He wanted to explain and decipher her unexpected presence here. He knew better than to depart early with his parents in attendance. Finally, dessert signaled the end of the dinner. He wolfed down his last bite, stood, and excused himself. He captured Kat's small hand in his much larger one, pleading with his eyes. "Please walk with me. I need to explain many things."

Standing, Kat smiled at the others before following him out the door. "Thank you for the wonderful dinner. I'm delighted to meet all of you."

Grigore strolled out into the courtyard, leading her down the trail to a more secluded rose garden. "Kat, what are you doing here? I thought I'd never see you again."

"It's your sister's doing," Kat explained how Elena had the town's sheriff detain her. She watched Grigore's face, her teeth nibbling on her lower lip.

"I didn't know you were here, but I'm glad. We need to talk. I should've told you, but I wasn't sure how you would react. Telling people I'm a werewolf isn't something that comes up in conversation." Grigore faced her and took both of her hands in his. He gazed deeply into her darkened blue eyes as he futilely tried to read her mind. Fire flowed through him from the touch of their hand.

Kat pulled her hands free, turning away from him. "I felt frightened and confused when I saw your transformations in front of me. Your sister and I had a long talk. She explained things. Grigore, I have nothing to offer you."

"That's not true. I know you can feel this. The connection we have. I've seen your reaction when we touch. Even now I heard your pulse race and detected a change in your scent." Grigore placed his hands on her shoulders and turned her back around to face him. Her citrusy fragrance filled the air, floating around him. His appetite for her grew more voracious each day as the full moon approached. She must leave, or he'd be locked away during the full moon. He would be unable to control his primal need to claim his true-mate.

"Yes, Grigore, I feel it." Kat gazed into his gray eyes. He saw the fire of desire glowing in their depths and her resistance melt away. The tangy scent of arousal filled the air. Kat licked her lips, stood on her tiptoes and brushed her lips against his. The tantalizing taste of the chocolate mixed with a fresh minty flavor from the dessert filled his mouth.

Growling, Grigore pulled her to him and deepened the kiss. His tongue slipped between her parted lips, dueling with hers like a sword. "Kat, I want you so much. I want you to be my true-mate, but our liaison may be dangerous. Our pack is in the middle of a battle. You could be a pawn. Once the knowledge gets out that you're the Alpha's mate and an empathic healer, you'll be in danger."

"What's the Alpha?" Kat looked up at him with confusion-filled blue eyes.

Closing his eyes and inhaling, Grigore took her hand and led her to a bench beside a little waterfall in the garden. "The Alpha is the ruler of the pack. A prince. I'm Alpha in North America. One day I'll become the *Regele Alfa* or King Alpha of all the packs. I will inherit the title from my father."

Kat stared at Grigore with wide-open eyes and gaped mouth as she tried to digest his revelation. This man, or werewolf, or whatever, who had been fixing her cabin and chopping wood had royal blood. She'd fallen in love with a prince. "You mean you're a... a...," she tried but couldn't even get the words out.

"A werewolf? A shapeshifter? A lycanthrope? Yes, to all the above." He sighed and gave her hand a gentle squeeze before he released his grip. "I thought…,"

Cutting him off, Kat spit out, "A king!"

Grigore suppressed a chuckle. His eyes twinkled with humor as he watched a variety of emotions dance across Kat's face, that finally settled into a look of horror. "Is that bad? Is that worse than being a werewolf?"

Jumping up from the bench, Kat paced back and forth. "This is surreal. I came to the mountains to get away. Boy, did I get away from an acrid reality into a fairy tale or is it a horror story?" Throwing her arms up in the air, she stood in a daze and stared into space.

Kat heard Grigore walk up behind her. He didn't touch her, but he was close enough that she could feel heat radiating from his body. She whirled and collided with him. He lifted her chin with his fingertip and gazed deep into her eyes. "Kat, my love, I wish things were different. I'm still the same person. I want you by my side forever, but only if you want to be there."

Kat turned, but he restrained her with an arm around her waist, placing a fingertip on her lips to silence her. "I won't pressure you. I'll accept whatever decision you make. There is more I need to tell you. After we talk, you can decide what you want."

"But your parents are here for your mating to Roxie." Kat blurted out, her voice filled with irritation and disbelief.

"No, my exuberant sister jumped the gun. You're the one she told my parents would be my true-mate. Tonight, you were introduced to them. My family isn't always so formal. If you decide the answer is no, I'll explain, and we will have had a delightful visit before they return home." Grigore lightly caressed her lower lip with his fingertips.

"You're still a king or prince or whatever. I have no clue what is expected of me in that role." She gazed into his gray eyes. Her doubt showed on her face.

"Just be you. I can't change who I am." He pulled her closer, wrapped his arms around her and rested his cheek against hers.

"Why didn't you tell me any of this?" Kat pushed away and glared at him, an edge of anger in her voice.

"When would I have brought it up in conversation? The day you nearly walked off the cliff and I helped you? Or maybe the night we played with those slippers of yours in front of the fire?" A smile played across Grigore's lips.

The blood flooded Kat's cheeks, and they blossomed into a bright red color of a nearby rose. Kat nibbled on her lower lip. She twirled out of his grasp and ran down the path, pausing at his words. "Kat, please wait. Those were wonderful times… the only way I could get close to you in the beginning. You wouldn't even look at me as a man without fear flashing in your eyes. You accepted my wolf without question. I experienced such a potent attraction that I wanted to learn more about you. Condemn me for that if you will." Grigore didn't move. He waited for what felt like a heart-stopping eternity.

"You're right. When could that have been brought into the conversation? It shocked me to witness the changes and hear the child call you uncle." Kat faced him. She shook her head and sighed. Her sad eyes gazed into his gray eyes.

Grigore inched toward her, and Kat saw his face soften in relief. "Now that we're past that, I must fill you in on the rest."

Kat stared at his outstretched hand for several long minutes. Glancing up, she saw the anxious crease of Grigore's brow. She reached out and slipped her hand into his grasp. They walked in companionable silence down the garden path. While they walked hand in hand, he explained about his cousin Moog and the renegade pack formed to overthrow the current system of Alt government. His cousin's vindictive, delusional nature made him the primary target. Moog wanted command of Grigore's dominion, controlling all the lycanthropes within. He informed her of the plan in place to stop him but didn't provide any details.

"My concern is that if you accept me as your true-mate, you'll become a target for Moog. He will try to use you as a weapon against me. Word spreads fast. He'll find out about you." Seeing her dazed look, he wrapped his arm around her waist and headed toward the house with the moonlight illuminating the pathway.

"I'll escort you to your room, my love. I have business I must take care of. I'll leave you to digest the day's events and what we talked about. Elena and the others will be available if you need anything. You've already met your maid, Ilinca." Opening her door, Grigore brushed his lips against her cheek before he headed down the hall.

Chapter 42

Kat entered her room and felt drained. Her mind whirled from the clash of two realities, the one she knew, and the one Grigore represented. Lying in bed, she stretched like a cat and snuggled under the lush blankets, savoring the warmth and comfort of the large, luxurious mattress. What would she do? Kat wanted a change, but did she want one this extreme? She expected a nice, simple life in a secluded cabin, more of a hermit lifestyle. Now a king–or a prince–and a werewolf wanted her to be his true-mate. She had a feeling that this wedding didn't entail a white wedding dress in some little church. Her father would be ecstatic that she married into the Lupescu empire because he could gain business connections. He didn't have a clue they were literal monarchs or the true nature of this family.

Kat's feelings for Grigore remained the most important consideration. She couldn't deny the attraction between them. He made her blood boil. She enjoyed both the man and the wolf's company. Happiness filled her days after she met him. She couldn't imagine going back. The thought of returning to that desolate existence only brought her sadness. There could be no other answer. She needed to find him and tell him. Throwing back the covers, she jumped off the bed and threw on her clothes.

She opened the door, and Ilinca greeted her. "Good morning, Miss. The others have eaten, but the cook will fix whatever you want."

Kat hadn't noticed the time. She had tossed and turned half the night, overwhelmed by her thoughts. At some point, she had dozed off, waking with the sun shining in through her window. "Thank you, Ilinca.

Do you mind showing me the way again? I must get acquainted with the house. Is Grigore around?"

"Yes, Miss, Grigore's been up for a while. He's out playing with the cubs. He said you were not to be disturbed." The maid ducked her head and led Kat through the mazelike hallways into the dining room. They passed several wolves and people who stared at her before they scurried away.

Bursting at the seams with excitement, Kat ate a quick breakfast of toast and juice before searching for Grigore. She stepped outside and saw three cubs and a half-grown wolf piled on top of an amber-colored wolf as they tumbled around on the ground. The wolf rolled over, and she recognized the beautiful, burnished color of Lupescu's wolf's coat—Grigore's, she reminded herself.

Kat watched him with affection as he played with the younger group. Seeing his compassion and joy filled her heart with even more love and brought a smile to her face. She wondered if they'd have children. She laughed when one cub growled and pounced on Grigore. He fell over prone. At the sound of her bubbling laughter, Grigore's head popped up. He shook off the attacker, lowered his snout and nuzzled the cubs. He communicated with the half-grown wolf before he trotted over to the porch.

Kat watched his body transform into human form. She watched in stupefaction and admiration as he approached her. His hair receded into endearing short, curly tufts. Bones elongated and shifted into the familiar shape of the man she loved. Muscles rippled and flexed with each step until he stood bare-skinned beside her. She blinked mutely, awestruck at his handsome, disrobed figure. Her mouth hung open, and she tore her eyes away from his groin and looked into his bemused eyes. "I don't know if I'll ever get used to that."

"I'll help you get used to that." Grigore's eyes flashed with mirth as he watched the telltale bright pink fill her cheeks.

"You know what I mean." Kat gave his shoulder a playful shove. Her cheeks grew redder.

Grigore stepped up beside her and brushed his lips against her cheek. "Good morning, my love, did you sleep well?"

"Yes, that bed is sumptuous." Kat tried to make herself keep eye contact. Her gaze kept wandering downward over his magnificent body.

Once more, Kat ripped her eyes away. She saw amusement in Grigore's eyes. "Good. I hope it helped you think."

"Yes, I have an answer for you." Out of habit, she worried her lower lip between her teeth.

Hunger flared in Grigore's eyes. He cut her off before she could reveal her answer. "Something I forgot to mention, lupines have exceptional hearing." They noticed that the wolves and humans had focused their attention on them. "Let's go into my office. I can soundproof the room."

Keying in the barrier code, Grigore grabbed a pair of jeans from a closet in his office, slid the zipper up and left them unbuttoned. He settled in a chair beside the one she chose. He faced her. "Now we have privacy. Lupescu Industries' high-tech security system is installed. It has a sound barrier that can block hypersensitive hearing. It's a necessity for privacy with all the nosy wolves around, especially when I want the news first."

Distracted by the play of his bare chest muscles, Kat's eyes followed the thin trail of hair. She gulped when her eyes reached the point where the hair disappeared beneath the unbuttoned jeans. Her imagination kicked in, and she groaned at the picture of the zipper slipping down. She closed her eyes and took a deep breath to calm her racing pulse. Opening her eyes, she gazed at him, trying to read his hooded expression. "I gave it a lot of thought last night since I couldn't sleep. One question kept coming to mind. What does it mean to become your true-mate?"

Grigore expelled a breath and carefully worded his answer. "A better word is wife. It's the more familiar term for humans. The difference is that to a lycanthrope, a true-mate is a lifelong companion. Not all lycans are lucky enough to find their true-mate. The scent is like pheromones for attraction but much stronger. Once the scent is found, the chemistry cannot be resisted. The pair become inseparable."

"So, it's kismet? Its destiny for the pair to join?" Kat felt disappointed. Thoughts raced through her mind. *What about love? Do you love me, Grigore, or is it the chemical reaction you're attracted to? You call me your love, but is it just an endearment?*

"Yes, but it's much more. It's hard to explain. A true-mate is a soul mate but much more. True-mates have a union for life. A mark will be shared to show others a true-mate has been claimed and that the true-mate is protected and cherished. A bite and exchange of body fluids are involved. The exchange lengthens the true-mate's life if they are not a werewolf," Grigore said. Kat saw a dark intensity in his eyes as he looked at her.

Grigore knelt on one knee beside her chair. He grasped her hands in his and gazed into her eyes. "The question, my dear Kat, is will you do me the honor of becoming my wife?"

Kat's eyes filled with tears at his tender proposal. She had longed for this moment. She hoped the man who asked her that question would love her. Kat gazed at their entwined hands and wondered about the meaning of love. He'd be a delightful companion, a good father if they could have children. His terms of endearment indicated he cared for her. Kat felt his grip tighten and gazed into his eyes. "Grigore, my love, yes, I'll marry you and become your true-mate."

Grigore jumped up, scooped her into his arms and swung around. He set her back on her feet. He bent down and brushed his lips against her earlobe. His breath caressed her neck like angel wings. "You don't know how happy you've made me. We can announce it tonight. I'll give you a chance to acquaint yourself with my family. We can have the ceremony in a week."

The auburn-haired man moved his mouth along her jawline and brushed his lips against hers in a tender kiss. The kiss deepened. His tongue teased and plundered her mouth to release an aching hunger she doubted would ever disappear.

Kat wrapped her arms around his neck and held on tight to keep from drowning in her turmoil of emotions. She sank deeper into overwhelming passion. Her hunger for him consumed her. A hunger she had never experienced before. His hands pressed her tighter against his chest, molding her against his body. Her knees turned to gelatin. Her toes curled in her shoes. She tilted her head back, and her tongue dueled with his. He tasted of fire and that unique hint of chocolate.

Grigore's hand slid down her back and cupped the curve of her behind as he pulled her tight against his hips. Kat felt their hearts thud in unison. A low guttural growl rumbled in his throat. He pushed her away without warning. A fire glowed in his silver eyes as he fought for control. Her breath escaped in quick gasps, and she stared at him in bewilderment.

Stunned, Kat gawked at him and wondered what she'd done for him to stop so abruptly. She fought through the lust-filled haze, and his comment hit home. "I can't make wedding arrangements in a week. My father needs to be notified." She had to notify her family. There were many things to arrange.

"You can work out the details with my mother and sister. There's a church in Wolf's Haven, or we can have the ceremony in a garden here." His voice was a gravelly growl.

A muffled rhythmic cadence, too steady a beat to be someone knocking, beat against the outside of the door. Grigore and Kat gave each other a curious glance. He placed his hand on the small of her back, guided her to the door, typed in the security code, and opened the aperture.

Sitting lined up in a row against the door were three cubs eagerly wagging their tails as they watched the pair emerge. Grigore burst into laughter at the excited trio. "What are you three rapscallions doing here?"

"They're such cute wolf cubs." Kat snatched up the smallest cub, scratching her behind the ears.

"Cute? These three fur balls were trying to listen into our conversation." Grigore choked back a laugh.

"But they're cute..." She started before Grigore interrupted her.

"Remember, things aren't always as they seem. If you're going to say cute little cubs, it's true, but they're also my nieces and nephew." He picked one up, ruffling the fur, while the cub licked the side of his face.

Kat's eyes grew wide at the reminder. The wolf cubs were human or at least could take human form. She sat the wiggling creature back on the floor. "Oh, I forgot."

Grigore enfolded her hand in his, squeezed and gazed into her blue eyes. His gray eyes filled with sadness. "Like a ship in a storm, rocks have smashed your reality." It must be hard to accept the existence of creatures from horror stories."

Kat's heart overflowed with love. Her heart went out to Grigore when she saw the concern in his eyes. He'd be a wise and compassionate leader for the lycanthropes. An excited yip reminded her of the three energetic cubs at her feet. Kat laughed at the rowdy trio, who almost knocked her down as they jumped around her feet with excitement. Catching Kat's elbow, Grigore prevented her fall, affectionately chiding the trio. His parents, sister, and brother-in-law surrounded them in the hallway. He laughed. "Your little spies need to be more careful."

"Spies? I don't know what you're talking about, dear brother. You're the one who encouraged them with the roughhousing." Elena teased Grigore as she slipped her arm around Kat's. Maricara took her other arm and headed down the hall. Kat blinked, speechless between them. "Come along, children. The men want to talk."

Chapter 43

Grigore watched his mother and sister hustle Kat around the corner, his protests ignored. Andre and Cristofer directed him back into the office. Filled with apprehension, Grigore keyed in the code and faced the two men already settled into chairs. "Has something happened to Kane?"

"No, nothing like that." Andre sat impassively in his chair.

"What's wrong then?" Grigore watched the pair with suspicion in his eyes.

Cristofer leaned back in the enormous leather chair behind the desk and scrutinized his son, his forefinger tapping his lower lip.

"Tell me what's going on? What's so urgent?" Grigore growled with impatience.

Leaning forward, Cristofer steepled his fingers and rested his elbows on the edge of the desk. The regal male watched his son for a moment before he spoke. "Patience, *fiul meu*, I have told you many times, you need patience in your position."

"Forget patience. What's going on?" Grigore gave a low growl in his chest and ran his hand through his hair.

"The waxing gibbous of the moon is affecting him more than we thought." Andre ignored Grigore and focused his attention on Cristofer.

"Perhaps. We both know once a true-mate is identified, the primal urges are stronger until after the claiming ritual." Cristofer sat back in the chair to observe his eldest son.

Grigore snarled and paced the length of the room and back. "I'm still waiting for an answer."

"*Fiul meu*, this is but a taste of what you will experience once you are mated. You will think you are in charge, but there will be times it is much easier to do as your true-mate wishes." The corners of Cristofer's lips twitched in repressed merriment.

"The ladies asked us to talk with you while they got better acquainted with Kat." Andre looked at Grigore with laughter in his eyes.

"There isn't a crisis to deal with?" Grigore's irritation turned into relief.

"None that the ladies won't take care of. Today they only require our presence at lunch but not before then. Maybe we have time for a run in the forest." Andre gazed out the window.

Chapter 44

The two women's constant gregarious chatter overwhelmed Kat. The announcement hadn't been made about their engagement, yet the women acted as if they knew. Their excitement spread to her. She liked these two ladies. Her mind worked through the events of the day, and she found herself not really listening to them. The pair were making plans of some kind, but the details were vague.

"What do you think, Kat?" Elena's question broke through her mental distraction

"What? Oh, I'm sorry I didn't hear your question." Kat gave Elena a blank stare.

Both women grinned and twittered knowingly. "That's okay. I remember my shock when Andre asked me to marry him. We had always been at each other's throats." Elena smiled and repeated her question. "Would you like the wedding in one of our gardens? Have you seen all of them?"

"We haven't announced anything yet." Kat gazed at the women in confusion. Everything moved too fast. Her father needed to be told.

Both women froze, stared at her, and asked in unison, "Did you say no?"

Uncomfortable in the sudden strained silence, she regretted her comment. She hastened to regain the affable atmosphere. "I said yes. We're announcing it later."

They sighed in relief and began the excited chatter once more. Elena hugged her. "Is that all? You can still announce it. The others will be as excited as we are."

Both women shot questions at her, like a machine gun firing. "Do you have any idea what style of dress you want? Will one of the gardens suffice? Do you prefer a church? How many guests do you have in mind? Who will walk you down the aisle?"

Kat's head reeled from the barrage of questions. The women were oblivious to the fact that the questions were unanswered. In a daze, she watched the two flutter around until a comment brought her out of her stupor.

"There is much to accomplish in a week." Elena bustled around the room in excitement.

"What? It'll take longer than a week to complete all the plans. My father will need time to re-arrange his schedule." Kat burst out flabbergasted. *Why did everyone keep saying a week? Too many things had to be done. How could a wedding be planned in such a brief time?*

The women stopped again and gave each other a knowing glance. Elena asked with a solemn expression, "When do you want the ceremony?"

"Maybe a month, maybe longer to complete the arrangements." Out of the corner of her eye, Kat saw the women covertly glance at each other.

Elena took the role of spokesperson for the women. "Do you want a big wedding?"

"No. There are still a lot of things that need arranged. I need a gown. My father's schedule will need to be re-arranged. He's busy. He can't do things on short notice." Her dad would be pleased she was marrying a Lupescu. He would come to the ceremony.

"We'll aid you with anything you need." Elena soothed and patted Kat's arm.

"Won't your *Tata* drop everything for his *fica's* wedding?" Maricara's accented voice chimed in. Kat stared at her blankly until the meaning of her words sank into her subconscious.

"Some things he can't drop." Kat swallowed hard and gazed at the older woman. That must seem to be a poor excuse since they had arrived in a helicopter to meet their son's intended. Maybe the real reason that she wanted to delay things was to give her time to come up with an excuse for her stepmother and stepsister not to be at the wedding. She didn't want them there. She knew Keisha would make a play for Grigore. Carolyn would see the situation as an advancement in her social status. "My father works a lot. I'll call him later to see when he can come. One garden would be great for the ceremony. I'm not sure which one."

"You can call him on this phone or go into Grigore's office for privacy." Elena stood to leave and gestured toward a landline on a nearby table. "If you'll excuse me, I'll go check on the cubs."

"I must check on lunch preparations. You will join us for lunch, won't you?" Maricara joined her daughter in the doorway, leaving Kat alone.

"Yes," Kat called after them, stunned by their hasty departure.

Kat stared at the phone, wondering what she would tell her father. It didn't seem right to say, Hi Dad, I'm inviting you to my wedding. I'm marrying a guy I've only known for a couple of weeks. Oh, by the way, he's a werewolf. Maybe he didn't need to know about the short time they'd been in a relationship since he was out of touch with her life. Kat took a deep breath and dialed his cell phone number.

"Kat, I'm going into a meeting. Can you call back later?" Her dad sounded distracted. There was never a good time to talk with him.

"Dad, it'll only take a few minutes. I don't know when I'll be able to call again." After Kat's mother died, he was always going into a meeting, in a meeting, or coming out of a meeting. Besides, she wanted to get this out before she lost her nerve. Her voice sounded strained even to her.

"What's so important?" Kat pictured her dad checking his watch impatiently.

"I'm getting married, Dad. I want you at the ceremony." There. Kat dropped the bombshell. She held her breath waiting for his response.

"That's great. I must go n... What did you say?" He snapped.

"I'm getting married." Kat winced at the tone of his voice and sucked her lower lip into her mouth.

"When did this happen?" His voice sounded tight.

"It hasn't happened yet. I want you to give me away." Kat spoke in a quiet, tension-filled tone.

"You know what I mean. I didn't know you were seriously dating anyone. Who is the young man? I want to meet him before you marry him." His tone was terse and impatient.

"I've already decided. His name is Grigore Lupescu. I'm sure you've heard of him." Her father was familiar with all the CEOs of the big companies, having done business with many of them. Kat thought her dad would be ecstatic when he heard the name of her betrothed. Instead, silence filled the line.

"Dad, are you there?" Concern filled Kat's voice.

"I'm here. Where are you?" Kat couldn't make out the tone of his voice. He didn't sound happy.

"I'm at the Lupescu estate, near the cabin. They will hold the ceremony in one of their gardens."

"I'll be there as soon as I can. I'll cancel my meetings and drive out. Don't do anything until I get there." She could hear the grim concern in his voice.

Memories of her father's stories flashed into her mind. Kat asked him in a soft voice. "Dad?"

"Yes, kitten?" His tone had softened.

A shiver ran down her spine at the endearment he hadn't used in years. "You remember the stories you told me about the big hidden house with all the special people? Now, I know they're real."

"Kitten, I'll be there as soon as I can." Silence came from the other end. Stunned, Kat hung up the receiver and stared off into space until she heard a noise behind her.

"Kat, what's wrong?" She saw Grigore leaning against the doorjamb. He watched her with guarded eyes.

Love flooded through Kat at the sight of him. The panic she felt at her father's reaction subsided. "My dad's coming for the wedding. He'll be here as soon as he can. There is so much to do."

"We will all chip in. You will be amazed by how quickly we can complete it." Kat buried her face against his chest.

"I came to escort you to lunch. I wanted time alone with you." Grigore nuzzled against her silken hair. Kat felt his warm breath against her neck. His hands traced over her curves as he cradled her against him.

Kat gazed at him with loving eyes and slipped her hands around his neck. Grigore said, "Shall we join the others?"

"If we must." Kat grinned and wiggled her eyebrows.

She heard Grigore release a little groan as he led the way from the room. "You little tease. It's a good thing we're running late, or you'd find out what I want to do."

Kat's eyes gleamed as a shiver ran down her spine, and she mumbled under her breath. "Promises, promises."

Chapter 45

Grigore ignored her comment and led her to the yard. "Lunch is on the veranda," he said. "The ladies thought you'd enjoy the view. The day is a little nippy. I hope it won't be too cool for you. Cold doesn't bother us much."

Kat stepped through a set of oak doors with glass inserts onto a marble floor. She looked across to see the family sitting around a large wrought iron table with a glass top. This massive table sat at the center of the roomy veranda with a dome roof. A white balustrade surrounded the rounded open-air portico supported with large columns. Rattan couches and chairs were evenly spaced on either side of the sun porch. Trellises with pink and red roses entwined on opposite edges close to the house's interior walls. Their sweet scent filled the room with delicate aroma.

Kat returned her focus to the table, laden with a sumptuous array of food. She approached the table with Grigore, and the conversation ended. The men stood, and the women greeted her cheerfully. The aroma of the roses mingled with the delectable smorgasbord, gave the crisp fall morning a fairytale atmosphere.

The welcoming atmosphere was nothing like the one at home. She had walked into a dream, and she feared a rude awakening at some point. Even her dad's reaction was unexpected. Kat glanced out across the expansive view, astonished at the beautiful scene. The view took her breath away. Gardens, forests, and grassy knolls surrounded the house as far as the eye could see.

Grigore's fingers glided up the length of her arms, coming to a proprietary rest on her shoulders. He guided her into a chair. His warm breath whispered against her ear, which brought her out of her trance. "Are you all right, my love?"

Kat placed her hand on Grigore's and smiled at him before she gave a cheerful greeting to the others. "Yes, I'm admiring the beauty of this place."

"I am glad you like it, Katarina. You will be mistress of the manor after the ceremony," Cristofer said in a no-nonsense tone. Her full name sounded like a song with his lilting accent. Kat admired his old-world manners. He returned to his chair after she took her place.

Kat gasped and gazed at the faces filled with reassuring smiles. "I never considered that possibility. I keep forgetting Grigore is royalty."

"I don't feel like royalty. My thoughts tend in another direction." Grigore gave her a devilish grin, his gray eyes flashed silver, and Kat could feel her face flush with heat.

Cristofer cleared his throat. "Alas, I have tried for years to impress upon *fiel meu,* my son, the correct behavior for the position he will take one day."

"*Inima mea*, my heart, you did a wonderful job. He is as you were when you were younger." Cristofer and Maricara gazed at each other with such adoration that Kat felt a shiver run down her spine.

"Really?" A lanky youth that Kat recognized as the youngest brother, Anton, jumped into the conversation eagerly. "Did you have lots of women around when you were younger, Pop?"

The foreboding-looking older man scowled ferociously. "Anton, mind your manners. These ladies do not wish to hear such things."

Anton looked like a whipped puppy after the rebuff but bounced back with exuberance when his sister came to his rescue. "Pop, I'm interested in hearing about your younger exploits. What about you, Grigore?"

"Sure, after all, Pop, you haven't told us much about your younger, wilder days. Back then I bet you could get away with anything, right Mama?" Grigore joined in the teasing and watched his father squirm with a scowl, his eyebrows knitting together.

Cristofer growled in feigned disgust. "Children do not respect their parents anymore. I will not respond to that word, Pop. It is something a balloon does. It is not appropriate to call one's father such a name." Mock disdain filled Cristofer's voice.

"*Inima mea*, is it not patience you teach that is so important? It might be interesting to hear those tales once more." Maricara's eyes sparkled with mischief the same way Grigore's did.

Smiling, Kat sat back to enjoy the amicable banter within the family. Her family never teased one another. Her stepmother was too worried about appearances. Kat would enjoy being part of this family.

Andre leaned forward in his chair, drolly commenting in a stage whisper. "Welcome to the family, Kat."

"Andre Louvel, you stay out of this. You'll give her the wrong impression of our family." Elena sent a mocking glare to her husband with her hands on her hips. Her eyes filled with adoration and laughter.

"Yes, dear." Andre sat back in his chair, with the corners of his mouth twitching.

"Let us eat before the food gets cold." Maricara silenced the group, and everyone dived into the food.

"Thank you for letting me call my father. He said he'd arrange things for his arrival at the ceremony." Kat took a bite of a luscious strawberry. Sweetness exploded in her mouth, and juice dribbled over her lip and down her chin.

Kat glanced up to see Grigore watching her with lust-filled hunger in his eyes. She licked the juice off her lips, and a silver flame burned in the depths of his eyes. His lips parted.

"How delightful. I will have a room set up for him. Will anyone accompany him?" Maricara beamed and exchanged a hopeful look with Elena.

"I'm not sure. I forgot to ask, and he didn't say. He was going into a meeting. My stepmother and stepsister will probably come with him." Kat had the uncharitable thought they would come to be nosy.

"I'll have three rooms prepared in case." Maricara motioned to Ilinca, the maid, who stood at the entrance. The lycan maid nodded and disappeared into the house. She had overheard the conversation.

"If it isn't too much trouble, thank you." Kat smiled at the beautiful older woman. Grigore had gotten his looks from her, including his expressive gray eyes.

All the men except Grigore excused themselves when the ladies started discussing the preparations. Grigore moved behind Kat's chair with his fingers splayed against her cheek. "Mama said you might use part of the estate for the ceremony. Will you walk with me to explore another garden?"

Kat leaned her cheek into his touch with a soft sigh. "I'd love to. If the rest of the gardens are as delightful, it'll be a tough decision."

Hand in hand, the pair followed the stairs off the terrace onto a pathway that led to the Great Lawn. On the horizon, the spectacular green lawn blended into the blue-green sky filled with rolling clouds. No painting ever displayed such vivid hues. Lost in the artistic beauty of the view, Kat didn't realize Grigore had taken a fork in the path until she felt a tug on her hand.

He guided her down a granite path through an ancient arched portal of intertwining branches and Hedera helix gold ivy. She gasped at the brilliant jumble of colorful and fragrant flowers that filled the beds along the path. A small fountain with benches flanking either side of the trail marked the garden's center.

"This is delightful. It reminds me of an old English garden." Kat released Grigore's hand and twirled around with her arms spread. The cool breeze caressed her skin, like butterfly wings, while a multitude of fragrances floated around her.

"The idea is similar with a few additions." Grigore smiled as he watched her wander around the garden with a radiant glow. The strategically placed decorations among the flowers enchanted her. He asked, "Do you pick this one or wish to continue your tour?"

"If they're all this dazzling, it will be difficult to make a choice." Kat ran back and slipped her hand back into his. "Lead on."

Chapter 46

Grigore gave her hand a light squeeze and proceeded with the tour. He enjoyed her childlike delight in the gardens he loved. Going around the fountain, he took her down a path through another archway and stepped back onto the Great Lawn. The mood had become light-hearted and companionable. They walked across the path to the Great Lawn, which gave way to a thicket that blocked the sharp rays of the sun from overhead. The trill of the bird's songs filled the air. Hand in hand, the pair broke into a small clearing inside a small thicket of trees.

A gazebo sat in the center. The little building appeared to be created of white flowers on the sides and roof. Walking closer, Kat noticed a wooden framework covered by flowers that twisted among the wooden slats and draped across the roof to conceal it. Boulders and other decorative pieces were sporadically placed around the clearing.

"This is a favorite area of cubs and whelps, a place for education," Grigore responded to her inquisitive glance. "They learn much here." He took a deep breath and reveled in her citrusy pure scent mixed with the flowers.

"I can picture them playing here. I bet it would be a safe place for little ones." Kat smiled, "I hate that your nephew was hurt by the trap near the cabin."

"Yes, Daniel should have been here instead of in the woods." Grigore furrowed his brow and scowled at the memory. "As the leader, I should've been here to protect him."

Kat cupped his cheeks and stared into his eyes. "You're not at fault. Adventurous children... cubs have a mind of their own and can be a handful. I hope he learned a lesson from the event."

"Luckily, you were there to heal his wound. You don't know how we all appreciate that." Grigore's arms slid around her waist and pulled her tight. He rested his chin on the top of her head. He nuzzled his nose in her hair, losing himself in the delectable scent. His muscular arms tightened around her as fire flashed through his body. Her fingers glided from his cheeks to interlock around his neck. His eyes flashed silver, and he growled before he shoved her away. He took off in a run, his voice husky as he called over his shoulder. "Race you to the trailhead."

"Hey, no fair," Kat called out. Her voice faded behind him when he gave a burst of speed to cool his heated body.

"All's fair in love and war. Didn't you know that?" Grigore reached the spot long before Kat jogged over. He sat on a rock and watched her with a smirk.

Reaching the rock, Kat gave him a playful shove, laughing at the great show he made of falling off onto the lush grass. She whirled and raced down the path back through the trees. Grigore caught her and covered her mouth with a kiss. He gave an animalistic growl of hunger and pressed her body tight against him. The taste put the sweetest honey to shame.

Grigore inhaled her unique feminine scent mixed with her innocence and a touch of arousal. His breath quickened, and he fought the primal urge that flooded through him. Against his better judgment, he ground against her. He fought his bestial instincts for control. He gritted his teeth and asserted his willpower to tamp down the primal instinct to claim his mate.

In a slow, deliberate manner, so he didn't scare her, he lightened his kiss until his lips barely brushed hers. Her harsh, sharp intake of breath filled his ears. She gulped in air trying to catch her breath. Arousal filled the surrounding air. He started to pull away but hesitated when he felt her weight lean on him for support while she struggled to regain her composure. Kat blinked unfocused eyes at Grigore as she fought an internal battle.

"Shall we continue?" Temptation ached inside him as Grigore eased her away and slipped his large hand around hers. He didn't want to do something he'd regret later. He led her around the estate, through the gardens one at a time, only holding her hand. The strong tingle of electricity between them kept the flame of carnal lust simmering deep inside him.

Grigore noted the moon edge upward across the horizon. He wanted to show her his favorite hideaway. Her reaction was important to him. They hiked down another path, through a small grove of trees, and he smiled at her exclamation.

"Oh my! This is fantastic." Kat exclaimed as she gazed out at the breathtaking vista spread out before her.

A grassy knoll lay in the middle of a grove of trees. On the far side of the clearing stood a cliff with the backdrop of the forest where she met Grigore. In front of the cliff ran a spring so pure the water flowed a blue-green and so clear anyone could see the bottom. On the bank of the river were flat boulders. Inside a small rock alcove was a natural rock bridge that crossed from one bank to the other with waterfalls flowing over the side. The most incredible part was the columns with wolves in various poses. They had been carved out of the rock of a rock cliff that sheltered a small cave. A waterfall fell from another section of the cliff. It all looked natural to the naked eye.

"Do you want to tour inside the cliff?" Grigore watched her with anticipation. This had been his favorite play spot as a cub.

"I'd love to," Kat said. He smiled as she gazed breathlessly around the alcove, enthralled by the beauty.

Grigore took her hand and used his natural balance to aid her across the bridge built by nature. "This has always been my favorite place when I needed time alone. I'm glad you like it."

"Like it? I love it. I can see why you'd want to be here. I've never seen anything so fantabulous, and that doesn't even describe it." Kat couldn't tear her eyes away from the beautiful scene.

"It's a good word." Grigore grinned. Even her movements among the carvings inside the cliff stoked the fire inside him. He wanted her. Not to appease his beast. She filled his heart with joy because she found delight in everything she did. He chuckled at her antics, as she examined and explored all the nooks and crannies of the statues and caves in the cliff's curvature.

Grigore lost time, oblivious to the moon rising higher in the sky, creating the dusky gray darkness before night reached full bloom. The flicker of his primal beast's hunger glowed in his eyes. He watched her movements with an overpowering awareness. Her scent increased his hunger for her.

Grigore's body acted of its own accord. His feet inched closer to the object of his desire. The predator inside him surfaced to claim his prey. Her animated laughter played on his nerves, fueling the internal fire. He would seize his target in his snare. With her back to him, Kat didn't see his eyes glow with luminous ferocity. The half-aware man reached out to pull her against him and to ensnare her in his grasp.

With Grigore's hand inches away from his prey, he felt a hand grip his shoulder, stopping him. Whirling around, Grigore snarled and crouched ready to pounce on the adversary who dared interfere with the attainment of his goal. He displayed his sharp fangs and snapped at the intruder. Unintelligible words broke through his mental fog. He shook his head, clearing it. The primal glow died down, and his humanity returned to expressive, gray-flecked eyes. Grigore recognized Andre as he stood in an alert defensive stance.

"There you two are." Elena's casual comment didn't fool Grigore. He heard the underlying tension and noted her guarded stance. Thankfully, the pair made an appearance. No telling what he would have done to Kat.

Kat's absorption in the statuary-filled alcove kept her oblivious to the scene played out before her. "Elena, Andre, I'm glad you could join us."

"Andre needs to discuss business with Grigore. I'll return with you to the house. We can discuss more details these beasts are clueless about." Elena stepped between Kat and Grigore. In a protective gesture, she slipped her arm in Kat's and headed toward the house.

"We can discuss the plans. I didn't realize the late hour. Grigore can return, too." Kat reached for Grigore's hand and jumped at the look on his face.

"No!" Grigore snapped in a guttural tone. Seeing the inquisitive look in Kat's eyes, he inhaled and softened his tone. "Kat, go ahead. I'll discuss business matters with Andre and join you later."

"All right, Grigore." Kat reached out to touch his hand, but Elena interceded and grasped her hand. She chatted and led Kat toward the house.

Grigore watched the two women disappear down the path. He heard Elena's comments to refocus Kat's attention. "Mama is flying in her Parisian seamstress tomorrow to fit you for the wedding gown. What color gown do you want?"

Chapter 47

Kat felt flabbergasted by the idea. "What? A simple white gown would suffice. I thought someone in town might have a gown, or I could take a trip into the city."

"Only the best will do for my parents' eldest son's wife." Elena laughed at Kat's shocked expression. "You might as well get used to it. You'll have the best of everything. My brother is a simple man, but I know he'll lavish you with gifts."

"I'm not marrying him for his money. My family has money. I love him." A wistful sadness filled Kat's blue eyes. *I wish Grigore loved me.*

As if reading her expression, Elena stopped and smiled. "Grigore feels the same. He doesn't express his emotions easily. You two make a perfect couple. You'll balance out some of his hard-headedness. Our parents brought him up with a focus on his training to become Alpha of the Versipellis. He is used to making hard decisions on the spur of the moment. Non-emotional split decisions. His position demands he keep our pack safe from Moog's renegades and other problems that arise."

"Alpha means he's the prince. What are Versipellis? Grigore mentioned Moog." Kat blinked and stared at Elena in confusion.

"We are Versipellis. Werewolves under the protection of my father, the *Regele Alfa*, the king over all the continents. We believe in honor and integrity. My brothers live in different regions, where they reign. They watch over the lycanthropes around the world and aid other Alt factions, if needed. Grigore rules North America. Each area has smaller clans. Each clan has a leader who reports to Grigore." Elena watched the emotions play across Kat's face and smelled her sudden apprehension.

Kat had no clue about Grigore's power. The woman needed to know. Grigore should have told her.

"What about Moog and his renegades? Grigore mentioned his concern about his cousin. He didn't want me in the middle of the problem. Is there more than a disagreement?" Kat's mind raced, her lower lip working between her teeth. How could she be a wife to someone this powerful? Panic built inside her.

"Moog's father, Dronel, was deposed as *Regele Alfa* for cruelty. My father took his place. My father and Dronel are half-brothers. Moog is determined to retake the throne from our side of the family. Grigore is afraid Moog will use you as a pawn against him." Elena's tone grew quiet as she observed Kat's reaction.

"If I marry him, that means I'd be a princess. Why would Alts accept a human to rule over them? Now, you say if Grigore marries me, he could get hurt because of this Moog. I didn't realize the significance. I can't marry him. I can't." Kat's blue eyes flared in panic. She put a hand over her mouth and fled to her room. She would leave and return to a normal life, if there were such a thing.

"Mama, what have I done? Kat can't leave." Elena gave herself a mental kick for frightening Kat. Elena spoke in a soft voice, knowing that the others would hear with their sensitive hearing. The guards fanned out and repositioned themselves to observe all exits.

Maricara heard her daughter call. She glided toward Kat's room while she admonished Elena. "*Fiica mea*, my daughter, Grigore should have been the one to tell her. Kat doesn't accept her own strength. I will talk to her. You are too impetuous. Go look after the cubs."

"Mama, Grigore will kill me if Kat leaves." Confident her mother would resolve the problem. Elena headed into the nursery to check on her children.

Cristofer intercepted his wife in the hallway and pulled her with tender care into his arms with admiration, he gazed down into her gray eyes with adoration. He said in his soft melodic voice, "Our daughter is too much like you were when we met, impulsive and willful and eager to expose all details. One should approach some things with more diplomacy. This woman is good for our son. She must not leave."

Maricara returned the look of adoration and caressed his cheek. "I have learned much over the years. I will talk with her and be diplomatic.

Losing his true-mate would wilt our son's heart and change him forever. Kat is a good woman, an Alt, regardless of her denial."

The elegant woman headed toward Kat's room but was pulled back into Cristofer's arms. His lips captured hers with a deep, passionate kiss. Her body trembled against him. Her love for him had grown over the years. A youthful voice broke their reverie. "Sheesh, Pop, you and Mom need to find a room. Aren't you too old for that stuff?"

Cristofer sighed in exasperation and released his wife, watching her walk down the hallway. The tall, regal man stared at his youngest son in disapproval before he walked away, shaking his head.

Chapter 48

Grigore's mother knocked on the door. "Katarina, may I come in?"

"It's unlocked." Kat sniffled. She wanted solitude, but the house belonged to this woman's family.

"Why are you crying, child? Elena said you were upset." Maricara glided over, stood beside Kat, and cupped her hand around the younger woman's.

"I can't marry Grigore. He should find another for his wife." Kat wiped her red eyes. She kept her eyes down to avoid connecting with the beautiful lycanthrope's gray eyes, which were like Grigore's.

"He has found the perfect wife. You will soften his edges." Maricara smiled and pressed her finger with gentle pressure lifting Kat's chin so she could look at her.

"I'm not a werewolf." Kat released a shaky breath that she didn't realize she'd been holding. Maricara released her, and Kat began pacing.

"Katarina, you have a magical healing touch. You are an Alt. Our people will accept you. You are true-mates. You make him happy, and the pack wants their prince to be happy." The older woman watched her with kind eyes. Maricara recalled her reluctance to marry the prince when younger. The handsome young Cristofer had his choice of any woman. The two had fought as a cover for their attraction.

"I'll never be as elegant and sophisticated as you." Kat stopped and looked at the beautiful woman.

Maricara gave a light musical laugh, eyes twinkling. "When I met Cristofer, I displayed wild and reckless behavior. We fought often. In those days, women were to be docile. Bowing to men's desires. I had a strong will, and Cristofer didn't understand how to deal with an independent woman. We fought the inevitable attraction of the true-mate metaphysical chemistry. He left the country to avoid contact with me."

"But you're married with several children. What happened?" Kat looked at the woman with puzzled interest.

"The full moon." Maricara's musical laugh encircled Kat, soothing her nerves. Confusion was evident in Kat's eyes. The older woman sighed. "I shall talk with my son. The full moon affects lycanthropes. If a true-mate has been found but not claimed, the reaction is severe, even when apart. Cristofer and I are both lycanthropes. On the night of the full moon, we fought our families and had to be restrained. I am told Cristofer's reaction became quite violent, and he caused a great deal of destruction. No one suffered any severe injuries. I too reacted, but my family took precautions."

"I can't imagine either of you out of control. You're both sophisticated and elegant." Kat shook her head in wonder. "Is that why Grigore wanted the marriage so soon? The full moon will be in a few days. Will he have a violent reaction?"

"Yes, it will affect him. He has not claimed his true-mate." Maricara gave a slight nod of her head. "Do you still wish to leave him?"

"I still think someone else is better for him. More capable of taking on the role of princess. True-mate pheromones or not, I love him." Kat sighed, sat in a plush chair, and stared at the fire.

"Love is a potent motivator, too. Sometimes the best princesses are the most reluctant to take the role. Does anything else bother you?" The sharp scent of anxiety had abated, but not completely. Maricara heard the younger woman's heart still beat faster.

"Grigore and Elena have both mentioned someone called Moog. I am not worried about myself, but I don't want Grigore to get hurt in a fight because of me." Kat brushed the last of the tears away and jutted her chin out with lips set in a grim line.

"Moog, my nephew by marriage to Cristofer, has been a problem for many long years. He will not be happy unless he takes the position of *Regele Alfa*, but he has no chance of ever gaining the title. He has caused problems for decades, and his father did before that. You and Grigore will be protected. All lycans have the ability for regenerative sleep if they are wounded. Soon, we will have you in the family to aid in healing. Grigore is strong and an excellent fighter. His father taught him well."

Maricara stood and smiled, holding her hand out for Kat. “Come, let us go have dinner. Whether you leave or stay, you need to eat.”

Kat’s hand slid into the slim grip. The woman gave a little squeeze of reassurance as the pair wandered to the dining room.

Kat noted Grigore’s absence throughout the meal and the rest of the evening. She assumed business kept him preoccupied. His mother and sister kept her busy until she made her excuses and headed to bed early.

Chapter 49

Kat tossed and turned until the wee hours of the morning. Shortly after she fell asleep, a horrible bellow in the distance woke her. Reclined in bed, she heard doors slam and a faraway muffled commotion. Suddenly, the commotion ceased, and Kat drifted back into restless slumber. Awakened once again by the saddest howl, she lay awake for what seemed like hours and finally fell into a deep sleep.

Kat woke with a start and checked the bedside clock. Longing to pull the covers over her head, she dragged out of bed, completed her morning routine. She dressed and went to join the others in the dining room. At home, Kat's family rarely ate together. Most of the time, Carolyn dragged her father to charity events. Any meal with her stepsister made her uncomfortable, so she dined alone in her room.

Kat walked into the dining room and noticed the occupants were subdued compared to the previous morning. Kat noted Grigore wasn't among the group. "Good morning."

"*Bună dimineața,* good morning, Katarina, did you sleep well?" Maricara smiled, playing the part of the ever-gracious hostess.

Kat debated whether to ask about the disturbance last night. Instead, she walked into the dining room with a smile. "Yes, the bed is comfortable."

"Good morning, everyone. It's a beautiful day." Grigore walked up behind Kat, placed his hands on her shoulders, and leaned down to kiss her cheek. "More explorations of the grounds today, my love, or do you have other plans?" His freshly showered scent mixed with manliness filled her senses.

Relief washed across the others' faces when Grigore entered. This behavior renewed Kat's curiosity. "I'm not sure."

Elena piped in while she filled her plate. "Mama's seamstress will be here later. You need to make yourself scarce, brother dear. You can't get a glimpse of the garment. That would be bad luck."

Grigore thanked his sister with a silent glance for giving him an excuse to disappear again this evening. "I thought that occurred on the wedding day. I won't buck tradition."

"Do you think you can escape the wardens for a little while today and spend some time with me?" Grigore gave Kat a conspiratorial wink.

"Wardens? Bah, when we were young, I found it almost impossible to court your mama. I had little time, and etiquette dictated that couples have a chaperone. Back then, we were not allowed to be alone." Cristofer joined in the good-natured ribbing of his son.

"You men don't understand all the preparations it takes to get ready. All you must do is show up." Elena laughed and glanced at Andre.

Andre joined in the conversation. "Grigore will need a tuxedo. I don't think Kat's family will be comfortable with the natural state."

The waiter came into the room, interrupted the meal, and whispered to Cristofer. "Excuse me a moment, please. Grigore, please accompany me." Both men left briefly.

When he returned, Cristofer kissed Maricara on the cheek and sat once more. "It appears we will have company soon. The sheriff called. Your family is on the way, Katarina. He will escort them. The staff has rooms prepared."

"Thank you. Did the sheriff say how many there were? Is it my father or the whole family?" Kat's sudden apprehension became palpable.

"There were four in the car. Two men and two women." Cristofer watched Kat out of the corners of his eyes as he took a bite.

"My stepmother and stepsister are here too. I didn't think she'd resist the opportunity. Dad's bodyguard, Gerald, must have come, too," Kat mumbled. The disappointment on her face was obvious.

The atmosphere in the room felt stifling, even when the others tried to recover the jovial mood. Once everyone finished, they retreated into different areas of the house, reappearing at a knock on the door. Kat saw her father enter the foyer, followed by Gerald. The bodyguard's eyes briefly locked with hers. He took a position just inside the door, standing rigid with hands held in front of him, one wrist held in his fist, and his observant eyes scanned the scene. When Keisha walked inside, Kat cringed at her stepsister's appearance. Keisha wore a short dress that showed off her long legs. She had meticulously styled her makeup and hair for her come-hither look.

Carolyn walked in behind her and immediately scrutinized Kat, paying particular attention to her stomach. Her squeaky voice grated on Kat's nerves. "We drove all night. What's the hurry? Are you pregnant? It's hard to tell. You still have too many extra pounds."

"It's good to see you, too." Kat gritted her teeth, feeling self-conscious, but resisted the urge to rub her stomach.

"There are rooms prepared. Allow Ilinca to show the way, so you can freshen up." Ever gracious Maricara said to cut the tension.

"Oh yes, the drive was dreadful and long," said Carolyn. "I don't know why we came by car. I saw a helipad as we arrived. Carter insisted we leave the moment he got home. He even cut his workday short. We had little time to prepare. I need to freshen up."

Keisha ignored the women and gave a megawatt smile to the men present, patting her short hair into place. Ilinca led the two women upstairs, while Gerald stood in the background as if he were a statue. Kat's father stayed behind. "We need to talk. Is there a place to go so we can have some privacy?" He gave a dismissive wave to Gerald. "Park the car and bring in the bags."

Gerald nodded and smoothed down his suit as he stole a glance at Kat.

"We can go into Grigore's office." Kat gazed over at Grigore for his approval. He stood rigid, his eyes stern. He gave her a slight nod in response.

Following her into the room, Carter Anderson barely waited for the door to close. He glared at his daughter. "What do you think you're doing? You don't know the man. I don't want you to get mixed up with this family. Come home with me."

"No, Dad, I love Grigore. I'm going to marry him." Kat was shocked at her father. His tone didn't show concern. Disapproval was more than evident in his fierce reaction. "You told me once I'd know when the right one came along."

"I said that in the past. You have no clue what you're involved in." Carter paced back and forth. Kat had never seen her father so highly strung.

"Yes. Yes, I do. I thought your stories were fairy tales. Your reaction tells me they're true. He's a lycanthrope, an Alt. You know too. How did you find out, Dad? You told me that someone being different isn't a reason to fear them. What changed your mind?" Kat saw the sadness in her father's eyes. His reaction astounded her. What did he know that she didn't?

"It was long ago, kitten. Your mother became sick and hid the illness from you. She developed into a shadow of the woman I married. She couldn't heal herself. You remind me of her." He gave a wistful smile, lost in memory. He touched his daughter's cheek and gazed into her sad eyes. "Things change. I don't want you to get hurt."

"I love him, Dad." Kat wrapped her arms around her father in a tight hug.

"Love will not conquer all. Has this werewolf told you how old he is?" Carter's frustration and anger were rife in his voice.

"I guess in his mid-thirties, but he hasn't told me. A few years older than me. Age is irrelevant. What does it matter?" Kat gazed at her father. Her brow and nose scrunched in confusion as she tried to figure out what he was trying to tell her. His strangled voice puzzled her more. He knew. Her father knew the Lupescus were werewolves. He never mentioned it.

"Has he told you about what is involved in this claiming ritual?" He spat out, his voice grating.

When Kat heard the term 'claiming' from her father, she realized he knew far more than he said. "It's like a wedding ceremony. I have a fitting for my dress today."

"There is more to it than that. The full moon will come soon. He must have the ceremony before then." The older man threw his arms up in exasperation and shook his head.

"You make it sound like it's a life-or-death situation." Kat pursed her lips and jutted out her jaw. Her father knew everything. How?

"No, not quite that bad, but ask him." Carter grabbed her upper arms, his fingers gripped tight in anger.

"Dad, you're hurting me." Kat felt him release his hold.

He gently rubbed over the spots. "Sorry, princess. Promise you'll ask him. I don't want you to go into this relationship blindly."

"I will, but I still plan to marry him." She hated defying her father because he hadn't shown this much interest in her for years. "Will you give me away?"

"Ask his age and about the claiming. Then you consider all the facts, after that, If you still want to marry him, yes. After all, you're my little girl. I've tried my best with you, even when I was away with work. When your mother died, I remarried for your sake." He sighed. "I wish I hadn't rushed into marrying Carolyn. I thought she would be a good mother for you." His eyes grew sad.

"You're a wonderful father who has always been there for me. You always wanted the best for me. I will ask him later. You're worrying needlessly. Let's get you settled into your room." Kat slipped her arm through his and led him from the room. Her father stopped as he walked out the door, his mouth dropped open, and he stared at a tall thin woman outside the door. Kat had never seen her before.

Chapter 50

The subdued beauty stared at Kat's father. "Car, is it you?" Her words came out breathlessly. Her trembling hand splayed across her chest. "I thought I smelled your scent and thought my mind was playing tricks on me. I had to find out."

"Hatya." Carter almost whispered as he stared in shock. "You haven't aged a day. You're as beautiful as ever. I thought you had returned to your homeland."

Kat glanced from her father to the strange woman in wonder. She hadn't heard her father called Car since her mother died. Her stepmother always chose the more formal version of his name.

"I came for the claiming ceremony of my nephew. What are you doing here?" The woman inched forward, hesitantly reached her hand out, and then pulled it back.

"I came for my daughter." Carter stared at the woman, took a step, hesitated.

Surprise registered on the woman's face as she noticed someone else in the hall. After a cursory glance, she gave Kat a tentative smile and returned her attention to Carter. "I never dreamed your daughter was my nephew's mate."

"Your nephew?" Carter glanced around, confused.

"My sister's eldest son." The woman's smile lit up her face.

The news registered through Carter's shock. He focused on Kat with an edge in his voice. "You didn't tell me your betrothed is the heir to the lycan throne."

"Does it matter?" Kat felt more confused than ever about her father's reaction.

"It makes things worse. Keep your promise to me, Kat, today." Carter's eyes pleaded with her before his gaze returned to the woman.

Stepping up and slipping his arm through Kat's, Grigore watched the nonverbal exchange between the older couple. "Kat, this is my aunt Hatya. She doesn't get out of her room much." He turned to Carter. "It seems you already know each other. Why don't you show him around the gardens, *mătușă,* aunt?"

Stiffly, the older woman turned with regret. "He has seen them. I doubt he wants to see them again."

"Dad, I'm sure they've changed over the years." Kat encouraged her father.

"Your stepmother..." He couldn't tear his eyes from the beautiful woman in front of him.

"... Is probably taking a nap." Kat finished for him. "She wants her beauty rest." He obviously longed to go with Grigore's aunt. Had she been wrong all these years? Did he stay busy to avoid Carolyn? He'd told her he remarried for her so that Kat had a mother.

Carter gaped at Kat, and then he nodded in acknowledgement. "She went to freshen up." Stepping to Hatya's side, he gallantly held up his arm. "Would you accompany me on a walk and reacquaint me with the gardens?"

Giggling like a schoolgirl, the tall woman looped her arm in his. "I would be delighted."

"I wonder if our favorite alcove is still intact?" Carter asked in a husky voice.

"I'm sure we can find out." The two disappeared around a corner. Kat's father seemed to have a spring in his steps.

"Well, who would have thought?" Grigore stared after them. His aunt had been torn from her true-mate, leaving her devastated. She lived a reclusive life, rarely coming out in public. His parents never explained what happened. Now, he knew what his life would entail if Kat refused him.

"Yes, who? I learned something new today." Kat rested her hand on Grigore's arm.

Placing his hand over hers, he turned, the glow burning in his eyes from the familiar tingle. Swallowing, he removed her hand and cupped it in his hand like a precious gem. "You didn't key in the code on the security pad."

"You didn't give it to me," Kat said softly, her eyes filled with love.

"You got away too quickly. Remember what I told you about werewolves having exceptional hearing? I heard your conversation with your father. Come, we need to talk so you can keep your promise." Placing his arm across her shoulders, he guided her down the hall.

"Grigore, don't you want to go into your office?" She hooked her lip between her teeth.

"It's no secret. The others can hear what I say. Let's find a comfortable spot where we can relax while we talk." For what he had to say, Grigore wanted little reminder of his formal position. He held Kat close as they walked down the hall. He felt as if he were going to the gallows. Outside, he took her into a little clearing near the rose garden.

Kat's father had told her the truth. This might end any hope he had for his future. She had become ingrained in his very being. He didn't know what would happen if she rejected him. His aunt grew into a recluse after being rejected by the one she loved—Kat's father, of all people. He cringed at the thought of telling her. He should have already given her the truth.

Chapter 51

The opening was in the shape of a triangle. At the top point an enormous, shining golden globe sat in the middle on an ancient brick foundation edged with decorative benches. Two trees standing across from each other. At the third point of the triangle, a row of five old, well-kept trees spaced methodically defining the edge of the forest. Kat's brow furrowed, and she released her grip on Grigore's hand so she could wander around to explore the large clearing. "Do you know what a syzygy is?" He asked.

"A what?" Kat glanced at him and blinked, her mouth open.

"A syzygy. It is an alignment of three or more planets in a nearly straight line."

"What does that have to do with your age or this clearing?" Kat ran her hand over the side of the golden orb. She felt the engraving on the side of a wolf and some words.

"Bear with me, my love." Grigore walked over and took her other hand in his, leading her away before she read the inscription. "When I was born, there was an alignment of five planets. The row of trees represents the planets, Saturn, Jupiter, Mars, Venus, and Mercury. They are not in a straight row." He led her to the end of the line, and she saw they were askew. Though the row seemed straight, two trees were angled a bit. "The trees on either side of the globe represent Earth and the moon. The globe is the sun."

"I still don't see what that has to do with your age." Kat faced him. Her brows furrowed, and a pout showed on her face. Grigore cupped her cheek and kissed her on the forehead.

"Patience. I'm getting to that. When I was born, astronomers considered the planets and eclipses as integral parts of life and events that would occur. In the first part of the twelfth century, a document called the Toledo Papers predicted the planets would align, causing the end of the world. The prediction was wrong. Otherwise, we would not be here now."

Kat huffed and pressed her lips together. "Grigore…"

Grigore cut her off with a rush of words. "I was born then."

"Oh, come on. Quit joking and tell me your age." Kat's laughter stopped when he didn't join in. She took a step backward and stared at the handsome man. Her mouth open.

Grigore walked to the sphere and continued, "My parents had gone through several miscarriages. They said the alignment was the beginning of something wonderful because I was born. In the old country, they created an identical garden. Once they arrived at their new home, they recreated this garden. The trees represent the planets, and the golden orb represents the sun and their newborn son." Grigore took Kat's hand and led her to the orb. He lifted her hand and placed it on the inscription. His gray eyes watched her expressive face for her reaction and said in a grim voice, "Read it."

Kat stared at Grigore a moment longer, snapped her mouth shut, and read the words, "Welcome into our world, Grigore Lupescu (our Watchful Wolf). Our son makes our world bright as the sun." She cleared her throat and closed her eyes. "You're not joking, are you?"

"No, I'm not," Grigore answered solemnly. His gray eyes intently observed her.

Kat gawked at him. Her jaw dropped open again. "But that makes you… that's not possible." She assimilated the information, shaking her head in denial. "You're in your thirties. What kind of prank is this?"

"I hadn't told you before. I didn't think you would believe me." Grigore sighed, stood dejected, staring at the golden globe. He reached out to touch her shoulder.

"You planned to marry me, letting me think you were only a few years older? What other secrets are you hiding?" Kat jerked away from his touch and strode several feet away, glaring at him.

"None. I'm not hiding information. It didn't come up. Ask anything and I'll answer." Grigore watched her with guarded eyes. The pungent scent of fear oozed from her pores. Her pulse raced. He could have said more but feared her reaction.

"No wonder my father wanted me to ask." Kat looked dumbfounded. "If you're that old, what about your parents? What about the cubs?"

When Grigore started to answer, Kat stopped him. "No, I don't want to know right now. Don't tell me."

"We age differently, my love." Grigore sighed, running his hand through his hair.

"Stop, I can't handle the endearments right now. I need time alone to think." Kat rubbed her temples as if her head ached.

Grigore exhaled a heavy breath and walked away, his head lowered.

"Wait!"

Hope sparked in his eyes, and Grigore took a step towards her. Kat put up her hand to stop him, extinguishing the spark. He said in a guarded monotone to hide the turmoil he felt. "Yes, Kat?"

"Is it true the claiming mark is like a wedding ring?" Overhearing her conversation with her father, he expected her to ask him.

"The ritual is like a wedding, with the mark showing others you have a true-mate. The wedding night would be different in some ways. A couple becomes one. The animal nature takes control. They bite each other's shoulders, savoring the taste of the true-mate's essence in their blood. Other body fluids combine at the climax of the event. The conjugated union makes them a whole instead of two parts. A wolf mates for life. Sometimes, bonding can be almost violent in the culmination of satiation for each other. The mixture of the fluids enhances the mates to lengthen the nonlycan's life." He tried to find words she'd understand without scaring her.

Fear flared in her eyes. She stammered, biting her lip. "What form is the mating completed in?"

Grigore looked puzzled as he tried to decipher what she had asked him. His eyes grew wide when he understood her meaning. "Our joining will be in the most comfortable and accommodating form. Wolf to wolf. Human to human. No intermingling."

"Oh." Kat breathed an audible sigh of relief, and she stepped back until the back of her knees hit the bench behind her. She plopped down. Fatigue washed across her face, and her body slumped. Her eyes darted as her brain went into overdrive. For a few seconds, her expression went blank.

"Kat?" Worried, Grigore stepped forward, feeling helpless.

"Please leave me. I have to think." Kat looked at him with pleading eyes. He saw the shimmer of tears in the depths. Torn between his desire to give her space and pull her into his arms to protect her, he left. She needed protection from him. He returned to the house, sending someone to watch her from a distance.

Chapter 52

Withdrawing into his study, Grigore felt fate plotted against him. He wanted solitude so he could sulk. Dropping some ice into a glass, he poured two fingers of bourbon and slumped to brood in a leather chair in front of the ornate fireplace. He neglected to close the door, but he didn't expect company, especially not Kat's stepsister. He recalled Kat had called her Keisha.

The willowy, bleached blonde slithered into the room, hips swaying. It must be illegal somewhere for women to gyrate like that. She glided past his chair. Her warm thigh brushed against his hand on the armrest. Her strong perfume suffocated him, unlike the fresh, sweet, citrusy fragrance of Kat.

In a breathless voice, she asked, "May I join you?"

"Sure, it's a free world, for most anyway," Grigore groused, staring at the wavering fire.

Keisha faced him and perched on the edge of the stone hearth. She wiggled her buns against the hard surface and leaned forward in a provocative position to highlight her enhanced cleavage. She placed her arms across her legs to show off her augmented assets. Her fingers made seductive little circles across her flesh below her knees.

Grigore thought her breasts would pop out of her low-cut top if she took a deep breath. Her voice came out breathy in a sultry coo. "I've seen you at some of the social events I attend. There's always a beautiful woman with you. I didn't know you were dating Kat. I felt mystified when my mother told me you were marrying her."

Grigore kept his expression bland. He watched her through hooded eyes, swirling the bourbon in his glass. "She's a delight. Fate stepped in for us to meet."

"Kat can be sweet in a childlike way. I'm not sure she understands a man's needs." Keisha said as she slid her hands slowly up and down the lengths of her bare arms, which caused her breasts to swell more.

"What are you getting at, Keisha?" Grigore focused his full attention on her face, not in the mood for her games.

"Nothing." With a coy smile, the bleached blonde batted her eyelashes demurely. She pursed her lips. "The women you date are much more sophisticated with more to offer."

Grigore raised an eyebrow. He deliberately acted obtuse to the meaning of her comment. "Kat hasn't said. Are you older? Is that what makes you more mature?"

"Age has nothing to do with maturity. I thought you should know. Poor Kat has difficulty pleasing a man. I've consoled the men she dated. The poor dear." Her voice was filled with pity and contempt. "My mother has tried numerous times to change her from a caterpillar into a butterfly. Kat fights her every step of the way. It's no wonder she has trouble keeping a man. I thought I'd let you know that if things don't work out for the two of you, I'll be there to comfort you, however you wish."

Keisha slid to the edge of the hearth, placed her hand on his knee, and locked eyes with him. She parted her lips. The tip of her wet tongue ran across her upper lip, receded between her teeth, and darted out again to skim across her lower lip. Her fingertips nimbly played across his knee. The firewood crackled behind her. A shower of sparks seemed to emphasize her comment.

Abruptly standing, Grigore stepped away from Keisha. He turned to glare at her. "Your definition of maturity is wrong. Those men sought you out for one thing. It wasn't for your maturity. Kat is wonderfully refreshing. You can be assured I won't be searching you out for comfort or anything else."

Grigore scowled and slammed his glass on the oak table. He ignored the wetness on his hand when the contents sloshed over the edge. He stalked out of the room. It wasn't lunchtime yet, and he longed for the day to be over. Marching out the door, across the Great Lawn and into the hidden garden, he heard voices from the alcove. He sniffed the air, catching Aunt Hatya's and Kat's father's scents. Kat's father shared the mingled parent-child fragrance with Kat. Grigore's aunt's odor triggered something in the back of his mind. He couldn't pull the memory from his subconscious. While he shared his love of the concealed niche with his aunt, he wanted to avoid everyone and everything at the moment.

The portal in the alcove's cave, on the other side of the couple, would be the shortest route into the forest. He needed to be on the other side of the man and woman without being seen. Skirting the alcove, Grigore stayed low in the trees. He started to bolt, and shift into his shadow form, but he stopped when his curiosity peaked by a comment from Kat's father.

"Why didn't you tell me?" The soft male voice was full of remorse.

"I tried. Would it have made any difference? Once, I told you the truth, but you thought of the worst possible scenario. You wouldn't listen to anything else." His aunt's melodic voice resonated with regret.

"My wife lingered on the brink of death. Her healing abilities couldn't help her. I had a daughter to worry about," Carter said.

"Yes. You had to get away from the monster to protect your daughter." Grigore could hear the hurt in his aunt's voice when she spoke.

"Hatya, I never thought of you as a monster." Carter's voice shook with regret. The woodsy scent of his arousal mixed with the musty aroma of sadness.

"Why did you leave and never return? You married a woman you never loved so your daughter could have a mother. Did you think I could not take that role?" Tears were in her soft, quivering voice.

"What if she had seen you change? How do I explain that to a child when I told her stories of such creatures?"

"I'm sure she would have accepted the truth. Look how easily she has accepted her relationship with my nephew. Now, you plan to ruin her love, too." Anger filled her voice, and a soft growl rumbled from her chest.

"I don't want to ruin anything. I want her to understand what she's about to walk into. I want her prepared because once she enters your world, she can't leave." Carter had a strained, matter-of-fact tone.

"You left without caring about the others your rejection affected. You didn't even say goodbye." Her voice wavered.

"I thought you'd find someone else." Sadness and sorrow filled his voice. Grigore smelled the truth.

"I told you once we find our true-mate, there is no other." Anger slipped into Hatya's voice.

Her words slowly soaked in. Carter asked. "Others? Who else?"

"Your son. The brother Katarina does not know she has. You never considered the possibility, did you?" With a howl of despair, Hatya ran from the alcove, leaving Carter alone and stunned.

Staggered by this new information, Grigore secreted into the nearby woods. He shed his clothes and shapeshifted into the billowing shadows around him to conceal his identity. Flowing with the wind into the cave opening. He hovered over the floor of the cave and disappeared through the aperture in the cliff side.

Grigore broke out into the trees that muted the light of day. He ran it safely out of Carter's and Hatya's eyesight. Energy surged through his body as he shifted from shadow into wolf form. The claws of all four paws dug into the earth as he ran. The wind blew through his hair as the tumult of emotions roared inside him, exacerbated by the phase of the moon. He craved solitude, a chance to think. To clear his head. He wouldn't blame Kat if she left, but he would be lost without her. Why couldn't his true-mate have been a lycan?

Since childhood, Roxie thought they were true-mates. Grigore had never had a bonded chemical reaction until Kat came along. Kat, full of sweet innocence. Kat, who made his insides boil like a cauldron. Kat mesmerized him when she drew her lower lip into her mouth, nibbling on the tender flesh.

Kat had been right about her sister. Keisha made her move the first time she found Grigore alone. The urge to physically throw her out of his house hit him when they made derogatory comments to Kat as they walked through the door. No wonder Kat felt so insecure. How could her father pass up his lovable aunt to marry a disagreeable harridan? Did Carter bear his aunt's claiming mark? Among all these thoughts, his heart ached at the thought that Kat might leave him.

This new information about his aunt's halfling by her father could scare her away. When did Hatya have the baby? It must have been about twenty years ago. About the time his parents and aunt went away for an extended vacation. His father gave assignments to the family in other parts of the world to keep them from Romania.

Where was the baby? It'd be a whelp by now. His family would never abandon anyone. That meant the youth lived with them. The only juvenile who was the right age would be Anton, his little brother. If his aunt told the truth, they weren't brothers. Anton would be the half-breed son of his aunt and Kat's father. His cousin. That explained why Anton's odor smelled a bit different from the rest of the family. No wonder Anton reminded him of Kat. Would this be another wedge between them?

Feeling smothered, he ran to clear his head. He crested the ridge at a trot. When he saw the wide-open expanse of thousands of acres of forest and meadows before him, he gave a burst of supernatural speed. A surge of power flowed through him. Energy raced through his veins as he stretched out his muscles. He ran hard and fast across the outstretched territory. Low-hanging limbs brushed against his hide.

The long grass brushed his belly. The stems broke, filling the air with an earthy, slightly sweet aroma. He dodged trees and boulders in his path. Inhaling, he could smell and almost taste the musty, rotted wood as he jumped over fallen logs. He surrendered himself to his feral side with every inch of ground he covered. Coming to a bluff overlooking the river, he stopped. His sides heaved from his exertion. His regal stance thrummed with dominant arrogance. He surveyed his domain for anything amiss.

Grigore loved this place. Although he traveled extensively, in his untamed wilderness he could be true to his nature without fear of being caught. If humans found out the Alts were more than myths and legends, they'd go on a rampage, worse than the Salem Witch hunts. His parents had told him stories. Grigore's grandfather, King Lupescu, had heard tales of Leif Erikson's exploits of finding a new land across a wide body of water. His discovery turned out to be North America.

The King had sent out a group of his men to discover and establish a colony to protect Alts before the humans encountered them. The explorers started in Vinland but traveled southwest inland. They came upon a wild forest land and claimed it for the king. They worked hard to turn it into a livable domain. Word got around among the Alts, who agreed to give their loyalty for protection. They had heard many stories from the old country about the benevolent and gracious king. Over the centuries, the claimed land became their current family home.

Duty called Grigore back to civilization, but he preferred to stay here. Howling with sorrow, he cleared his head with a shake and resumed his lope. He tested his endurance as he raced across the rugged terrain. The gamey scent of a rabbit filled the air. Giving chase, he dodged under a cedar with low-hanging leaves that infused the air with a pungent fragrance. The burbling river caught his attention, and he crashed through the rushing bed, letting the rabbit run free. The chilly water invigorated him as he dove into a deep spot. He tasted the sweet ambrosia of the water and drank his fill. Like a lighthearted pup, he raised his front legs high, splashed with each paw and pranced to the bank.

Trotting out of the river, Grigore shook the water from his fur. He spotted a sunlit patch of ground and plopped onto his side, rolling and scraping along the clear section of verdant meadow to dry his coat. He stretched out on his side and dozed in the heat of the sunbeam that reflected on his pelt.

Distracted, he luxuriated in the brief detachment from the day. Dozing in the heat, he didn't hear the intruder approach. He felt a heavyweight hit his side and roll him onto his back. He drew back his lips to display razor-sharp teeth as he snarled and snapped at his unseen opponent. Wagging her tail, his foe jumped off his side.

"Elena, what are you doing here?" Grigore rolled to his feet with a glare directed toward her.

"Looking for you." Elena dodged around him, nipped at his heels, and pushed against his side.

"You found me. Now go away." Grigore stood, hung his head, and wandered away.

Cocking her head, Elena picked up his morose mood. "What's wrong?"

"I want to be left alone for a while." He sighed and stared ahead.

"Grigore, you've always confided in me. Something's wrong. So, talk." Elena prodded his side with a nudge of her muzzle.

"You overheard the conversation, too. He placed doubt in her mind. Now, she'll leave," Grigore groused, running his paw through the grass.

"You don't know that. Give her a chance. Her heart will tell her the truth. The stepsister has good taste in men. She picked the wrong one this time. He's taken." She smirked at the look of surprise on his face. "What? Just because you're my brother doesn't mean I don't know what a catch you are. You have money and power, and some might even say, looks. After all, you're my brother, so some attractiveness had to rub off over the years."

Grigore grinned, pushed her with his snout and jabbed her with his paw in a frolicsome manner. "I'm the oldest, so you got your looks from me."

Prancing around, the pair wrestled on the bank, stirring the dust on the ground, splashing the water, rolling into the edge of the spring. Grigore's mood buoyed. He nipped at her tail as he chased her around the clearing. "You always could boost my spirits."

"Good. Are you ready to return? Others will start looking for us." She butted his side with her head and ran for the trees.

Chasing her, Grigore easily caught up, tagged her back, and dodged her attempt to tag him. They whisked back through the forest toward home. Back and forth, the two made a game of tag on their way back. Approaching the cave portal in the cliff side, they cautiously slipped through the opening. They slowly approached the niche and hoped they weren't disturbing anything. It was empty. They continued toward the house. They had been gone most of the day, and the sun dipped low in the sky.

Grigore stopped at the edge of the thicket and stared at the trail to the house. "Elena, don't forget your promise to keep Kat safe after dark. Get her as far away as you can if she says no."

"I won't forget. She'll marry you. How can she resist you?" Elena hated the thought of what would happen to her brother if Kat refused him.

The pair gathered up their clothes, dressed quickly, and returned to the house. Normally, they would have walked up nude, but they didn't want to shock their visitors.

They spotted Keisha on the veranda, reclining on one of the wicker divans. Regardless of the cold, she still wore the skimpy mini dress with her legs stretched out on the sofa. She looked up and spotted Grigore. A smile spread across her face, giving her the appearance of the cat who stole the cream. Moving with the grace of a tiger on the prowl, she moved toward him. She stopped beside him, practically rubbing her side against his. "There you are, Grigore. I hoped you'd show me the gardens. Kat said they are beautiful."

"Elena will show you the gardens. She knows them like the back of her hand. I have a pressing matter to attend to." Grigore circumvented her and disappeared into the house.

Elena hid her smile at the frown that creased Keisha's brow from Grigore's evasion. "Which garden would you like to see first?"

"Oh, I've changed my mind. It's a little chilly out here. I'll go in where it's warmer." Keisha dismissed Elena and walked away.

Chapter 53

Grigore walked into the house and looked for his father. He found him in the study. His father enjoyed spending his time here or outside in the gardens when he was at this estate. Most lycanthropes preferred being in the wilderness. Grigore stood in the doorway and debated how to approach the topic.

Inhaling Grigore's scent, the older man took a sip from his drink. "*Fiul meu*, my son."

"*Tata*, I wish to talk about something I've discovered." Grigore entered and stood in front of his father.

"Speak of it, *Fiul meu*." The older man leaned back in his chair, eyes alert.

"I went for a run and overheard a conversation between Carter Anderson and Aunt Hatya." Grigore paced the distance of the room and back, pausing in front of his father to see his reaction.

"I wondered when this time would come. Your mama should be here for this discussion." Giving a low resonant howl, he took another sip and waited.

A few minutes passed before Maricara floated into the room. "You called *inima mea*?"

"*Iubire, love*, the time has come to explain some things to our *fiul*. He overheard a conversation between Hatya and Carter." Taking Maricara's hand, Cristofer wrapped his arm around her as she settled on the arm of the chair and leaned against her mate. "Grigore, please set the sound system. This is not a conversation for all to hear."

Punching in the code, Grigore settled in a plush chair across from his parents. His patience ended, and he blurted out, "Is Anton their son?"

"As always, you do not beat around the proverbial bush." Cristofer chuckled, placing his drink on a nearby table.

"*Tata…*" Grigore's annoyance tinged his voice.

"Anton is the son of my sister, Hatya. She did not wish people to know of her indiscretion with a human. He left her after the claiming." Maricara closed her eyes, heaving a heavy sigh. "We agreed we would raise Anton as our son, your brother. It has been a struggle for Hatya. It is for any of our kind rejected by their true-mate. Over the years, she overcame some difficulties. Her condition prevented her from raising a cub. I hope she does not have a setback with him here."

"It is amazing how fate brought two more members of the same family together." Cristofer gave his wife a supportive squeeze.

"You cannot tell anyone about this. We promised Hatya." His mother locked eyes with her son, gray eyes staring into gray eyes.

"Kat should know. I hope she can handle the news that she has a half-brother who is a werewolf. She has already been through so much. I'm not sure how she'll handle this information." Grigore paced to the door and back, facing his parents. "I'm not sure she will stay after the latest news I told her."

"True, Katarina should know. It is up to her father and Hatya. We cannot break a promise. I will have a talk with Hatya. I am sure she will understand the need to tell Katarina." Maricara arose from the arm of the chair and patted her son's arm. "Have confidence in your love for each other. Katarina is stronger than her father."

Chapter 54

Elena chuckled and wandered back into the house, nearly plowing into Kat, who was lost in thought. Kat didn't notice Elena. "Kat, are you alright?"

Blinking, Kat gazed at her in surprise. "Elena, I'm sorry, I didn't see you."

"That's obvious. Anything I can help with?" Elena hoped to ease Kat's concerns as she kept pace with the woman. She liked her and wanted her to be part of their family. Besides, she wanted happiness for her brother. Grigore and Kat were meant for each other. She smelled Kat's anxiety increase.

Kat stared at her for a moment. "Thanks, I have to figure it out for myself."

"I don't mind listening." Elena shrugged as she followed the healer.

"Thanks. The problem concerns your brother." Kat walked down the hall, lost in thought.

"Then who better to ask?" Elena placed her hand on Kat's arm.

Kat gave her a suspicious glance. "I don't know. You might be on his side."

Stopping beside her, Elena took Kat's hand and gave it a supportive squeeze. "Kat, he's my brother. I'm ferociously protective of him, but I can still listen to your concerns. I hate to see you this unhappy. Let's talk. Maybe it'll help."

Kat followed her into a room she had yet to explore. A vast library filled with volumes of books, was lined with shelves from floor to ceiling. An ornate fireplace with a marble mantle covered one wall. In front of the hearth were two large nutmeg-brown stuffed leather chairs with a small wooden table and a Tiffany lamp between them. Behind the chairs sat a matching couch and large desk. A Persian rug lay over a hardwood floor. It looked like a comfortable room, she'd love to spend many hours in.

Kat settled in a large leather chair in front of the blazing fire. She faced Elena, who sat in a matching chair. "I appreciate your listening. I must express my concerns to someone. The thought of leaving him fills me with sorrow. I don't want him to tire of me and leave. I feel he's withdrawing from me. For the past couple of nights, I haven't seen him after dark."

"Grigore's preoccupied in the evenings, so he enjoys his time with you in the gardens." Elena watched as relief spread over Kat's face.

"Grigore told me how old he is, but he seems so young. They explained the danger from Moog. I'm confused. Maybe I'm taking up too much of Grigore's time." Kat grasped her lip between her teeth.

"You worry too much. Right now, Grigore is busy. He'll let you know if there's pressing business. As for the age difference, wolves mate for life. He'll always be there for you." Elena had promised her brother she wouldn't tell Kat that his nights were spent locked away until the full moon.

"What about the claiming? I'm not sure about letting him bite me until I bleed. I can heal from that, though. He said it could be violent and would mark me. Will I be disfigured?" Kat stared into the fire.

"Once the true-mate is located, the bestial side of our nature grows stronger, until the mating occurs. During the claiming, or what you'd call the wedding night, he'll bite you. This bite identifies the mated pair to other lycanthropes and Alts. It will break the skin, and the saliva will mix with the blood during the climactic passion of the mates. The mixture of the body fluids has a distinct and distinguishable odor to all other Lycans. They'll identify the mated pair by scent. The preternatural sight of the lupine and most Alts can see the mark. There is rarely a scar." Elena smiled as disbelief etched Kat's features. Elena folded back the collar of her shirt and pointed to the vee spot on her neck and shoulder. "There is no scar from Andre's claiming mark."

"Grigore said all of you have extraordinary hearing. I didn't think of the rest of the senses, but I guess they are superior to human senses." Kat gaped at Elena.

"Exactly." Elena gave a bubbly laugh.

“That still doesn’t solve the age problem. I’m afraid that as I grow older, he will lose interest in me.” Kat’s brow furrowed.

“Ah yes, you see that’s another advantage of the exchange of fluids in the ritual. We’re not immortal. If you stay with him, a periodic bite acts like a potion to extend your life. You’ll live longer than typical humans. Plus, it is one of the strongest emotional highs a person can have.” A look of bliss crossed Elena’s face as she talked about the mating ritual.

“Have you seen him?” Kat stood and looked out the window.

Blinking out of her reverie, Elena looked confused for a moment, then realized Kat meant Grigore. Elena glanced out the window. The gray of eventide filled the sky with the moon angled overhead. “He went into the west wing right before I stumbled into you. He had to take care of business. I doubt you’ll see him until morning.”

“I’ll have some more time to decide then.” A faraway look filled Kat’s eyes.

“In the meantime, what can you tell me about Keisha? Seems she came on to Grigore, even knowing you’re getting married.” Elena took in Kat’s reaction. Kat hissed a breath through her teeth, her heartbeat speeding up.

Kat sighed and shook her head. She told Elena about life with Keisha. Then Elena told her stories of growing up with Grigore. They were interrupted by the call for dinner.

Chapter 55

Gerald heard Kat's stepmother and stepsister excuse themselves and retire to their bedrooms for the evening. Kat told her father this would give them an opportunity to visit before they both went to bed. They planned to meet in Grigore's office, so he waited in the shadows of the hall outside the door, standing as still as a statue against the wall. The familiar, delicate citric fragrance drifted down the hall before he saw her approach. Her light footfalls on the hardwood floor were like music to his ears.

As her hand touched the doorknob, he stepped out of the shadows. "Kat, can we talk?"

Kat jumped at his sudden appearance. She put her hand over her heart as her breath caught in her chest. "Gerald, you scared me." She released her breath. "We have nothing to talk about."

"Kat, I've known you longer than he has. I thought we had something special." Gerald stood stiff and threateningly as his rock-gray eyes watched her.

"If we had something between us, you ruined it when I found you in Keisha's arms." Kat inched toward the door.

"Keisha set me up. I never cared about her. She saw you approaching the front door. At the sound of your key in the lock, she wrapped her arms around me and kissed me when you walked into the house. I couldn't stop her." Gerald's large fingertips brushed her arm, and he frowned when she stepped out of his reach.

"Grigore stopped Keisha when she flirted with him. Meeting him made me realize I have never felt anything for you. Dad's waiting for me." Kat disappeared into Grigore's office.

Gerald's jaw tensed as he watched Kat disappear inside the room. His heated gaze glowed dark gray with hungry anger. Kat should have been his. With long, silent strides, he returned to his post outside her stepmother's room.

Chapter 56

Going into the office, Carter sat in a chair across from his daughter. "Kat, did you ask Grigore?"

"Yes, I did. It took me a bit to process the information, but age is relative. My biggest concern is how he'll react when I grow old, since he will age more slowly. My discussion with the family helped calm my concerns." Kat hoped her father wouldn't try to talk her out of the marriage.

"Good, you have always been smarter than I am." Carter walked over and gave her a hug.

Returning the hug, Kat saw a hint of the father from her childhood. "You're the one who taught me to accept people for who they are."

"One of my lessons I wish I had listened to. I must tell you something important. Can you turn on the security system in this room?" Carter glanced around with his lips pursed and brow furrowed.

Kat typed in the numbers Grigore gave her. "What's wrong, Dad?"

"You remember how we came into the mountains to camp when you were younger?" Carter fidgeted as he tried to decide where to begin. He paced in front of the ornate desk.

"Yes, we had so much fun. Your stories were genuine, not made up." A dreamy smile played on Kat's lips.

"They were real. I met a wonderful woman, Hatya. We fell in love and mated. We completed the claiming. I didn't know until today, but when we talked again… she told me, it is rare but..." Carter swallowed to gain courage. He continued, "She became pregnant, and you have a half-brother."

"What?" Kat blinked and stared at him with her mouth hanging open. She took a step back, felt the edge of the chair, and she sat down.

"I didn't know. Hatya never told me. I ran like a coward before she could give me the news." Carter wrung his hands and dropped his head.

"I have a half-brother?" Kat stared at her father, her mouth opening and closing. No words came out.

"Yes." Carter raised his head to gaze at her.

"Is he here? Have I met him?" Kat's blue eyes grew dark with emotion as she searched his eyes.

"Yes, and yes. It's the young man, whelp, whatever you call him, named Anton." Emotions from confusion to elation to horror flash across her face.

"Anton? Grigore's little brother, Anton? But how can that be?" Kat felt confused. "How can Anton be my half-brother and Grigore's brother? Are Grigore and I related? Oh no, I can't marry him." She stood, took a step toward her father, and then backed up.

"Yes, but he isn't Grigore's little brother. His mother is Hatya, the aunt. She had difficulties after I left and couldn't raise him." Carter watched as relief swept across Kat's face.

"I have a little brother." Kat staggered and fell into a sitting position again.

"Does Grigore know? He never told me." Anger played across Kat's face.

"You can't blame him. In fact, he's the one who insisted you be told. He found out this afternoon accidentally. He overheard Hatya telling me and went to his parents. I didn't know until she told me."

"Where is Anton? I want to talk to him." Kat jumped up and headed for the door.

"You can't tell him. Hatya and I must be the ones to break the news at the right time. He'll still be your brother when you and Grigore marry." Standing, Carter walked over and placed a hand on her shoulder. He cupped her chin in his other hand, lifting her face to peer into her eyes.

"I must think about this." Kat sighed and shook her head. "Since I came to the cabin, my world has turned upside down."

Carter wrapped his arms around her in a tight hug. "My poor baby. I haven't been a very good father to you. I want the best for you, but I haven't made the best choices."

"Dad, you've done everything you could. I guess things kind of happened. I'm tired and need to sleep." Kat disconnected the code, and

Carter escorted her to her bedroom. He kissed her forehead before the door clicked shut. Her head was muddled from the blast to her reality that had hit her since the time she had first arrived at the cabin.

Chapter 57

A forlorn howl pierced the night, awakening Kat in the early hours of the morning. Loud bangs and thumps between howls continued for an extended time. Curiosity won. Kat slipped on some sweats and her bunny shoes and headed down the hall toward the noises. Her search for the source ended when Marcus stepped in front of her, his clothes and hair ruffled. He was far from the pristinely dressed man she had seen earlier. He gave her a weak smile. "Having trouble sleeping?"

"Yes, there's a muffled noise coming from somewhere outside my window. I thought I heard a wolf in trouble." Worried, Kat's brow furrowed.

"Outside your window? I'll go look. If a wolf is in trouble, you're better off in your room. No telling what a hurt wolf might do. Lock your door for protection." Marcus escorted her back to her room. She heard her lock click from the outside, followed by his footsteps fading down the hall.

Something wasn't kosher. Kat would be no match against a fortress filled with werewolves. She climbed back into bed, pulled the covers up under her chin, and listened to the distant sounds. No other sounds broke the night. Kat slipped back into a fitful, dream-filled sleep.

Grigore stood in the distance, just out of reach. He watched Kat with sad silver eyes glowing in the distance. She reached out a hand but couldn't get to him no matter how hard she tried. A force blocked her approach. Shackles hung from Kat's wrists, preventing her from moving. Her stepsister popped out of the shadows with hips swaying as she moved toward Grigore. She laughed. She gave Kat a devilish grin and bit

Grigore on the shoulder. His blood flowed across his chest, and he embraced Keisha in his arms. She gave a maniacal laugh before she faded into a foggy mist, floating through the darkness.

Like a shroud, the darkness enveloped Kat keeping her immobile. She stood in front of a mirror and watched lines fill her face as wrinkles covered her body, her hair gray. In the reflection, she saw handsome young Grigore watching her metamorphosis into an old hag. Keisha, still young and beautiful, wrapped her arms around him.

The scene shifted once more. Grigore broke free of Keisha's avaricious clutches. He pushed Keisha away and walked toward Kat with sluggish movements. He dragged his feet as if mired in mud and a bog sucked him down with each step. The shackles disappeared from Kat's wrists, but her stepmother appeared to hold her back. With a wicked grin on her face, Carolyn told Kat that she didn't deserve any man, especially a handsome billionaire.

Kat fought to free herself, inching closer to Grigore. Before she reached him, he transformed, not into the wolf she'd seen but into a rabid half man and half animal. His fangs grew six inches long. White foam dripped from his mouth each time he snapped at her. Other wolves flanked him with bared, snapping teeth to keep her away from him. All around were little half-human and half-werewolf cubs, snarling and nipping at her ankles.

Suddenly, a whirling vortex swooped down from the sky, picking her up. It twirled her in dizzying movements like the tornado in the Wizard of Oz. The impetuous wind lifted her higher, until she could see the roof of the house, upward until she saw the forest, all specks far below her. The wind stilled, and Kat fell when the ground had disappeared beneath her. Her arms flailed around wildly in search of something to stop her from plummeting into the unknown.

Kat saw a pit filled with gorgeous women. Their teeth gnashed as they spat venomous words, saying no man or wolf would ever desire her. She screamed when she landed in the chasm. Her hands lashed out to fight off the creatures. One woman pinned her down and laughed in her face. In the distance, she heard Grigore call her name. His soft voice soothed her. She knew he would come to rescue her and to stop the others from destroying her. "Grigore, where are you? I need you."

"I'm here, my love." His fingers brushed her hair as he cradled her in his arms. "Wake up, Kat, you're having a nightmare."

Kat's eyes flew open to see Grigore's worried expression. He held her in an embrace. "Grigore. What are you doing here?"

"I heard you cry. I came to check on you. Are you alright?" Concern filled his eyes as his fingers brushed the hair from her eyes.

"I had a dream—just a bad dream." Kat shook her head. She placed her trembling hands on his chest and pushed him away.

Grigore released her and stood to leave. He tried to show no emotion, but she saw the hurt from her rejection. "I'll send Ilinca in to check on you."

"Grigore," Kat called out.

"Yes?" His voice filled with sadness.

Grigore turned his back on her, his shoulders stiff. She felt her heart shatter at his aloofness. "Will you walk with me one more time in the gardens?"

Still turned away, he inhaled deeply to gain fortitude. "If you like."

Kat felt doubts assailing her. Maybe he changed his mind. Maybe her stepsister seduced him already. So many maybes. She'd come this far and planned to prevail. "Can I look at them one last time…"

Before she finished, he paced to the door and grasped the handle. He spoke at the same time that she finished her statement. "We can after breakfast. When you leave, I won't be able to escort you to the door. I'll have one of the others see you off."

"-before I decide where to have the wedding." His words sinking in, Kat fought back tears. "I'll get my stuff together and leave afterward."

Gyrating around to face her, Grigore, bound toward the bed. "What did you say?"

"I said I'll get my stuff together." Kat's voice quivered. She refused to meet his eyes.

"No, before that." Grigore put his finger under her chin to tilt her head up and look into her eyes.

Kat squirmed on the bed. Her blue eyes brimmed with tears. "I planned to pick the garden for the wedding. I'll pack to leave."

"Leave? Never! Kat, I want you by my side forever, the sooner the better." Grigore scooped her out of the bed and pulled her into a tight embrace. His mouth dipped down to capture hers in a passionate kiss. His hands slid down her back in a caress through her nightshirt.

With a laugh, Kat pushed on his shoulders. "Let me go. I need to get dressed. We can go tell the others."

"You tempt me beyond belief, woman." A growl came from deep in his chest. Silver glowed in his eyes as he fought the predator back into the depths and regained his senses.

"Soon, I'll show you temptation. We can't dally. The day will be full of things to accomplish. I'll meet you in the dining room, or you can wait outside." Kat smiled at him. Love filled her sky-blue eyes as they locked with gray eyes.

"I could stay and watch you get dressed." He wiggled his eyebrows and gave her a suggestive grin.

Kat threw a pillow at him with a laugh. "If you stay in here, I won't get dressed. Now go. It won't take me long."

Chapter 58

Rushing through her morning routine, Kat stumbled into Keisha on her way to the dining room. Her stepsister gave her a look of disdain. "Isn't this place magnificent? I should be the one who lives here, not you."

"You're lucky they've invited you to stay after your shameless display yesterday." Kat shook her head in disgust.

"What are you talking about? You're jealous I can catch any man I want." Keisha tossed her peroxide blonde locks back with a flip of her hand.

Kat didn't realize how much her involvement with Grigore and the lycans had changed her outlook on life until she interacted with her family again. "Maybe in the past. This one is mine. Keep your claws to yourself. You must dislike yourself to think the only way you can be happy is by making others miserable. I feel sorry for you, Keisha. I hope one day you can find someone to love." Kat looked at her—really looked at her for the first time.

Keisha's face scrunched with pain for a second before rage flashed in her eyes. "How dare you say such things to me? Because you've bagged someone with more money than you, there is no reason to belittle me. I'm surprised he'd give you a second look, as ugly as you are. You don't even have any enhancements that can entice him. You're lucky you are family, or I'd leave right now."

"I can call a car for you." Elena joined them, looking at the woman with distaste. "I wouldn't want you to stay where you're uncomfortable."

Ever the diplomat, Andre walked down the hall to intercede.

"Good morning, ladies. May I have the privilege of escorting such a lovely group?"

Cooing, Keisha latched onto his arm, giving him her most dazzling smile. "You're so sweet. I haven't learned my way yet. I don't want to get lost. Thank you for being gracious and escorting me." She flipped her hair back in dismissal of the women.

Keisha turned her back to the two women and didn't see the feral look in Elena's eyes as she took a step toward her. With a telling grin, Kat tapped her on the arm. "I see what you mean about the natural protective instinct of the mate. In this case, you have nothing to worry about. He's totally devoted to you."

Elena stopped mid-stride to gaze at Kat. She took Kat's arm, and they followed the duo at a discreet distance so Keisha couldn't hear their comments. "You're right. She gets under my skin. How have you lived with her this long? I'll wait to rip her throat out until after dark." Seeing the look of horror on Kat's face, Elena chuckled. "I'm joking. Don't worry, I won't kill her unless he responds to her overtures. Then he'll be the first to die."

Andre's sensitive ears picked up the conversation behind him. He turned, winked at Kat, and opened the door for Keisha to enter the dining room before him. He waited to escort Elena to her chair with a flourish. Sitting attentively beside her, he gave her a peck on her cheek.

Grigore watched the proceedings with amusement. Keisha moved to sit beside him, earning a glare from Kat. She sat beside her father. Her stepmother occupied the chair on the other side. Both men rose to assist the women into their seats. Banal chatter passed the time during breakfast. Most of the conversation was guardedly mundane.

After Kat finished her meal, she excused herself. Grigore hastily joined her. "If you'll excuse us, I promised I would show Kat the gardens once more. She wants to decide about the place for the ceremony."

Keisha jumped up and latched onto Grigore's arm as she joined the exiting pair. "What a delightful idea. I've wanted to see the gardens. I bet they're as magnificent as this estate."

"I believe Kat wants to discuss some details for the ceremony." Grigore tried to brush her off. She clasped his arm tighter.

"I'm family. I'm sure Kat will want me to accompany the two of you. She has abysmal taste in events." Keisha squeezed his arm, pressing her body against his side.

Carolyn piped up, "Keisha has a penchant for soirees. Her input will be needed. Poor Kat tries. She has no taste, especially for social events."

Everyone stopped talking and stared at Carolyn. Cristofer cleared his throat and spoke in a deceptively soft, authoritative voice. "Kat has exhibited impeccable taste. I have no doubt she'll display the same in her wedding choices. If she wants help, Kat can let someone know. Keisha, please have a seat. The betrothed wish to have some time to discuss matters."

Keisha gaped at the older man and then gazed at her mother. Her lower lip quivered slightly before she developed a full blown pout. "Mother?"

"You can't talk to my baby like that." Carolyn, threw her napkin down. She stood and glared at Cristofer.

"Keisha, you're making a spectacle of yourself. Carolyn shut up. If you'll excuse us, my wife, stepdaughter and I need to have a discussion." Carter aided them from their chairs and guided them out of the room.

Kat noticed the stillness of the room's occupants, as if everyone were listening to a conversation. She couldn't hear anything with her human ears. Embarrassed, she tried to redirect their attention. "Maricara, will you and Elena do me the pleasure of helping compile the guest list later? There are a few people I wish to invite. I want you and Elena to invite all the guests you wish to include."

"I would be delighted to help." The older woman smiled.

"We've started the list already. Mama and I can go over it while you and Grigore take your walk," Elena chimed in. "There's so much to do today. Be prepared to see very little of her today, brother dear."

Kat breathed easier at the others' attempt to lighten the mood after her family's dramatic scene, but the atmosphere remained stifled, even with the lighter conversation.

Grigore took her hand and squeezed it. "We'd better go before they say we're out of time and don't make it to the gardens." He whisked her outside.

Chapter 59

The rest of the day passed like a whirlwind. About mid-morning, Ilinca appeared in the rose garden saying the ladies of the house wished her presence for a dress fitting. Afterward, they discussed the guest list. Kat was amazed by the A-list of actors, authors, politicians, and other famous names on the list.

They discussed the menu, the design of the cake, options for the wedding band, and the décor and flowers. She didn't realize the late hour until Andre interrupted them. He instructed one maid to bring sandwiches and other treats for them.

Kat wanted to see Grigore before his business dealings occupied him after dark. Looking for him, she wandered fruitlessly through the house, starting into the garden. Standing on the veranda, she spotted Elena's children playing in the bushes below the balustrade. She peered over and opened her mouth to call out to the cubs, but their words drifted up to her. The two oldest were talking in the way children do.

"How come Unca Grigore don't play wif us no more?" The five-year-old girl, Lucia, pouted.

The seven-year-old boy, Daniel, puffed out his chest with his superior knowledge. "Mama said he and Kat are gonna be true-mates. The full moon makes his fairy moans too strong, and he can't control his wolf."

"Why are the fairies moaning? Cuz they like Unca Grigore and they don't like Kat?" Lucia asked.

"No, don't you know nuffin? Mama said it wudn't those kinds of fairies. She said some kind of chemical make men and women like each other. Sumthing stinky but only to the other person kinda like... like a fly goes to a pile of poop."

"I get it. Unca Grigore is the fly and Kat is the poop." The five-year-old said with an epiphany.

"Uh-huh," piped up Ana in her three-year-old wisdom.

Choking back her laughter at the comparison, Kat realized the fairy moans must be pheromones. Hearing the noise above them, the trio stared up at her.

"Hello, do you know where Grigore is?" Kat smiled and called down to the three.

"Uh-huh," was the stereophonic answer.

"Is he nearby?" Kat glanced around.

"Uh-uh." They answered in unison.

Kat had forgotten when dealing with young children how important it was to word the questions right to get the answer. "Can you tell me where he is?"

"Not s'pose to tell ya," replied Daniel.

"Why not?" Kat frowned, puzzled.

"Mama said he don't want you to know he gots to be in the cellar." Daniel nodded sagely.

"In the cellar? Why is he in the cellar?" The conversation gave Kat a headache.

"Acause he don't want you to see him at night." Daniel shrugged, looking at her like she should know the obvious answer.

Their answers confused her more. "He goes into the cellar where I don't see him?"

"Uh-huh."

Closing her eyes and praying for patience, Kat tried again. "Can you show me where in the cellar?"

Looking from one to the other, the children shrugged their shoulders. Daniel bounced up the stairs. "Sure, Mama didn't say we couldn't show ya the cellar. You're gonna be our aunt, aren't ya?"

"Yes, I'll be your aunt." Kat smiled down at the three faces staring up at her. With a dimpled smile, the cherub face of the three-year-old smiled back as she slipped her sticky hand into Kat's. Lucia followed suit and slipped her hand into Kat's free hand.

"Good cause we like you. Mama says it don't matter if you are human." Daniel trotted through a door leading the expedition on their journey. With a tug on both hands, Kat started behind him.

The children headed into the empty kitchen and led the excursion through a wooden door into the bowels of the house. The trio went downstairs and across an extensive wine cellar to a blank wall. Daniel pushed a hidden spot on the door facing. The wall slid back to reveal a room with a second door on the farthest wall. It reminded Kat of the Edgar Allan Poe story, "The Cask of Amontillado."

Kat came to a thicker, heavily reinforced second door with an ancient padlock hanging loosely. The door opened with a loud creaking moan as the stale, oppressive air inside pushed out, filling the small room with a musty odor. The girls pressed themselves against Kat's legs. Daniel dropped back from the door, looking up at her with wide eyes.

"Are you sure Grigore's in there?" Kat stared at the door, as she gave the girl's hands a reassuring squeeze.

"He's not there now. You asked, where he goes at night." Daniel said.

The faint sound of voices from above. Elena's voice could be heard over the other voices above them.

The distinct rise of Elena's voice calling the children was heard above the other voices. "Daniel, Ana, Lucia where are you? Come here now."

"Uh-oh, we gotta go." The trio tugged on Kat's hands and released her when she didn't move. They fled toward their mother's voice.

Chapter 60

Kat released the girl's hands and watched them scurry across the cellar to the other door. She faced the open door. It seemed to beckon her with a chilly dread of what she would find below. Picking her way down the old, steep stone steps of the stairway, Kat clung to the slick, moist rail until she came to a landing. Feeling around on the cold, damp walls, she found a light switch and flipped it on, illuminating the room in a dusky half-light. The dull light revealed a dark, moldy corridor covered in cobwebs. She took a deep breath to build her courage and inched down the dimly lit passageway into a large, cavernous room. She blinked at the sight of a dungeon, just like those in the movies of medieval knights.

Kat gasped and gazed around at the contents. She stared in morbid fascination as she recognized the objects that filled the space. An inquisition chair covered with spikes sat in a corner. A Judas cradle occupied the opposite corner. A rack stretched out along a far wall beside an Iron Maiden. Shivering, she turned to see a wheel hung with shackles and whips near the door.

Kat felt a chill run down her spine and drew her arms tightly to herself. The gray mist of the pending night swirled outside a row of small, barred windows, which added to the eerie atmosphere. She spotted another corridor and followed it a short distance into an area with two cells with large, reinforced bars that assured no escape.

For the most part, thick layers of dust and cobwebs covered the torture devices, the tables, and most of the surfaces in the confined space. The items appeared untouched for a long time. A small, clean table near one cell showed recent use. She crept forward toward the farthest cell and peered through the bars. The dust and webs had been cleaned from the cell. Claw marks dug into the walls, and some fresh bits of rubble were on the floor beneath a small window. A large animal had ripped the bedding to shreds.

Surely the cubs were wrong. Grigore couldn't spend his time here at night. What protected him from the vicious animal in the cage? It made no sense. They had to be playing a joke on her, but they seemed sincere. Lost in her introspection and exploration of the room, she didn't hear anyone enter.

"The cubs said you were down here." Elena spoke in a hushed tone filled with sadness. She stood in the doorway to watch Kat.

Kat squealed. She whirled around, to see Elena behind her. "I didn't hear you enter."

"It's not a very pleasant room. Shall we go back upstairs?" Elena frowned and gestured toward the stairs.

"Don't blame the children. I insisted they show me where Grigore spends his evenings. I wanted to say good night before he locked himself away." She chewed her lower lip at the irony of her statement.

Elena snorted.

"I didn't mean that. I didn't know he truly was locked away. Why is he locked away? What's going on?" Kat looked horrified at her comment.

"I promised him I wouldn't tell you. I can't break my promise." Elena sighed, leading Kat back upstairs to the kitchen. Twilight had receded to fill the room with darkness.

Andre and Cristofer walked into the kitchen with two other men escorting Grigore. When Grigore spotted Kat, his eyes glowed silver like pooled mercury. He gave her a feral smile and started toward her. The two men interceded, grabbing his arms. Elena stopped Kat's approach toward Grigore.

Snarling, Grigore tugged his arms to break free of their grip. He shook his head. A red glow flickered in his eyes for a moment. "Kat, I didn't want you to find out this way." His eyes glowed once more, and his words were more a growl than speech. "Come join me, Kat, be mine now."

Closing his eyes, Grigore shook his head again. He regained a semblance of control. A grimace of pain crossed his features. "Elena, take her out of here. Tell her."

The glow sparked to life again. Brighter, fiercer with each return. Growling, he struggled against the guards, fighting as they dragged him down the stairs. In this state, his adrenaline flowed into the beast, and his ferocity required four men to get him into the cell below. Kat watched dumbfounded as his dual nature possessed Grigore.

Chapter 61

Kat stared into space, oblivious to the hand on her arm that dragged her from the kitchen and into the family room. She stumbled when her knees touched the edge of the chair, and she stiffly sat down. A faraway voice repeated her name several times an floated into her subconscious before realization struck. She blinked back to reality.

"Kat, are you alright? Kat, talk to me, please." With fear in her eyes Elena knelt in front of Kat, patting her hand.

Blinking, she focused on the voice, bringing her back to earth. "Elena?"

"Oh, Kat, I thought for a minute we'd lost you. I'm so sorry you found out this way. I told him he should tell you, but he didn't want you to know." Elena paced the floor, scared of the woman's reaction.

"Tell me what? Know what? Please, Elena, explain what's going on. I'm so confused right now." Tears glistened in Kat's eyes as she tried to grasp any reality. Any reality she could comprehend. "I overheard the cubs say something about fairy moans and the full moon. What's going on?" Kat sobbed and pulled her hand across her face to wipe away the torrent of tears.

"Fairy moans?" Elena looked confused.

"*Mon Amour,* I believe your discussion about the birds and the bees with the cubs has gotten turned around. She is talking about pheromones." Andre strolled through the door, taking his place beside his wife.

"The little rascals, they twisted it all around. I must talk to them again." Elena grinned at her husband.

"I hate to interrupt this family moment, but what's going on?" Kat demanded.

"Oh, sorry." Repentant, Elena faced Kat, pulling up a ottomon beside her. She clasped Kat's hand, patted it gently, and handed her a box of tissues to dry her eyes. "I should've told you this the last time we talked. Grigore demanded I promise not to say anything. He has released me from the promise. It is long past time you knew."

Kat became aware that Grigore's family had all filed into the room. They found a seat or stood in silence in the periphery of the room. Maricara served tea from a tray. She handed Kat a cup, and then settled on the couch beside Cristofer, who laid his hand on her knee in support. "We will help Elena with the explanation, if needed."

Kat sat back in her chair and surveyed each couple: Cristofer and Maricara, Andre and Elena. She saw the devoted adoration they each had for their true-mates. The porcelain cup rattled in her shaking hands.

Elena gazed at Andre for encouragement. He gave a barely discernable nod, and she calmly started the explanation. "Kat, do you remember our conversation about the bite exchanged during the mating ritual? And how wolves mate for life?"

Kat nodded and took a sip of her tea. Her body trembled.

"Some of the lycanthrope legends are accurate. Some aren't. Unless a silver bullet goes through the heart, it can't kill us but can cause damage. Wolfsbane doesn't affect us. In fact, you probably saw some in the gardens. We can change at any time, not just when the moon is full." Elena squeezed her husband's hand for encouragement.

"What does that have to do with Grigore and the cage in the basement?" Kat refused to call it a dungeon.

"Patience, Elena will get there. You are getting to the point, right?" Andre caressed Elena's cheek.

"Yes, I'm getting to the point. I thought she needed some background. Speaking of which, you saw the implements in the dungeon. At one time the Alpha wolf used the dungeons, but not for decades or even centuries." Elena's eyes flashed to her father.

"Let me *prețioase fiica,* precious daughter." Cristofer joined in the conversation. "My older half-brother, Dronel was the Alpha of our pack before me. My *tata*, King Lupescu was the *Regele Alfa* over all the continents. He sent Dronel to North America. *Tata* wanted my half-brother to establish a home and rule over the domain with *Tata's* guidance. Dronel would become *Regele Alfa* if something happened to

Tata. One day, after Father became ill, the minister of Father's cabinet sent me here with word that Dronel must return to the old country. Dronel claimed he didn't want to abandon this part of the kingdom. He instructed me to remain here and supervise. Dronel would send for me if something happened to our father. I would return home and attend the coronation. Father was killed after Dronel returned. While it could not be proven that Dronel committed the murder, people thought he had paid for an emissary to do it. Again, there was no evidence."

Cristofer took a deep breath and glanced at Maricara when she squeezed his hand. Sadness filled his eyes as he continued, "No one informed me of our father's death. Dronel became *Regele Alfa.* He ruled with a sadistic streak. There were reports from people here about his cruelty. I didn't realize how extreme it was until I found this dungeon filled with torture devices. If someone did not do as he wished, he brought them into the dungeon and tortured them until they changed their minds or died."

"The people, Alts and lycanthropes, feared Dronel. He became so extreme that the people instigated a revolt to overthrow him. Back then travel was burdensome without the conveniences of today. It took months for me to receive news about my brother's viciousness. By the time I arrived home, Dronel was captured and given a taste of his own torture devices. Those who led the revolt were going to torture me, but trusted individuals came to my defense. They made me the *Regele Alfa.* I adopted my father's first name as my last, Lupescu. I dropped Dalca to escape the negative association of our subjects. Our father had been a benevolent king. I kept the devices here as well as back home as a reminder to never use them again. Now, the cells are used for emergencies."

Kat's head spun with the deluge of information. She blinked several times as she processed the information. "How is Grigore an emergency?"

"Explain the effect of the full moon on Versipellis," Maricara interjected softly.

Andre continued with the explanation. "As Elena said, we can shapeshift at will, but the moon phases still influence us, especially the full moon. Once a true-mate is identified, the desire to complete the claiming intensifies as the full moon approaches. The full moon is a time of love, attraction, fulfillment and desire. The gravitational pull draws out our beast. If we don't fulfill our needs, the beast inside fights for control once the moon rises in the sky. Tonight, as the sun set, you saw a small sample of the internal battle between humanity and the primal beast. Grigore fought his beast to stay in control. When he saw you, the feral beast wanted to claim his mate. To protect you, he ordered us to lock him up at sunset. He made us promise not to tell you where he went at night."

"Why wouldn't Grigore tell me?" Kat gazed from one face to another.

"Grigore feared you'd change your mind and leave. He didn't want to frighten you. You know little about the beast in us," Elena interjected.

Kat sat straight and pushed her chest out as her mouth gaped and her eyes widened. "The growling and mournful howling I've heard at night is Grigore, isn't it?"

"Yes, we should have placed you in a room away from the dungeon because you are above the windows." Maricara explained and leaned into her husband for strength.

"Are you going to leave?" Anton asked the question on everyone else's mind.

All eyes stared at Kat, who licked her lips while her glance moved from face to face. She loved him and knew his wolf but hadn't considered that a vicious animal lurked beneath the surface. "How can we mate if the beast, as you call it, escapes and tears me to shreds?"

The group gazed at each other. Andre answered, "The best time will be during the day when he can control the beast. Kat, you're human. We're not sure what will happen. If you want to leave, we understand. It's your choice. You must determine how much you love him and want this to work."

"Grigore got control of the beast when he saw you." Anton piped in with a smile.

"Yes, Grigore controlled it for a short time. My brother is strong." Elena added.

"What about the wedding? My family? I can't have them see a—what is it, a mating ritual." Kat fretted her lower lip.

"If you decide to stay, we will have the wedding as planned. Your dress is almost finished. Other plans have been completed. Your father is familiar with the claiming ritual. The rest of your family won't have a clue." With her brow furrowed, Elena glanced at Andre.

"Car sent your stepmother and stepsister home today," Hatya said softly.

"What?" Kat exclaimed louder than she meant to.

Hatya repeated and then added, "You need to ask him why."

Kat felt dizzy with the flood of information and events. A few weeks ago, she lived a mundane life. She closed her eyes and rolled her head around, feeling a headache crawl up the back of her neck. "I hate to be rude, but I'm going to my room. I need time alone to think."

"Certainly. I'll escort you to your room." Andre offered his arm to her.

"No, that's alright. I can find my way." Kat didn't look back as she left the group. She left the room to dead silence.

Like a zombie, Kat walked down the hall into her room. She fell backward onto the bed. She tried to sleep but heard an anguished howl. Groggily, she stumbled to the window, which she struggled to open. A gust of cold air hit her in the face, waking her from the stupor. Kat poked her head out and looked down at the wall but couldn't see the dungeon window. The mournful howling filled the air, hanging on the light breeze. Unsure about what she would accomplish, she spoke into the air in a normal tone. "Grigore, I don't know if you can hear me. You told me you have exceptional hearing."

The lamentable howl paused.

"I love you, Grigore. Somehow, we'll work it out with the beast. I still want to be your mate." Kat slid to the floor with knees drawn up against her chest.

A sharp barking growl erupted into the night air.

"Grigore, I don't know if you can even understand me. Hold on until tomorrow. They said you have more control during the day." She leaned her head against the window frame and released a breath.

Kat heard the bars rattle, followed by an ear-splitting bellow. Leaving her window open, she crawled into bed and pulled the blankets up tightly under her chin. "Tomorrow, Grigore, tomorrow."

Kat heard another howl before she drifted into a deep sleep.

Chapter 62

A droning buzz outside her door awakened Kat from a dreamless sleep. She stumbled out of bed, dressed, and slipped her feet into her bunny slippers. Shuffling to the door, she opened it to see three small fur balls standing in the hall outside her door. Shocked that they were caught, the three scattered and ran in different directions down the hall.

Daniel and Lucia turned left, running for the stairs, while Ana turned right into a dead end under a window. With a yelp, she realized her mistake and whirled around to head in the other direction, colliding with Kat's leg. With large innocent eyes, her head flew up to stare at Kat.

"Ana, what were all of you doing outside my door?" Kat reached down to scratch behind her ears.

Sheepishly skulking back up, Daniel transformed into human form and scooped his sister into his arms. "We didn't mean nuffin', Kat. We're 'cited bout the day's activities. Mama told us you and Uncle Grigore are gonna have the claiming ceremony this afternoon. She said we had to ask you if we get ta be part of it."

Lucia rejoined the pair outside her door. "We didn't mean ta wake ya. Please don't tell Mama we did, or we'll be in big trouble."

Ana nodded vigorously, nearly tumbling from Daniel's grip. Daniel tightened his grasp, making her yelp. Holding her securely, he set her on the floor. "Sorry, Ana, but ya gotta be still."

"Can we Kat?" All three turned their large, pleading eyes toward her.

Kat's head was still fuzzy, and she didn't get the full gist of the conversation. "Can you what?"

"Can we be part of the claiming ritual?" Lucia repeated.

Elena walked down the hall and rescued Kat before she answered. "There you three are. Are you disturbing Kat?"

"No, Mama, we didn't ask her 'til she opened her door. We waited right here, and we didn't 'sturb her." Daniel played the spokesman for the group.

"We waited." Lucia nodded in confirmation of her brother's statement.

"Uh huh," Ana added as she stared at her mother with wide eyes.

"Kat, I'm sorry if they woke you. You had a stressful day yesterday." Elena mollified Kat before turning to the cubs. "Run along, children. Go find your father."

"But Mama, she was gettin' ready ta tell us," whined Lucia.

Elena tapped the girl on the bottom. "Do as I say. Go find your father. It's time for breakfast." The threesome disappeared down the hallway, grumbling under their breath.

"They don't mean to bother you. It's hard for them to contain their excitement. Are you sure you are going through with it? We understand if you don't. It must be hard since you're not used to our ways." Elena chattered nervously as she watched Kat.

"I'm sure. I can't stomach the idea of Grigore being in that horrible cage for another night. What do I need to do?" Kat shut the door behind Elena after she entered the bedchamber. Ilinca had laid out her clothes and performed her morning duties.

"This afternoon will be the claiming ritual. Later, we'll have a wedding ceremony to appease the press. They'll be hungry for information about the merger between two such prestigious corporations. If we don't give the press some information, they'll never leave the two of you alone." Elena frowned, shaking her head.

"You should have seen what a number they did about Andre and me when they found out we were a couple. The large wedding will be for the lycanthropes to gather and see the new Alpha female of the pack. Mama will still be the *Regal Alfa* over all the lycans."

"Late this afternoon, long before sunset, everyone will gather in a spot of your choosing. There'll be a ritual like a wedding but different in some ways. Everyone but the two of you will leave. The rest is up to you two." Elena grinned.

Capturing the essence of her words, Kat blushed. She chose not to dwell on that aspect of the claiming. "Will there be a part for the cubs? I hate to disappoint them. They have their hearts set on being a part."

"If you wish, they can have a part. It's very thoughtful and kind of you to ensure they can be a part of the ceremony. This will be their first mating ritual. They're very fond of Grigore." Elena smiled and squeezed Kat's hand. "Thank you for last night, too. It was a private time for the two of you, but lycanthropes have superior hearing. You were benevolent in reassuring Grigore in his state of mind. It shows you truly love him."

"I do love him. I hope I'll be a worthy wife… true-mate for him." Kat sighed and jumped when someone pounded on the door.

Elena suppressed a smile. "I'll have to remember you don't hear as well and you can't pick up everyone's unique scent."

Turning toward the door, Elena called out. "Go away, Grigore. You can't see her until the ritual, you know that."

A growl came from the other side. The knob turned. "I'd like to speak with Kat for a moment."

Kat watched in open-mouthed astonishment as Elena moved in a flash to lock the door before he could enter.

Elena leaned unfazed against the door when it shook and rattled as he tried the handle. "Nope, go away. I already thanked her for last night. If you have anything else to tell her, you can tell her tonight."

Another growl burst from the other side of the door. "My, what big ears you have, Grandma."

"Watch it, buster. I'll come out and bite you to show you what big teeth I have. Go away before you scare her off with your growls and snarls." Elena casually examined the ceiling as if this happened every day. "Besides, you'll get Mama and *Tata* up here, then you'll be in trouble."

"I'm a grown male. I'm not scared of what they'll do." Grigore growled, thumping against the door.

Kat's ears perked up at the sound of unknown voices murmuring outside the door. She tried to hear the conversation but couldn't make out any of the words.

"I told you so," Elena mumbled under her breath with a triumphant grin.

Chapter 63

Grigore snarled in response to his sister's childish gloating. He dared not do more with his parents standing so close, chastising him like a naughty child.

"We have other guests, *fiul meu.* Carrying on like this is serving no purpose." Grigore's mother linked her arm through his to lead him away from the door. "You have waited this long. Surely you can wait a few more hours."

Grigore wanted to hear her voice directed at him, if only for a few minutes. The beast became overpowering last night. Her words floated down to him like a lifesaver. "Mama, I want to thank Kat for keeping me grounded last night."

"Then tell her." Maricara released his arm, stepping closer to Cristofer.

"I'm trying, but knot head..." Grigore growled, stalking back to the door.

Cristofer scowled. "Be respectful, *fiul meu.* You must have patience as the Alpha. Her methods may leave something to be desired, but she is your sister."

Grigore took a deep breath and counted to ten, regaining his composure. "Yes, *Tata* I forgot myself. Elena won't open the door so I can speak to Kat."

"Then speak through the door. You know the tradition. Seeing a true-mate on the day of the ritual is bad luck." Cristofer's soft, commanding voice soothed Grigore's nerves.

Grigore leaned his ear against the ornately carved panel of the door.

His hand splayed across the wood beside his face, his voice like a caress, "Kat?"

"Yes, Grigore?" He heard her soft footsteps move closer.

"Soon, my love, we'll be complete. Thank you for giving me strength last night." Grigore closed his eyes and imagined her wrapped in his arms with her head against his shoulder. He inhaled her unique, light, refreshing scent. Even through the door, the natural citrusy fragrance filled him with longing.

Grigore felt a hand on his shoulder and turned to walk away. A picture flashed through his mind, and he paused. "Kat?"

"Yes, Grigore?" Kat's breathy voice was by the door.

"Do you still have those bunny slippers with you?" Grigore scowled at the questioning look on his parents' faces.

"Yes, my love, I do."

Grigore ignored the snort from the other side of the door and the odd stares from his parents. "Can I take them with me?"

A burst of laughter from the other side of the door followed his question.

"Shut u…" Grigore stopped at his father's glare. He altered his statement. "Be quiet, sister dear. This is between my true-mate and me."

"Whatever you…"

"Elena!" Maricara hissed, silencing her.

He heard shuffling on the other side of the door. It cracked open enough for the fuzzy pink slippers to be pushed through the fissure. Grigore snatched them from Elena's hand and held them against his chest. Kat's warmth lingered in their depths. She had pulled them off her feet. He inhaled her fresh scent that clung to the soft, fuzzy fabric.

Cristofer's eyebrow shot up at the sight of the fluffy oversized pink bunnies.

Maricara smiled and poked him in the ribs. "You wanted my silken scarf to hold the day of our claiming." Cristofer returned her smile. He took her by the elbow and led her down the hallway.

"Take your son and go. I will stay with the ladies." Maricara gave her husband a gentle smile. She gestured to the maid lingering in the shadows. "Ilinca, please have the cook send up three trays to Kat's room. We will need sustenance before we tackle this day. The day guarantees to be hectic."

"Yes, ma'am." Ilinca gave a slight dip and disappeared down the back passage.

Maricara tapped on the solid wooden door. "*Prețioase fiica*, the men are gone. Let me in so we can confer about the day's events."

The door swung open. "I knew he'd try something. He doesn't know the meaning of no."

"All men are the same, dear. They do not understand why superstitions exist. I recall your *tata* and husband did the same thing." The older woman glided through the door.

Elena hugged her mother and laughed at the memory. "Andre tried to scale the wall. You stopped him dead in his tracks."

The women smiled, their eyes filled with mirth at the memory. "Have you decided on a garden, Kat?"

"I think so. I'd like to take a quick stroll before I commit to a location." Kat hated being indecisive. All the gardens were so beautiful, she wanted to make sure of the perfect spot.

"We'll discuss the details before we take a stroll." The women discussed various aspects of the ritual, nibbling at the trays of food.

Chapter 64

About mid-morning, each woman had a list to accomplish before the ritual. As they left the room, Kat and the ladies ran into Anton in the hallway. "Anton, just the person we wanted to see. Would you show Kat around the gardens again?" Elena drafted the young whelp.

"Sure, Sis, I'd love to show her around. I want to know her better." Anton chatted in his cheerful, expressive manner as he chaperoned her outside. Along the path, he pointed out some of his favorite things in the gardens.

"Anton, I want to see the hidden alcove garden, to check something before the ceremony." Kat had fun learning more about her newly discovered brother. She liked Grigore's brother, or rather, her brother, a gangly youth. Amid his identity crisis, he was polite and gallant. Some young woman would be lucky to catch him one day. She giggled when he became sidetracked from his conversation by a caterpillar making a cocoon on a tree leaf.

"Isn't it amazing how they create their own dressing room to change into their flashy new guise?" Anton gazed at Kat's amusement-filled eyes and sheepishly reverted into his role as escort. "The bosquet is one of my favorite spots. The hidden alcove garden is a good choice, too. I think that's Grigore's favorite garden. He even helped with some carvings there."

"He didn't tell me. They're amazingly lifelike." Goosebumps covered Kat's arms as she walked through the alcove opening. She crossed the rock bridge into the cave and examined the statues carved out of the cliff face. Her gown didn't have a pocket, so she searched for a small niche where she could hide a small gift box for Grigore. She wanted to surprise him. The idea of being nude still made her uneasy. Nudity was a natural state to the lycanthropes, but her upbringing trained her to always wear clothing. Sexual arousal had nothing to do with nudity.

Bent over, Kat slid her hand along one column, exploring the base for an indentation. She jumped, with her heart racing, at a muffled cry behind her. Her position behind the statue hid her from view. Twisting around, she peeked around a column and saw two men attack Anton. She stormed out of the cave. "Let him go, you brutes."

"What do we have here?" A hulking beast of a man said in a raspy voice. He had a shock of uncombed red hair protruding from his head. A matching scraggy beard sprouted on his warty chin. He had a huge bulbous nose and pointed ears, one of the ugliest men she had ever seen. He reminded her of a troll from her childhood storybooks.

The other had a thinner, wiry build. His beady eyes and head constantly bobbed around. He had a nervous twitch of his nose, reminding her of a weasel or similar rodent. "Sure, doll, it's you we want, anyway. How about a good tumble before we take her?"

Kat moved across the clearing, searching for an escape route. The weasel-like man blocked her path. She pushed her shoulders back and bolstered her courage, glaring at the men. "You're on private property and should leave now."

"That's our plan, doll, as soon as we grab you." The rodent-like male dodged toward her at the same time the hulk did.

They ignored Anton and turned their backs on him. He snarled and jumped onto the back of the weasel, changing in midair into his wolf form. His claws sliced down the weasel's back, shredding his shirt and flesh. Anton's teeth sank into the thin man's throat, drawing blood. The weasel reeled at the weight of the whelp and bucked to knock him off. Clinging to the creature's back, Anton sank his teeth deeper into the creature's throat, ripping off a chunk of flesh. His claws shifted from his back to dig into the man's sides. The hulk swiped at Anton as another wolf appeared from the edge of the forest, attacking the young werewolf with unbelievable speed. He pounced on the younger male, knocking him off the wiry man's back. The powerful impact sent Anton reeling across the clearing.

Anton yelped and hit the ground with a thud. He rolled over and sprang to his feet, snapping at the grown wolf. Anton's body transformed into the shape of a wolfen, half-man, half-wolf shape. The larger wolf launched forward with a warning growl for the whelp. He hit Anton in the chest with his shoulder, knocking the younger wolf flat on his back.

The larger wolf mutated into his wolfen form and loomed over the prone younger lycanthrope. Emitting a low rumble deep in his chest, he pounced. His razor-sharp fangs sliced into the whelp's throat. He shook his head, exposing shredded muscle and bone. Kat shivered at the sound of flesh ripping from Anton's throat. The metallic smell of blood filled the air. Anton lay limply in the older werewolf's grasp. The breath rattled in his chest. Kat spurred into action at the sight of Anton's life-force ebbing from his body. She just found her sibling and couldn't lose him. Grabbing a fallen tree limb, she slammed the branch against the strange wolf's head as hard as she could. "Leave him alone."

Kat stood over Anton, waving the branch. She flinched when they snickered. Shaking his head, the wolf reverted into human form, glaring down at Kat with cold, brown, dead eyes. He ran a hand through his dirty brown hair over the spot she hit. A scar marred his left cheek from above his eyebrow down across his lip, leaving his mouth in a perpetual sneer. "You think your pathetic attempts can stop us?"

Kat ignored his question and responded with one of her own. "What do you want?"

"You are what we want." The wolf responded as he took a step closer, extending his hand toward her.

"I'm human. Why would you possibly want me?" Kat stood her ground and braced her feet to guard Anton. Her hands gripped the branch.

"Bait for Grigore." Weasel man smirked.

"No, not Grigore." Kat gasped as she waved her stick at the men.

"Enough of this!" the barrel-chested man bellowed. He grabbed the stick from her hand and threw it to the ground. "We need to get out of here." He yanked her arm.

Kat dug her heels into the dirt. She hit and kicked the man in a pathetic attempt at resistance. Latching onto the nearest tree, she wrapped her arms around the base. The bark dug into her flesh. In desperation, she clung tighter to the massive tree trunk and winced at the snap of fingernails breaking.

The wolf snarled in disgust and pried her from the tree. "Let go or I'll hurt you. Grigore will still come as long as he can sense you're alive."

"Please wait. I promise I'll go peacefully. Let me check on Anton." Kat pleaded in despair. She released the tree, holding her bloody, scratched palms up in surrender.

"The woman is wasting time, Deave. Moog is waiting for us. I can get her to move." The weasel snickered, stomping toward her.

Kat didn't refuse to be a lure for Grigore. If she saved Anton, he could warn him. She could hear the death rattle rumble in his chest as each breath grew more shallow. If she could focus on his neck wound, he'd live. She'd go with the ruffians to protect Anton.

"Shut up, you idiot," Deave growled at the weasel. "You'll come without a problem?"

"Yes, if you let me go say goodbye." Kat could hear Anton gurgle as he struggled to breathe. "You can hear it. He won't last long. Let me say goodbye."

Deave waved his hand dismissively. "Very well, you have five minutes, no more. We can't hang around all day."

Kat crawled across the ground and cupped both her hands over Anton's neck wound. She sprawled across his neck and upper chest so the others couldn't see her actions. Leaning over, she whispered in his ear, hoping he heard her words. She had to be careful. Deave had sensitive hearing, like the other lycanthropes. She didn't know if the other Alts had preternatural hearing too.

Kat focused. The healing energy built inside her hands to create warmth and a tingling sensation. The energy flowed through her body to radiate a heated, pulsating friction, electrifying the air around the wound. Her touch began to heal the tissues deep inside Anton's throat. His breaths were less audible as the wound healed his air shaft. The warm blood stopped flowing from the mended carotid artery in his neck. She felt the tissue beneath her fingers become more solid instead of a shredded mush. "Please stay still. Don't give me away."

Without warning, the brute's large, meaty paw encompassed her arm. He yanked her to her feet. The air crackled around her bloody hands, and she hastened the cessation of healing energy. On her feet, she stumbled from weakness. The wolfman gave her a strange look.

"What's the matter, doll, can't ya walk?" The sneering weasel-man shoved her shoulder.

Kat jerked her shoulder out of the weasel's grip, speeding up to cross the clearing to the cliff wall. She said, "I can walk fine when I'm not knocked off balance. Back off, I'm coming peacefully as I said I would."

Deave stepped between them. His large hand wrapped around her upper arm as he led her through a hidden fissure in the cliff wall. He motioned to the other two to walk into the forest. He hastily dragged her beside him. "We must hurry. No telling when they'll miss her and the whelp. I'd love to see the high and mighty Alpha's face when he finds his brother laying in his own blood, dead and his precious mate missing. Good thing Moog knew about this secret entrance."

A chill of dread ran down Kat's spine at the look of sheer bloodlust on Deave's face. She kept pace with the men but stumbled over fallen trees a couple of times. The brutish troll lost his patience, grabbed her, and threw her over his shoulder. He trekked down the trail with her as if she weighed no more than a feather.

Kat hung over his shoulder in an undignified position. With a grunt, she kicked him with no effect. He placed his hand on her rump to hold her still. She grumbled, "Do you mind? Don't manhandle me."

"No, I don't mind. It's quite nice, soft and round." The troll's voice sounded like a rusty hinge.

Kat blustered and hit him ineffectually in the back. Finally, she addressed Deave. "Can you tell your trained bear to put me down? I can walk by myself."

"We can move faster this way. Besides, Bog's enjoying himself. Not as much as we all will once Grigore's killed." Deave gave a maniacal cackle.

Kat cringed at his words. *Grigore, what have I gotten you into? I won't let him kill you. I don't know how I'll stop it, but we just found each other.* The group moved through the forest in a blur with their preternatural speed until they arrived at a dark green sports utility vehicle hidden in the brush. Shoving her roughly inside, the three Alts climbed in and sped down the road. Kat heard gravel grind, the wheels slinging the rocks into the trees behind them.

Kat watched for landmarks to remember, counted the number of turns, and was desolate when she lost track. The werewolf behind the wheel drove farther and farther away. She wondered how Grigore would ever find them. She didn't see them leave a note.

Chapter 65

Elena and Maricara threw the door open and burst into Grigore's office where the men were meeting. "We've looked everywhere and can't find Kat."

"When did you last see her?" Grigore jumped up from his chair, striding over to the two women.

"Kat went with Anton to the hidden alcove over an hour ago. She wanted to check something. Anton accompanied her while Mama and I finalized arrangements for the ritual today. They should have been back by now." Elena frowned, paced the length of the office, and rubbed her hands together.

Cristofer leaned forward in the chair at the desk. "Calm down. Elena, did you check the alcove? Maybe she lost track of time?"

Elena gave a sheepish glance around the room. "No, *Tata*, I didn't. Kat said she'd be right back. That was an hour ago. Something happened to her."

"The first thing is to go check the alcove garden. Andre, please go investigate. Have them return to the house immediately." Cristofer delegated to his son-in-law. He tapped his lower lip with a long, slender finger. "Anton gets sidetracked easily."

"I'll go check." Grigore started for the door, but Elena blocked his path. Before he could circumvent her, Andre left.

Within a few seconds, a howl of distress split the air, spurring the occupants of the room into action. Each transformed into their wolf form as they galloped at full speed to the alcove. They hovered over Anton's prone figure on the ground. Maricara nudged his face with her nose and licked his cheek.

Moaning, Anton stirred and opened his eyes to stare at the wolf. "Mama." His memory slammed into him. He sat upright, looking around desperately. "Where's Kat?"

"Anton, what happened? There's blood all over you." Grigore bent, checking Anton's wounds.

"What?" Gazing down, Anton shuddered when the memories flooded back. "Grigore, I tried to stop them. I fought him. He was bigger and stronger. Kat helped, hitting him with a stick. Another one grabbed her. I'm sorry, Grigore. I'm so sorry." The whelp broke into tears.

"Anton, it's okay. I can tell you did your best. It's a wonder they didn't kill you." Grigore placed his hand on his brother's shoulder and examined his neck. There was a large pool of blood under Anton. His shirt was shredded by wolf claws. Sniffing, he smelled new flesh around his neck. The teen's wounds had been deep.

Grigore's gray eyes zeroed in on several sets of footprints. Three distinct scents mingled in the air besides those of Kat and Anton's. A sign of leg prints indicated someone knelt beside Anton. The light impressions must belong to Kat. The distinct citrus fragrance mingled with the overwhelming stench of fear.

"Anton5rt, what are you talking about? Who got her? Who attacked you?" Elena hugged him and then pushed him back to stare into his eyes.

Grigore stood alert and sniffed the air. "The scents belong to Deave, accompanied by the troll, Bog, and the rodent, Waso." Deave and Waso were Moog's right-hand thugs.

"Take a deep breath, my *fiul.* We must understand what happened so we can help." Cristofer laid his hand on his youngest son's shoulder, easing him to lean back against his side in his weakened state.

Anton closed his eyes and took a deep breath as he filled the others in on what had happened. He finished with Kat risking the thugs discovering her ability to heal his wounds. "I would have died without her intervention."

"Grigore, he's using her as bait. Moog wants access to you," Elena exclaimed in horror.

"I'll accommodate him." Grigore stood, a feral gleam growing brighter in his eyes. He stepped toward the portal.

"Grigore, stop. I forbid it." Cristofer eased Anton to the ground, moving with werewolf speed in front of Grigore.

"If they had taken Mama, you would've already been gone." Grigore glared back at his patriarch.

"We will go after her after we have a plan. Without one, you will die. I nearly lost one son. I will not risk losing another. Control the beast, my *fiul.* It will be harder on the night of your claiming. You must dominate it instead of allowing it to dominate you. Have you forgotten Kane is there? He will not allow any harm to befall Kat." Cristofer held his ground, prepared if he needed to attack to make his point.

Posed to fight, Grigore stepped back and bowed his head in submission. "Your ageless wisdom prevails, my father, my king."

"Good. Let us return to the house with your brother. We will implement a plan before the trail gets cold." The men carefully lifted Anton's battered body. Maricara walked beside him, holding his hand. They walked back to the house, overshadowed by a morose mood.

Chapter 66

Kat's senses were assaulted when they forced her through the door of a run-down warehouse. The intensity of a booming bass playing in the background hurt her ears. She bent her arm over her mouth and nose to shield against the stench of stale smoke, alcohol, and dirty bodies that filled the air. Another unidentified sulfuric aroma mixed with the other scents.

Moog had converted a large section of the abandoned warehouse into a bar. There were several unkempt men scattered inside. Some were sitting at tables on one side. Others were at a shabby wooden bar. In a corner, there was an empty section of floor for dancing. A lone couple swayed to the booming bass. Men were playing pool at a couple of tables in the middle of the room. Three or four other men were leaning on the edge of the tables, sneering at her with lust-filled eyes.

Kat shuddered. The brute's vice-like grip on her arm made her wince in pain. He drug her across the expanse of the cavernous building and pushed her into a chair near two tables in a darkened corner. A gigantic man equal in size to her mountainous beastly guard sat at the table across from Kat. The man wore black—black jeans, black T-shirt, black boots and black sunglasses that matched his black hair. He leaned back in a chair with his booted feet crossed at the ankles and propped on the table. His arms were folded across his massive chest.

Feeling her gaze on him, the man lifted his sunglasses and winked at her with ice-blue eyes before he resumed his sleeping pose. Kat jerked her eyes away. She observed the weasel getting a drink from the bartender. Nodding toward her table, he disappeared through a door behind the bar. The bartender grabbed a glass of water, took it to Kat's table, and slammed it in front of her with a loud clunk. "The boss says you's thirsty."

"Thanks," Kat reached for the glass, quailing at the black blob at the bottom.

The man grunted in response, returning to the bar. She shivered and tried to keep a brave front, hoping they didn't know she was scared witless. Kat stared at her blood-covered hands and prayed Anton still lived. She tugged down her shirttail and noticed for the first time that it had been ripped in the earlier altercation. Tearing off a small piece of the ruined shirt, she dunked it into the water to wash off some of the blood.

Kat heard hissing sounds as the men whispered. Occasionally, she caught a few words. What she pieced together didn't bode well for her. She casually leaned back in her chair, making a mental map of the layout of the building. She saw three exits, one she came in, and two others on opposite walls. She seriously doubted she could make it to any of the exits.

Two men skulked over to her table. One dressed in grease-stained jeans and a ripped T-shirt, leaned over, resting his palms flat on the tabletop. He grinned contemptuously at her chest and greedily licked his lips. The other one wore leather pants and an open leather vest over his hairy body. He ran his fingers through her hair, twisting a lock around the tip of his finger, giving a little tug. She smelled his fetid breath near her ear. "I can't wait to taste what you've got to offer."

"Yeah," panted the other slimeball, "I want first go. She smells so fresh and looks so pretty."

"She won't when we finish with her." The man with fetid breath sniggered and released his hold on her hair with a jerk. He reached down to squeeze a breast through her top.

Kat cringed in disgust as she pushed his hand away. "Get your filthy paws off me."

"You'll be begging for my touch before we kill you." He grabbed her neck in his fist, squeezing.

Chuckling, the other one moved in on her from the other side. "Paws. That's funny coming from the mate of a wolf."

"She needs to know what a real werewolf can do, not to mention some trolls, demons, vamps and other creatures." Fetid breath glared into her eyes as he lifted her partway from her chair by her neck. He gave a feral smile as she tugged at his hand.

"Go ahead," said the man leaning back. "Moog won't be upset he didn't get first chance at Grigore's juicy morsel." He never moved. His voice had a soft caress like black velvet.

The man stopped dead in his tracks at the soft baritone words. He glared at the sleeping man, released her neck, gave a hard squeeze to her breast and slunk back to the other side of the room with his companion. He spat out over his shoulder, "When he finishes, we'll all get a taste."

Kat took a deep, rasping breath but didn't move. She didn't want anything perceived as encouragement to this depraved group. Her breasts ached, but she resisted the urge to rub the tender flesh. She bet the cretin left a bruise. Kat glanced over her shoulder toward the voice. The man still appeared to be sleeping. Perhaps she only imagined the voice.

A dark-haired man of medium height appeared from the back room and walked to her table. He stared at her with a shake of his head. "All the she-wolves Grigore can choose from, and he picks you. What's the attraction?" The man slid his hand across her nipples, shaking his head. "Can't be your small breasts. They're not even a handful. Maybe it's what's between your legs." He moved his hand down to cup her mound as he sniffed her chaste purity.

Kat gasped as she tried to squirm away, held fast by his hand on her shoulder. Folding her arms over her chest, she refused to satisfy him with a response.

The man gripped her arm, ripped her from the chair, and pulled her tightly against his body. He captured her mouth in a harsh kiss with a nip to her lip that drew blood. He licked it off with his tongue. The acrid smell of her fear mixed with the coppery scent of blood spurred him on. He growled and ran his hands down her back, cupping her butt-cheeks. He pulled her hard against him, grinding his arousal against her.

His voice husky and his breath noxious, he bellowed out between clenched yellowed teeth. "Won't he be surprised when he finds his mate claimed by his enemy? How I long to crush him. You'll be the end of him."

The silky baritone broke through his reverie. "I applaud you, Moog. He will be drawn by the first ones defiling scent on his true-mate."

Snarling, Moog gave Kat a rough shove away from him and stomped to the other side of the bar. Kat hit the concrete floor hard, knocking the breath from her. She observed the man in black's furtive glance before she struggled to her feet. She rubbed her derriere, settling back into her wooden chair. The man extended his arms outward to stretch, shifted in his chair with a yawn, and resumed his nap.

Moog grabbed two beers from behind the bar and rejoined the mountain of a man at the table beside Kat. "How long do you think it'll take for him to show up?"

"It shouldn't be long. You nabbed his mate, like we planned. Lycans will do anything to protect true-mates." The man sat up with an indifferent shrug.

"True, the need to protect the true-mate is innate. Good thing we haven't found one. It would be a weakness." Moog laughed and slapped his companion hard on the arm. He chugged his beer in one gulp.

"Yep. Waso, bring us another beer." The man in black called across the room.

"I have interesting plans for her once he shows up, and we kill him." Moog gave a demonic chortle. "I'll test her tolerance level in all kinds of sordid ways. It'll be interesting to see what she can tolerate. When I get bored, the others can have her. You can have a go after I finish. Maybe we can both teach her a thing or two together. Maybe even claim her in front of him before we kill him."

"Quite a picture." The large man said flatly. He gave the smaller man a stoic glance.

The outside door flew open, spilling bright light into the oppressive bleakness of the room. A dark figure entered the building. His square-shouldered silhouette in the door seemed familiar to Kat. She watched him approach and gasped when she saw his features. "Gerald! Have you come to free me?" Bounding from her chair, she moved closer to the large man.

"On the contrary. He's how we located you." Moog gave her an evil grin, chuckling at the look of betrayal and disbelief on Kat's face.

"Gerald, tell me that's not true." Kat gasped, took a step back and stared at the large man.

"Kat, I wanted to talk. You wouldn't listen. You picked a werewolf over me. He has money and power. I'm a lowly bodyguard and chauffeur." The square-jawed man looked at Kat, his voice matter-of-fact. He stood as still as a statue by the table. His dark gray eyes bored into her.

"Gerald, you were my friend. You succumbed to my sister's advances. I love Grigore. He rejected Keisha. Money and power mean nothing to me. You've known me for years and surely knew that." Kat's voice caught as she fought back tears from the deception of a man she thought was her friend. She didn't know why it hurt so much. He had stabbed her in the back with Keisha, too.

"If you hadn't found Keisha kissing me, would we still be together?" Gerald watched her reaction.

"No, you are... were my friend. Why betray my trust? My father's trust?" Kat gazed into stone-gray eyes in search of her answer.

Moog chortled behind her, making her look at him. "Money and power. What else? Don't let him fool you. Who do you think told us where to find you on that dark road?"

Whirling back around, she glared at Gerald, her words venomous. "You were in on the kidnap attempt? You came to my hospital room to guard me."

"You were never supposed to get hurt. Still aren't." Gerald brushed her cheek with his rough fingertips.

"They're talking of raping me. How does that keep me unharmed?" Kat jerked away, crossed her arms over her chest, and glared at him with loathing.

"We have quite a catch. She will lead us to the hostile takeover of Carter Anderson's business and provide the bait to lure my enemy, Grigore, to his death." Moog rubbed his hands together, cackling with glee.

Seeing the loathing in Kat's eyes, Gerald watched her and added with his jaw set. "You won the trifecta tonight, Moog. She can heal with her touch, too."

"Grigore's woman could come in handy during battle. We won't kill her. She would make a handy pet!" Moog gave a sinister smile. His eyes glowed red in contemplation of what owning her would achieve.

Kat shivered, feeling Moog's cold eyes on her. She turned to look at the enigmatic man. He didn't give the same creepy-crawly feeling the others gave her. On the contrary, he had a calm air of reassurance. Somehow, he felt familiar. Her shoulders sagged. She hunkered over the table and wrapped her arms around her body. She wished for rescue yet dreaded the thought of Grigore walking into this pit of vipers, ready to strike him with their venomous bites. With a sigh, Kat settled in to wait for fate's outcome and hoped for a happy ending.

Chapter 67

Grigore paced across the office to keep his nerves from snapping. He slammed his fist on the desk for the third time so hard the windows rattled. He glared at the others through luminescent eyes. "I can't wait any longer. Dark is approaching. No telling what they're doing to her."

"We know time is of the essence. It will do no good to rush in unprepared. If you weren't fighting the beast for control, you would be cognizant of that, my *fiul*." Cristofer reasoned as he acknowledged the pain his son experienced.

Grigore snarled, his teeth bared and lengthened. An internal battle raged deep inside him, causing him to exhibit physical manifestations of his beast within. His breathing became labored, and he hunkered down, prepared to attack whatever kept him from protecting Kat..

"*Prețioase fiul* do not let the beast take control." His mother placed her hand on his shoulder. "The beast cannot win against Moog and his mob." Her soft lyrical words in his ear stopped Grigore in mid-crouch, and sanity gained control once more.

Grigore stood, ran his hand through his hair, hung his head, and the glow in his eyes briefly subsided. "Mama, I'm trying to stay in control. Truly, I am."

"We know." She embraced him.

"Moog can't be too far away. Anton said they had been in the garden for about thirty minutes when they were attacked." Andre hastened to business, knowing that the longer the delay, the worse things could be.

"Thankfully, Kat thought fast and used her healing powers, or we'd have lost him," Elena exclaimed.

"They must be in the city. We can fly the helicopter into the area where Kane said their headquarters are located. Kane is incommunicado. Otherwise, we'd know the exact coordinates. Grigore will follow her aroma to the location. Acting together, we can surprise and overtake them. Once we find them, nature will take over. Can you control the beast that long, Grigore?" Andre gazed at his brother-in-law.

"I can't promise. The beast is strong. Once the sun goes down, the moon will magnify the primal powers. He won't be satisfied until he destroys the usurpers of his true-mate." Grigore exhaled and rubbed the back of his neck. At this point, the beast was taking on its own identity.

Andre ended a call on his cell phone. "I've contacted Marcus. He'll have a vehicle standing by at the helipad to transport us."

Cristofer nodded with approval. "Good. Once there, we will strike hard and fast to take them by surprise. Elena has developed a new chemical to mask our scent. The lycanthropes and Alts inside won't be aware of our presence. How long will the effect last, Elena?"

Astonished, Elena stared at her father. "*Tata*, are you sure? There's been no tests, only localized experiments. I'm not sure how long it will last."

"We have no choice. This will be the first big test. We must get in." Grigore's eyes flashed silver.

"True, *fiul meu*, even if it is long enough for us to burst through the doors, your discovery will give us an advantage." Cristofer gave a reassuring smile to his daughter.

A wolf's howl broke through the tense momentary silence. Andre agilely stabbed a button on his phone, listened, and ended the call. "Marcus says some of our pack will meet us at the helipad to aid in the raid."

"Excellent. Elena, get Andre the concoction. Andre, meet us at the helipad. Grigore, I will fly since you are having difficulty keeping control. The helicopter holds seven. I will get some guards. We can fill them in on the way. There is no time for your brothers to arrive." Cristofer keyed in the security code, and everyone headed for their tasks, pausing when Anton rushed through the door.

"*Tata*, I want to go help rescue Kat. She saved me." The young whelp pleaded, his eyes filled with worry.

"Anton, you are still healing. You will stay here and watch over the women." Cristofer soothed the young man with a fond gaze.

"What?" screeched Elena. "You're not leaving me behind. I'm going too."

"Elena, my dear…" Andre stepped toward his wife, love shining in his eyes.

"Don't my dear me. I'm going. I must monitor the experiment. They hurt my brother and my friend," Elena growled with hands on her hips. She glared at the others.

"I agree. You will need all the help you can get. I shall go too. It has been years since I have been in a good battle." Maricara smiled, taking the side of her daughter.

"I forbid it as your husband and as *Regele Alfa*." Cristofer commanded, hands fisted at his sides. He glared at his wife.

"As your wife, I will do as I wish." Maricara lifted her chin and glared back, nose to nose. Her tone softened. "As a loyal subject, I will respect the word of the *Regele Alfa*. Be careful. I do not know what I would do without you, *inima mea*." Her soft voice was filled with concern as she glanced at each member of her family.

Cristofer cupped her cheek in his palm and gazed into her eyes with adoration. He disappeared through the door with the others.

"Mama, someone needs to talk with Kat's father. He will want to know where everyone went and why the nuptials were delayed." Elena reminded her mother before she left to join the others.

"True, we have forgotten that he will be concerned." Maricara left the room to intercept her sister and their guest.

Grigore thought the ride in the helicopter was endless. The dark sky succumbed to the lambent glow of the nearly full moon rising in the sky. His primal instincts created internal havoc. His agitation escalated to explosive levels as the helicopter began its descent, hovering above the ground. Grigore inhaled the barest whiff of Kat's scent. With a growl, the primordial pulse throbbed through his veins. His beast took over.

Ripping the door open with his superhuman strength, Grigore plummeted to the ground and transformed mid-air into his wolf form. He landed on his haunches. Once his clawed, padded feet touched the ground, he took off in a full run.

"Andre, no!" Elena shouted at her husband as he followed in hot pursuit. He couldn't lose sight of Grigore. Grigore would be killed in his present state of mind.

Grigore ran at full speed, oblivious to his surroundings. His only thought was to reach his mate. He didn't hear Andre call him. Andre did his best to keep pace but still dropped behind. Andre's powerful night vision kept Grigore in sight. Panting, Andre jumped through the open door of a Durango that sped by.

"Marcus, four blocks up. He turned left. Grigore's heading for those abandoned warehouses on Seventy-Second Street," Andre uttered through panting breaths. "I couldn't catch up with him."

Running. Heart racing, Kat's scent was closer with each step. Grigore growled at the terror that was in her fragrance. Focusing, Grigore heard her heart pounding. Another strong, familiar scent caused the hair to stand up on his back. His hackles rose. His enemy, Moog. He snarled and pushed his body to its limits, running faster as his true-mate's fragrance intensified.

Grigore's ferine instincts primitively overtook any humanity left within him. His body metamorphosed into a half-human, half-wolf physique. He covered ground on two feet. A burst of super-speed cut the time in half. The claws on his hind-paws dug into the asphalt. His teeth lengthened into razor-sharp weapons any samurai would envy. The radiant shimmer in his eyes changed from silver to a rabid blood red. He had a vague awareness of his name being called from a distance behind him. The reverberation of a motor chased his heels. His only focus to reach his mate burned inside.

Chapter 68

Punching a selection into the jukebox, the brutish troll lumbered over to Kat's table. He grabbed her forearm and yanked her from her chair. "Dance."

"What?" Kat stared at the troll, stunned by the tight grip hurting her arm. She tried to hide the terror on her face. Her feet skidded as the troll dragged her onto the dance floor.

"You dance." Bog grated out with a rough shove.

Feeling like a cornered mouse, Kat sought a hiding spot to avoid being the center of attention. All the men stopped their activities to contemplate this fresh development. A movement in the corner of her eye diverted her interest for a split second. One man at the pool table had a snake—no, not a snake, a long thin tail with a barbed point. He whipped it snakelike in excitement. He leered at her showing his pointed teeth. His slanted eyes gave him a devilish appearance.

A meaty paw shoved her shoulder, and Kat lost her balance and concentration for a moment. "Forget the demon. Dance."

Kat stumbled onto the cleared section of the floor. She got a glimpse of horns protruding from the demon's head. Her reality had been obliterated beyond recognition. Furtively glancing from one man to another, she pondered what hid underneath their human guises.

Another jab destroyed her preoccupation with the surrounding beings. She glared at the ogre. "What do you want?"

"Bog bored. You dance. Entertain him. He watch." The troll towered over her.

Obviously, he wasn't the most literate person, Kat stood self-consciously in the middle of the room. The occupants stared at her with lust and licked their lips. She looked for an escape route. Her eyes paused on Gerald, who sat on a stool at the bar. He lifted his drink in salute with a grim smile. The troll poked her in the stomach with his large finger. "Dance."

Kat's hopes were dashed when the others started chanting, "Dance. Dance. Dance."

Kat slowly moved her feet to the rhythmic beat of the song that blared from the speakers. Fear flashed in her eyes. The static, stale air filled with energy fed the occupants of the building. Kat trembled as she gyrated and inched closer to the edge of the dance floor, toward the metal door she had arrived through. She didn't know what she'd do if she reached the door. Even if she did, she seriously doubted she'd survive these creatures' retaliation.

From behind her, a hand encircled her forearm, like a shackle. The unseen captor drug her away from the door with the black velvet voice whispering in her ear, "Not a good idea if you want to live, Kat. Move back to the table." The words continued softly in her head. She glanced up at the bear of a man. His mouth barely twitched. His ice-blue eyes locked with hers, impressing the words into her. "Kat, when the time comes, the door will open. Run. Don't stop. Don't look back. Run!"

Kat stared at him open-mouthed. How did he know her name? She saw something familiar in his eyes that she couldn't quite identify. "Do I know you?"

The giant of a man shrugged and guided her toward her chair. "You know what they say. One werewolf looks like another."

The sharp-toothed, tailed creature from the pool table stepped into the pair's path, stopping them. "Breaking up the entertainment, lycan?"

The man's grip on her arm tightened. Visually, he appeared relaxed. Kat observed an infinitesimal tilt of his head and a flare of his nostrils as if he had caught a scent in the air before he released his grip.

The man's blue eyes fixed on the demon. He motioned toward the door with his head. "Pulling her away from the door. Don't want her to escape. Wouldn't want Moog's prize to get away."

A hiss of laughter escaped from the creature's hideous mouth, leaving a sulfuric aroma. He latched onto his prey and pulled Kat against his chest. His tail wound around her leg, slithering upward. Kat wrinkled her nose at the invasive sulfur smell. She jumped when the spade-shaped barbed tip of his tail patted her bottom. Repulsion flooded through her.

He dipped his mouth closer to hers. His tongue snaked out to lick her lips. Kat nearly retched at the smell of putrid sulfur.

An earsplitting bellow came from the opposite side of the door. Seconds later, the sound of metal screeching filled the air. The door burst inward, ripped from the hinges. A large panting creature threw it to the side as if it were a feather. A humanoid wolf filled the doorway. Silver-tinged eyes glowed with a demonic red flare as the shapeshifter glared at Kat's wrist in the demon's grasp. He snarled, stalked over, and slashed claws down the demon's back. The demon screamed as deep gashes oozed blood. The furious creature grabbed the demon's wrist, ripping the offending arm from his body. Then the creature pried Kat from his grip.

The wolfen humanoid scooped her against his chest and headed toward the door. Something slammed against his back, causing him to stumble. Kat squealed, and he tightened his grip, squeezing her before he carefully set her to the side. The creature whirled, roared and galvanized into action against his attackers. He lunged and grabbed the nearest enemy by the throat. His claws dug in, crushing the windpipe. Blood gushed from the wounds.

Realization dawned. Kat recognized Grigore. She saw a barbed cut on his back from the chair someone had slammed against his back. Bog bumbled into the fray. He wrapped Grigore in a bear hug from the back and tightened his enormous arms to crush Grigore. The troll shook him like a rag doll.

Emitting another bellow, Grigore dug his claws into the troll's forearms. He raked deep furrows into the flesh. The troll loosened his grip from the pain slicing into him. Grigore slammed his head back into the troll's forehead. Blood spurted from a jagged cut. More creatures jumped into the fray. Kat saw fur and blood flying across the room. Screeches, howls and yelps filled the air. She felt helpless. Fear for Grigore filled her. The enemy outnumbered him. She searched for a weapon of her own to help.

Bloody claws and teeth shown in the dim light. Bodies stumbled from blows. Kat winced when claws gashed Grigore's arm and chest. The others piled on top of him on the floor. He gave an explosive roar. He strained until a surge of adrenaline flowed through his body. His eyes glowed red. The primordial beast overtook his consciousness. He bellowed again as he threw his aggressors across the room and shook them off his body. A fresh group of creatures assaulted him. Men ran from all directions, shedding their human forms for their natural state. They knocked Grigore to the floor, continuing to attack him.

Kat's mouth gaped open in shock when Gerald transformed. His body solidified into stone, making his movements slower. Wings sprouted from his back. Kat shook her head. *Weren't gargoyles statues, not living creatures?* He stalked across the floor toward her with his heavy footsteps reverberating in the large bar. Kat broke from her stupor in time to dodge his large hand as he grabbed for her arm.

Kat saw others transform into werewolves and other creatures she didn't recognize. The troll and demon attacked the newcomers from the Versipellis pack as they stormed through the door. The cavalry had arrived, storming into the building in wolf and Alt form. Without hesitation, they executed a counterattack. Each wolf retaliated against the thugs as they surrounded their fallen champion. She thought she recognized some of them but had never seen them after they transformed.

Grigore's family and pack had arrived in their alternate forms and immediately jumped into the fracas. Bodies flew in every direction. Kat had to figure out the good guys from the bad guys. One black wolf had a streak of white hair across his head—Cristofer.

Kat accounted for all the men she encountered earlier except for three: Moog, the weasel man called Waso and Deave the werewolf with the scarred face. They were nowhere to be seen. Her eyes scanned the room. She spotted Moog leaning against the bar as he sipped a drink, cheering on his minions.

The man in black stood near Grigore. His lips twitched, and his voice—the velvet voice whispered—hit her from across the room. "Kat, now. Run. Don't stop." She refused to leave as long as Grigore remained in danger. Kat dodged the slow movements of the gargoyle when he lunged for her again. His solid arms could crush her without trying. The man in black came between them and shoved against Gerald's chest, sending him flying backward into the wall.

"Kat, run," the man in black said aloud this time.

"Not while Grigore's in danger." Kat renewed her search for a weapon. She dodged a flying table leg and retrieved it from the floor. She swung it with all her might. The enemy was unphased. Grigore grew weaker. His assailants were weakening too, but they outnumbered him. That'd give them the advantage. They could last longer. Cristofer lunged into the battle and ripped into the back of one of the attackers, knocking him from Grigore's back.

"Run." Kat recognized Elena's voice coming from a werewolf that circled her, snarling at anyone who approached. Kat looked around for the man in black but didn't see him. He must have run. She aimed the chair leg to clobber a half-man and half-goat on the head. A faun? A satyr? Elena dived for the man's throat.

She looked around. A motion by the bar caught her attention, Moog and his goons were slipping through a hidden opening behind the bar. One by one, some members of his pack threw the villains off Grigore's prone body. Kat gasped at his bloody torso, covered in lacerations. He lay unmoving. His flesh was shredded. Running over, Kat knelt beside him and examined his wounds. Laying her head on his chest, she heard the slow, erratic beat of his heart. He gulped for breath. She barely detected a pulse. The pool of blood beneath him continued to grow.

"Kat…" escaped his mouth in a rattle.

"Hang on, Grigore. I'm here for you. I won't let you die." Kat smothered a sob and placed her crossed palms over his heart. She focused on blocking out the chaos to concentrate on her task. Out of the corner of her eye, she noticed the man in black off to the side.

Kat closed her eyes and fixed on a focal point in her mind's eye. The telltale warmth started in her body, flowed down her arms and into her hands. Her body tingled as energy gathered around her hands. She gave a mental push of energy that surged from her to encompass Grigore's body in a cocoon of white light. A body flew past her, but the man in black stood guard over them and knocked it to the side.

Inhaling a deep breath, Kat descended deeper into a somniferous state of mind. Energy surged from her hands to envelop both she and Grigore in metaphysical armor of anodyne power. Grigore's body took over the natural healing process. The blood flow from his wounds stopped, and the wreckage to his tissues began to repair itself. Blood cells multiplied a hundred times faster than normal. Veins intertwined to grow back together. Ripped muscles mended. New flesh grew in place of skin ripped from his body.

The carnage around them continued as the battle raged on. Kat's mind was so absorbed that she became oblivious to the bodies and pieces of furniture flying by. The man in black shielded her with his body, knocking any creatures away from the two prone bodies. Screeches, howls, bellows and screams reverberated across the room.

The bedraggled family encircled Grigore, watching Kat work her magic. They were tense with fear of what would happen if something broke the connection. The battle had moved outside as the pack tried to capture the fleeing enemy. Other members of the pack came to guard Kat and Grigore. The man in black left his position to join the others outside in pursuit of the enemy. One by one, they returned to encircle the pair. Some of the lycanthrope guards gathered the living prisoners. The man in black trotted in through the door behind the bar. His shirt was torn, and blood dripped from a wound on his side. "How's Grigore?"

Chapter 69

Elena leaned against Andre's chest as he stood behind her. "We're all thankful to Kat." She filled in Ronald, one of the industry's scientists. He worked with her and had joined the group to monitor the cloaking serum's effectiveness. He had joined the mission to monitor the results of the cloaking serum. The results were inconclusive with the way things played out.

"You said the woman encased him inside some kind of insulated second skin, accelerating the healing process." Ronald had joined the group guarding the duo after the battle. He examined and took notes of the empath's healing trance as he observed from different angles.

"How long will she be able to continue?" Andre stood guard in wolfen form, glancing from Grigore to the scientist and back.

"I'm not sure. He's at the point where his internal healing abilities should take over. The other question is, if we break contact, what harm will come to either participant?" Ronald watched the interactions, making studious notes.

Emotion filled Elena's shaky voice. She poked Kane with her wolfen finger, careful not to cut him with her claw. "Where were you? Why didn't you help in the fight when they first jumped him?"

"I had orders to follow. Grigore told me that no matter what happened, I had two priorities. Kat's safety and keeping Moog from escaping. I failed on the second assignment. Moog escaped through a hidden passage behind the bar. One of Moog's goons jumped me. The goon is mincemeat. I'll track Moog. I wanted to make sure Grigore and Kat both safe before I leave." Kane's tone reflected his frustration. "I'm just worried."

"We all are." Andre stood beside his wife and placed his arm around her waist, pulling her against him.

Cristofer barked out orders, overseeing the action at the scene. "Time is of the essence. Canvas everything quickly. Once completed, we will have to risk moving Grigore and Kat." The others obeyed Cristofer's calm, commanding voice instantly. He patiently observed his pack and friends followed his instructions in the organized chaos around him.

The team removed proof of the Alt's existence. Marcus and Kane examined the files and inventory of the entire establishment for evidence of where Moog might have disappeared. For now, the family remains in control against Moog. Cristofer remained *Regele Alfa*. The Versipellis wolves fought the odds and conquered their adversaries. Many of the enemies were dead or captured. Some had escaped the building to run for their lives. Gerald made it outside into the alley and used his wings to take flight.

The cleanup crew performed their job with swift precision. They disposed of the dead bodies, cleaned the blood, and removed files and other evidence. The crew put any remnants of the fray into a reinforced security van.

Once they finished, they conversed with Cristofer and agreed to report any tangible information obtained. A team appointed by Cristofer, got into the van and drove to Paladin's Portal, where they would imprison the criminals in the Alt security prison using the interdimensional portal. The information gathered would be secured in an evidence room for examination. Later, they would interrogate the survivors for information. The occupants left in the building were those who had arrived by helicopter before the carnage and Marcus who had driven. They gathered around the prone pair on the floor once more, deciding what action to take.

Kat's body trembled. Her shoulders heaved with the effort of maintaining the restorative bond. The very air charged with electrified particles culminated around her, buzzing as if alive. The luminescent glow around the pair intensified when Kat absorbed the gathered particles. Everyone had to shield their eyes. After a bright flash like a supernova, the light burned out, Kat crumpled into a heap on top of Grigore.

Elena rushed to her side. "Kat is alive. Her pulse is faint." Moving to check Grigore's pulse, she smiled in relief. "His pulse is strong. His body has healed, but he needs to rest. Everything will mend through his natural healing process through regenerative sleep."

"Good, let us go." Cristofer motioned for Marcus and Kane to take charge of Grigore and Kat. He and the others had shifted back into human form during the cleanup. They changed into spare clothes kept in all the company's vehicles.

Kane hefted Grigore over his shoulder and waited for Marcus to scoop Kat's limp figure into his arms. They followed the others to the helicopter and settled their burdens carefully and securely. Everyone scrambled into the helicopter as the blades whirred overhead. Kane stood outside the door as it closed.

"Kane, get in," Andre called out over the noise of the motor.

"Those two are in excellent hands. I've got a job to finish." Kane closed the door and ducked out of the way.

"Kane, I'll return to help." Marcus yelled, knowing his friend's sensitive ears would hear him. He tossed the large man the keys to the SUV he'd driven to the scene. The chopper became airborne.

Chapter 70

At the estate, Grigore, Elena, Carter, and others gathered in Kat's bedroom. Carter fretted about his daughter's health. He didn't know what to do. He wished he had fostered her gift instead of fearing it and making her repress it. The Lupescu family called in one of the best Alt doctors for help since he knew the true nature of the family. Waiting was the only option now.

The doctor examined Kat once more, while Grigore hovered in the background. "Will she come out of her coma?"

"Kat is exhausted and in a deep sleep. I don't know how long this will last. I wouldn't advise waking her." The doctor watched the pale woman closely. Earlier, the doctor told them that Kat had given too much of her energy to save Grigore's life. Her sacrifice left her weak and fighting for her own existence.

"Is that all you have to say?" Grigore growled helplessly and moved to Kat's side, encompassing her small hand with his large one.

"The doctor is doing all he can. Give it some time." Cristofer's soothing melodic tone filled the room. "Kat used a a great deal of energy to heal your wounds. Even after she restored her life force, you slept twelve hours. You're much stronger than she is."

"Tonight's the full moon. After hearing what carnage, the beast created at the bar, I'm not sure the cage can contain him." Grigore gazed at the surrounding faces. "What happened to Kane? I haven't seen him since we returned."

"Kane went after Moog," Elena answered in a hushed tone. Her hand rested for support on her brother's arm.

"What? Kane can't go after Moog alone. We must reconnoiter, plan, and then go after him again." Grigore's helplessness turned into anger. Kane was one of his best friends, not just a member of the pack. He couldn't bear it if anything happened to him, too.

Marcus stepped into the room. "Kane felt he had failed his assignment. You know he won't let a failure go." Elena slipped out along with Carter and Andre.

"Much like another lycanthrope I know." Grigore gazed at his friend, the Arthurian knight. Marcus and Kane both gave everything they had on every assignment.

"Yes, I'll join him on the hunt. I had to get a few things before I returned." Marcus's sedate gaze locked with Grigore's. He leaned back in a chair.

"Marcus, I don't want you or Kane to risk your lives for mine. We can go together once we have discussed logistics." Grigore ran his fingers through his curls as he watched the door.

"A knight protects his monarch at all costs. You're much more important than either of us. Stay with our future queen. I have equipment to prepare. I'll leave after the strategic planning meeting." Marcus moved toward the door, hand on the doorknob.

"Marcus, my duty is to my people. Keeping them safe means destroying Moog and..." Before he could finish, he felt a hand on his shoulder to silence him.

His father whispered, "He needs to do this."

"I should be with them. Moog's vendetta is with me." Grigore's tone was determined.

"They both have their own reasons, too." Cristofer's soft remark showed his patience. He squeezed his son's shoulder in support.

"My world is falling apart. What will I do if she doesn't come out of her coma?" Grigore felt defeated. He slumped in his chair with his head down.

"You will do like others before you. You will go on. She will wake up and become your true-mate. Her will is strong. Her love for you is stronger." Grigore lifted his head and gazed into the depths of his father's eyes. He bowed his head to Cristofer's centuries of knowledge. Calmness overtook him. Bowing his head slightly, he acknowledged his father's wisdom.

A soft moan claimed Grigore's attention. He sprang from the chair to the bed and grasped Kat's hand. He heard the soft click of the door as it closed. Everyone left them alone.

"Kat, my darling, wake for me. I need you." Grigore sat on the edge of the bed and brushed the hair from her face. He closed his eyes and rested his forehead against her hand with a silent plea for her to awaken. "I love you so much, Kat." Grigore leaned his head into the soft caress of fingers on his cheek. A soothing touch. His eyes popped open, his head flew up, and he looked into her smiling face.

"Grigore, I love you, too." Kat's soft voice was barely a whisper.

"Kat!" Grigore wrapped his arms around her. He pulled her against him, covering her face with soft butterfly kisses. "I thought I'd lost you. You scared me when you drained all your energy to heal me. Promise you won't do that again."

"I felt a little fatigued, but I'm rested now and ready to become your true-mate. I never want to lose you, Grigore." Raising her head, she brushed her lips against his. The kiss deepened, mouth pressed against mouth. Lips parted slightly, tongues danced together in an intimate familiarity. Hands pulled each other closer. Grigore's beast awakened, causing his eyes to glow silver.

Grigore's hand slid around her back. His nails grew longer, sharper and raked down the sensitive flesh of her arm. He kissed down her jawline. His mouth teased along the back of her neck. He licked the saltiness from her flesh. His incisors lengthened in preparation to claim his true-mate.

Grigore snarled at a tap on his shoulder. Elena said, "Come up for air, brother dear."

Grigore closed his eyes and took a deep breath to rein in the beast once more. Releasing Kat, he stood. "Were you lurking outside the door?"

"Nah, if I were, you wouldn't have gotten as far as you did. I came back to see if you wanted dinner. It's a good thing I did too." Elena pushed him out of the way and smiled at Kat. "I'm so glad you're awake. We were all concerned about you."

"Elena, do you think we have time for the ceremony before nightfall?" Kat bit her lip and looked from Grigore to his sister.

"Kat, are you sure you feel like it? You've been unconscious for seventeen hours." Elena squinted and looked at her with concern.

"I'm more than ready and able." Kat smiled and pushed into a sitting position.

"We have things to finish from yesterday. Everyone will be so excited." Elena said.

"Kat, are you sure?" Grigore stepped in front of his sister and helped Kat out of bed.

Elena frowned at him. "Kat says so. Get out. You know the superstition. Go let Mama and the others know. There's a lot to do with little time to do it." Seeing his hesitation, Elena grabbed his arm and tugged him toward the door. "Go on, time is wasting. Make sure Marcus hasn't left yet."

Muttering, Grigore left the room to spread the word, although he knew the others had overheard the conversation, all except her father. Grigore ordered two guards to secure the hidden garden and then joined Andre, Cristofer, and Marcus in a discussion of the previous evening's events. Grigore had difficulty concentrating because his nerves were on edge. He paced back and forth. "What's taking them so long?"

"They'll be ready soon." Andre chuckled, exchanging a knowing glance with the other men.

"Now is the true test of your patience, *fiul meu.*" Cristofer gave his son a knowing smile.

"Forget patience, it will be dark soon and the full moon will fill the sky." Grigore grumbled as someone knocked on the door. He switched off the security system. "Come in."

Ilinca peeked into the room. "The ladies asked me to give you a message. Meet them at the hidden garden at three this afternoon. That is when and where the ceremony will take place."

"Thanks, Ilinca." Grigore glanced out the window at the position of the sun. "That gives us less than an hour to get ready and be there."

"Shall I tell them we need more time?" Andre offered in amusement.

"Very funny. Go get ready. Marcus, you're still standing by my side." Grigore headed for the door.

Chapter 71

In a daze, Kat went through the motions of getting ready while she waited in her room alone. Elena and Maricara left Kat alone for a while. If she were going to change her mind, it would be now. Once joined, only death would end the union. They both heaved a sigh of relief when she walked into the clearing.

She jerked at the knock on the door. "Come in."

Carter walked into the room dressed in a black suit. "You're beautiful, kitten."

She decided to save the bridal gown for the public ceremony. Kat straightened the bodice of her cream-colored, knee-length dress she had chosen for the claiming. She gazed at her father with her brow furrowed and lip between her teeth. "Do you think so, Dad? I'm so nervous. I'm not sure I'm doing the right thing. Maybe you were right, and I should run far and fast."

Carter took her in his arms and hugged her. "Do you love him?"

"Grigore's not like any man I've ever known. He says he loves me, and he accepts me with all my flaws. He rejected Keisha." She leaned her head against her father's chest, her eyes misting over.

"Grigore isn't like any man you've known. He isn't a man." There was no derision in his voice when he touched her cheek with his fingertips.

"I know, yet I still love him." Kat gazed up into his eyes with a wistful smile.

"Love is the key, then. You can make your union work if you have love. Your mother and I had that key element. I haven't been the best of parents, but I want your happiness." Carter cupped her cheeks in his hands and kissed her on the forehead.

"You've taught me well. You were there when I needed you. I'm glad you are giving me away today." Kat hugged him. Tears of happiness slid down her cheeks.

Pulling a handkerchief from his pocket, he wiped her tears away, tilted her chin up with his finger, and gazed into her face, smiling. "None of that. This is a happy day. Now let's go into the garden."

The few invited guests at the intimate union were gathered in the alcove. The cubs were standing near the rock bridge that spanned across the river from the caves. Kat and her father stood in the entrance of the caves behind a column. A guard was posted on the other side of the forest portal.

Cristofer stood before the crowd in the clearing. Soft music played in the background. Grigore, Andre and Marcus stood in front at the side of Cristofer. They all wore dark suits. Elena gave the signal, and the music changed to the traditional "Here Comes the Bride" by Wagner from Lohengrin. Kat walked from behind the column with her arm looped through her father's. She had a bouquet of fresh flowers clutched in her hands.

Ana and Lucia walked in front of her, moved across the clearing toward the men as they tossed petals from baskets of flowers. Daniel followed behind with a proud smile on his face. He held a small box tightly in his hands.

As they joined the men, Carter squeezed Kat's arm in reassurance before he offered her hand to Grigore. Grigore extended his hand, caressing Kat's hand in his, gazing into her eyes. Cristofer laid his hand on top of the clasped hands before him, which was Daniel's pre-arranged signal. Daniel puffed out his chest, strutted forward, and opened the box. Cristofer retrieved a long, wide red ribbon from the box before he returned to his spot. He wrapped one end around Grigore's wrist, weaving the ribbon around the couple's entwined hands. The *Regele Alfa* wrapped the end around Kat's wrist. Energy flowed from the magical ribbon into the couple's bound hands.

"With this ribbon, two shall be joined as one. Never parting. Always understanding. Love reigning eternally for both. Power exchanged is power given." Cristofer's words droned on, mesmerizing Kat. The ribbon glowed.

From that point, Kat went through the rest of the claiming ceremony became a daze. Kat executed the motions without remembering much of what happened, not even when Cristofer removed the ribbon from her hand and replaced it with the simple gold ring on her finger. When Grigore kissed her, she focused on him, unaware the others had left the hidden garden. His lips brushed against hers in a soft, feathery caress. His mouth lightly nibbled and licked her lips, which parted in invitation. The kiss deepened. His tongue explored the depths of her mouth, tasting her sweetness.

Grigore's arms slid around Kat, pulling her into an embrace. His need was obvious as he pressed his bulge against her. One of his hands slid the zipper down on her dress. The other caressed her bare back exposed by the open dress. He nibbled from her chin up to her earlobe and sucked the little piece of flesh into his mouth. His warm breath tickled her ear.

Grigore moved slowly and with care. He struggled with the monster inside that fought for release to conquer her. Now. Breathing hard, he stepped back to watch the dress drop onto the ground. His gray eyes devoured her flesh. She looked more beautiful than he'd imagined. Her curves were exquisite. Her pear-shaped breasts were a delightful handful.

Grigore shed his clothes before he lifted her into his arms. He buried his face in the vee of her neck, and the pure citrus fragrance filled his lungs. Her silken skin scalded him like a hot iron. He carried her to a spot in the alcove that he had prepared earlier. He didn't want her delicate flesh harmed by the rough ground, so he had ensured a comfortable spot for the claiming. A plush blanket was laid across the grass near a clear pool. Rose petals were scattered around the alcove and across the blanket. Lanterns lit the area, giving it a soft glow. A picnic basket and a bottle of champagne was set to the side by the edge of the pond.

Lying her on the blanket, Grigore played his fingers across her chest. His tongue flicked out to lick between her breasts. She moaned and arched her back. The salty-sweet taste of her rolled around his mouth. He craved more. He teased her flesh with caresses soft as the kiss of a cloud. Giving a low growl, he covered her mouth with his, unable to get enough of her taste. Her fingers teased the coarse, curly hair on his chest. With a growl, he captured both her hands in one large hand and held them above her head.

Grigore lowered his mouth to her breast, circling the tender mound with feather-soft kisses. His tongue flicked out to tease her tender, creamy skin. Reaching the hard tip, he sucked it into his mouth. His teeth scraped lightly against the hard nub. Kat gasped, arched her back, and pushed her breast deeper into his mouth. His teeth lightly scraped against the sensitive flesh. She moaned and squirmed at his touch. His trail of kisses felt like a lit match against her skin. He avoided her shoulders, doubting his willpower would be strong enough to stop an abrupt claiming.

Kat writhed beneath his warm mouth as he taunted her. Each wet lick of his tongue tormented her, sending a lightning bolt straight to her core to ignite a fire deep inside. His mouth traveled down along her flesh in a scorched trail of need with each spot he touched. Her desire built deep inside, creating a need she longed for him to fill. Releasing her hands, Grigore slid his fingers down her sides, dragging his nails to leave a trail of fire along her nerve endings. Kat released a hiss at the sensations as his warm, wet mouth and hands teased her body.

Grigore growled with desire when she moaned. Kat lifted her freed fingers and ran them through the curly hair on his chest, setting him on fire. She slid her hands up across his shoulders, along the back of his neck, and into his thick, soft hair. She gasped when his hand touched her inner thigh, tantalizing the smooth, sensitive flesh there.

Daylight faded into the crisp glow of the moon-filled night. The couple continued to embrace and explore each other's bodies. The sensual caresses built to an acrimonious crescendo of need. Grigore shifted positions. His hardness pressed against her thigh. A hand dipped between her legs to nudge her thighs further apart. His touch awakened a hunger deep inside Kat. His fingertip flicked her clitoris. She cried out and bucked in his arms. Shifting positions, he pressed his shaft against her slit and slid inside her opening. His hips moved, and she gasped with a soft mew as he pushed her near the edge.

Feeling her body jerk beneath him, he denied her orgasm time and again until the moment felt right for his possession. He pushed in deep, burying himself inside her. She groaned and stilled, but he held her tight, paying homage to her breasts with his tongue. His finger tormented her clit until the pain faded, and she gasped in pleasure. He moved his hips a little at a time while he adjusted to her tightness. Her hips moved to meet his. The thrusts became faster and deeper.

Grigore increased the speed as the beast took over. He snarled and held her down to assert his dominion over his true-mate. The silver in his eyes morphed into glowing red orbs as he prepared to take possession. He stilled when Kat called his name. Her hand brushed his cheek with a tender caress as she gazed into his eyes.

"Grigore, come back to me. Grigore, I'm yours no matter how you take me. We'll always be together." Kat's soft voice reached out to him. Her eyes wide. Her breaths shallowed as her orgasm grew closer. Kat moaned.

Grigore tossed his head back. He cried aloud as he fought the internal battle. The beast succumbed to the strong desire to protect his mate, allowing Grigore to regain control. He captured her mouth once more and pushed her to the edge again and again with slow strokes inside her. He kept her on the precipice until she whimpered with frustration and begged him to take her.

Nibbling her earlobe, he whispered into her ear. "My love, the mark will cause some discomfort."

"I don't care. I need you so much. Please. Now," Kat cried out through gasps of breath.

"Bite my shoulder, now." Grigore snarled with a low guttural growl. His thrusts sped up. His incisors grew longer and sharper. Kat entered a world of euphoria when he sank his teeth into her shoulder at the same time he gave a hard, deep thrust. He sucked and licked the bite. His true-mate screamed as he sent her over the edge into a climactic explosion.

Kat gasped for air and sank her teeth into his shoulder. The metallic taste of blood filled her mouth. Her fingernails dug into his back. She moaned at the mixture of pleasure and pain. Her mind and body opened to a new world. She felt orgasmic bliss had swallowed her whole. Fire spread from Grigore's bite to flow through her system. The inferno invigorated her. The depth of her passion changed her, making her stronger. Her senses awakened. A deep rumble in his chest built into a roar as Grigore filled her with ever deepening pleasure.

In the radiant moonlight that filled the night the couple explored new sexual positions in the nooks and crannies of the alcove. They fell asleep several times only to awaken to renew their joining. When their passion was sated, Grigore cradled his true-mate in his arms and rested his chin on top of her head. "You're amazing."

Sore and tired, she moved against him and splayed her hand against his chest. "We're amazing together. I almost forgot the reason I came here yesterday. I have a gift for you." She placed a kiss on the wound she'd made on his shoulder. Then she shimmied out of his embrace, padded across the bridge, and ducked into the cave to retrieve the box she'd hidden. On her return across the stream, her feet slipped on the rock. She lost her balance and fell over the brink.

Running to the edge, Grigore dived in and scooped her into his arms, the box still clasped in her grasp. His gray eyes twinkled with laughter as he gazed down into her blue eyes. "Promise me you won't go for a walk alone near any streams."

"Oh you. I just lost my balance." Kat playfully hit him on the arm. She wrapped her arms around his neck, shivering from the cold.

"Don't forget how many times I've seen you lose your balance around rivers. Maybe you have an affinity for getting wet." He grinned at her and wiggled his eyebrows, laughing at her reaction.

"Only if you're the one making me wet." Kat grinned, her cheeks turning red at the implication.

Loosening her grip around his neck, Kat opened the soggy box to show him two chains with matching halves. Connected, they depicted two wolves snuggling together. "I feared I wouldn't get this before the ceremony. Like us, the two halves are not complete without the other."

Grigore smiled and kissed her. Feeling her shiver, he tightened his hold and retreated to the house. Stashing her in his bedroom. No, their bedroom. The pair finished the night wrapped in each other's embrace.

Chapter 72

Grigore awakened early to see Marcus off. He kissed Kat on the cheek and left her tucked in bed. He went down to the helipad to see some of the other members of the pack depart to return to their sectors and lives. They would return for the wedding. The pack would continue to use all their resources to track and derail Moog's plans. Kane had remained in the city to continue his search for their nemesis. In a meeting, the pack decided Marcus would do a cybersecurity deep web search for any details. He may have been an Arthurian knight at one time but now he was a technological wizard. Grigore's parents planned to return to the old country until time for the public wedding ceremony.

Hatya had a long conversation with Carter about their future. She remained at the estate waiting for his return. He had departed with a promise to return soon after he took care of business and dealt with the situation at home. He needed to finalize his divorce with Carolyn. While at home he would make arrangements with his company to conduct business long distance so he could have a honeymoon with her. His attorney had been contacted about the attempted hostile takeover. Hopefully Moog had been distracted and would focus on keeping a low profile for now.

Carter had wanted to tell the police who instigated Kat's kidnapping, but Cristofer convinced him to let the pack deal with him as an Alt. The Alt laws were more stringent and the humans had a tendency to find loop holes that could end up with the release of the criminal. Before he left, he transferred the information he had about Gerald to the Lupescus. Gerald had escaped their clutches the night of the fight, and they didn't want that to happen again. Cristofer had already set a team on researching and locating the gargoyle.

Kat came down to join the others. "Dad, thank you for coming and being there for me."

"Of course, kitten, you are my only little girl and I wouldn't have missed it for the world." He hugged her and kissed her cheek. Turning to Grigore, he shook his hand and placed his other hand on his shoulder. "I better not hear you have mistreated my daughter."

"I could never mistreat her. I just have to make sure I keep her away from any bodies of water outside." He grinned and pulled her close to his side when she slapped at his shoulder.

"I'll be back to give her away at the wedding." He glanced at Hatya. "I'll return for you to, my love. I promise. It won't be like last time." He smiled and squeezed her hand.

When Carolyn and Keisha left, they were driven home in the car by Gerald. Elena and Andre offered to give Carter a ride in their helicopter. Elena wanted to return home to continue her research. Since Grigore's beast went into attack mode, the test of the scent neutralizer had been undetermined. This would give her a chance to test the product before their next mission. At this point its effectiveness was still questionable. If the Versipellis scent could be nullified, they would be able to sneak up on their foes without detection.

"Give your uncle and aunt hugs so we can get on the road children." Elena hugged both and lifted Ana up to kiss their cheeks. The cubs clambered around Grigore and Kat giving hugs and kisses before they left.

"Bye Unca Grigore. Bye Aunt Kat." They called out in unison as they clambered aboard the helicopter.

"Can we be in the wedding? Ana and I wanna throw more flowers." Lucia called out the door.

"Uh-huh." Ana agreed while sucking on her thumb.

"We'll be back early to help finish up any details." Elena squeezed Kat's hand. "My brother doesn't know how lucky he is to find you."

"Yes, I do. I'm the luckiest man in the world." He gazed at Kat with love in his eyes.

"*Non*, that would be me, *mon ami*." Andre said. The two men grinned at each other.

"I believe I beat you both to the most wonderful woman." Cristofer's melodic voice said from behind them. "Even if it took some training, *Pasăre mica*, Little bird." He gave a low grunt when Maricara jabbed him lightly in the ribs with her elbow.

"You are right *dragă*. It took me a while but I did finally train you." She smiled with humor in her eyes. Kat and Elena laughed.

"Ah, Pop, are you and Mom getting mushy again?" Anton groaned causing the others to laugh again.

They all loaded into the helicopter under the whir of the blades. Andre held the handle of the door closing it. Grigore and Kat moved back and waved as the copter lifted into the air. They had scheduled the wedding to take place in three months. That would give the family plenty of time to make an announcement and post it in the press. Arrangements would be made to accommodate the paparazzi with photos and information. Grigore wanted little reason for them to sensationalize their wedding and traumatize Kat.

He had already discussed with Kat and the guards which reporters and photographers would be allowed in for the occasion. They were all Alts. The others would be allowed onto the property but would be monitored closely and kept at a safe distance. He had contacted the witches guild about removing and replacing the protective wards and spells around the property to allow the guests and media to attend. They would add a spell that would confuse the location if they tried to return without permission after the wedding.

A suitable story about how they had met and maintained a hidden courtship would be created. It would be similar to the real story with a few details left out. They had both been in attendance at the same charity events on several occasions so it could be believable they had met at one of those. Later in the day Kat sent out the invitations to the five-star and other guests.

Chapter 73

Kat stood in her room, smoothing nonexistent wrinkles from her wedding dress. The three months gave Kat time to work on her wedding plans. Grigore's parents had returned from the homeland about two weeks before, so Maricara and Elena could help finalize all the details. The rest of his family arrived a couple of days before the ceremony.

Grigore took pride in introducing each of his brothers to her. He came from a large family, and she found it difficult to imagine the thin, elegant Maricara having nine sons and a daughter. Grigore had told Kat that his mother had lost some cubs before she carried him to term, making him the heir apparent. Grigore's brothers arrived from their kingdoms around the world. They all had the good looks of their parents and brother. Kat thought Grigore was the most handsome of them, but she acknowledged her bias. They were all gentlemen, accepting women as their equal, and precious to their existence. Sadly, none of them had found their true-mates. They hoped they would one day, especially now that their oldest brother had found his.

Kat knew Grigore held a royal title but remained clueless about what that entailed until she became his wife. She still had to get used to the term true-mate. Before the marriage, she thought him more of as a figurehead, like the monarch in the United Kingdom. Sense she married, she learned the Alpha had a much more active role in ruling the pack.

Geofri, Alpha of Europe, the next oldest after Grigore, seemed more urbane and reserved than his older brother. Next came Nandru, from Asia, accompanied by Codrin, the Australian Alpha. Wadim flew in from Africa with his three youngest brothers, Bogdan and the twins Aerian and Darius. The youngest were more gregarious. They had no realm to oversee, so they talked about their travels. Darius ruled Antarctica. He voiced that even with his fur coat, he hated the cold, so he visited his brother, Florin, in South America when he could.

Kat grew more anxious about the star-studded wedding than she had been about the claiming ceremony. In the past, she had met many A-list celebrities at charity events, but that didn't compare to having them at her wedding. At those events, she stayed in the shadows most of the time, letting her stepsister take the limelight.

She also had to become accustomed to her father and Carolyn's divorce. That wasn't bad, just different. Kat didn't have contact with her stepmother or stepsister since her dad made them leave that day. Keisha had reached out. In typical form, she blamed her unacceptable behavior on her mother. She dramatically professed that she missed seeing Kat and would love to attend the wedding. In other words, Keisha wanted to be part of the star-studded event in case there were photo opportunities.

By Versipellis law, her dad and Hatya were married before he married Carolyn. After his human divorce from Carolyn was finalized, he returned to Hatya. The soft-spoken woman brightened his life, and he seemed happier and became less of a workaholic. They were seen in tabloids together with their arms wrapped around each other and big smiles on their faces. They informed Anton about the truth about his parentage. He decided he would stay with Cristofer and Maricara and visit Carter and Hatya.

Kat caught her breath at the knock on the door. Elena smiled and opened it. "It's Mama and Hatya."

"Katarina, you're trembling." Maricara floated over to take Kat's cold, shaking hand in hers. "You're already married. This is a formality."

"This is going to be a spectacle. I'll mess up somehow and embarrass all of you." Elena grabbed Kat's arm before she threw herself on the bed and messed up her wedding dress.

"Nonsense. You could never embarrass us," Maricara said with a musical lilt in her voice as she patted Kat's hand. "We all love you. You are perfect for our family. Cristofer and I are glad you are our daughter."

"A daughter to be proud of." Hatya admired her new step-daughter.

A new knock sounded on the door. Carter called from the other side. "It's time, ladies."

When the door opened, the other ladies disappeared to take their spots while Elena stayed with Kat as her matron of honor. She took one last breath and shakily placed her hand on her father's arm as she gazed into his loving eyes. "Dad, I'm not sure I can go out in front of these people."

"Kitten, you're the most beautiful woman here. Everyone is envious that you caught one of the most eligible billionaire bachelors. They think it's a merger of our companies, but we know it's true love. All they must see is the love on your faces when you look at each other. I wish I had been as smart as you, and I wouldn't have lost time with Hatya. Let's go." Her father kissed her on the cheek.

Kat's long sleeve wedding dress of white Duchesse satin floated around her. The endless floral embroidery, embellishments and pearls glistened in the light with her every step. Her twelve-foot-long train spread behind her as she glided down the navy blue and gold runner with an interwoven Lupescu monogram interspersed along the length. The veil covered her face, and dipped down to hide the sweetheart neckline. One of Kat's hands rested on her father's arm. The other held a bouquet of white roses that signified her true love and devotion to Grigore.

Ana and Lucia led the procession in their identical pink dresses, tossing rose petals from white baskets. As the ring bearer, Daniel repeated his performance from the claiming ceremony. Their mother and father walked behind the children. Marcus stood beside Grigore. Both dressed in formal attire. A stunning arch decorated with pink and white roses from the gardens served as a backdrop at the end of the aisle. The delicate fragrance of roses filled the air, adding to the fairytale atmosphere of the event.

Kat glanced at the guests. There were few in the bride section reserved for her family. Hatya chose to sit on the bride's side. She smiled and gave the bride a nod of encouragement as Kat walked past her. Her father would join Hatya once he passed her into the care of Grigore. People packed Grigore's side of the venue. His mother and father sat in the first row. Behind them were his brothers, filling two rows of seats.

Pack members and extended family filled the pews behind his family. Four large men with broad shoulders filled one pew. They played the part of ushers but were the lead members of Grigore's security team. Kat met them after the claiming. She learned that the dark-haired, blue-eyed man who had protected them during the fight was none other than Kane. She was indebted to him for his protection and for stopping her departure from the woods. Otherwise, she wouldn't be so happy with Grigore. When she thanked him, he shrugged a shoulder and told her cryptically that Grigore made a perfect keeper, but he might need to buy a leash. When she asked Grigore what he meant, he said to ignore the large man.

Kat stumbled, and her breath caught at the sight of Grigore dressed in his dark blue, single breast formal attire. He wore the Lupescu medallion of a wolf intricately entwined around a graphic L, along with half of the necklace she gave him on the night of the claiming. His gray eyes gleamed in adoration for his bride. He caressed her hand with his thumb to soothe her raw nerves and to stop her trembling.

Kat relaxed at his touch, and the rest of the ceremony went by in a blur. Grigore kept her tucked under his arm, holding her up. She spoke her vows without stammering. When Grigore raised her veil and kissed her the crowd cheered, she felt as if she floated on a cloud. The pair disappeared down the aisle into another room for the reception. That evening, they danced, took pictures, and greeted celebrity guests for what seemed like hours. Kat planted a smile on her face through a shocked daze at some of the well-known faces.

Finally, the guests departed. The paparazzi flashed pictures from everywhere. The hosts invited a select few photographers into the foyer. Most lined the drive or stood outside the gate taking pictures. After most of the guests left, a small group of the pack and close friends gathered in the library for a private get together. Her father and Hatya were lost in conversation with Anton.

Maricara sat in a plush chair. Cristofer leaned against her, propped on the arm, his arm across her shoulders. Both sipped champagne. Cristofer raised his crystal flute, followed by the others in the room. "Let us raise a glass to the bride and groom. To find your true-mate is a true blessing. You will always have each other. Your pack and family beside you will offer support along the way."

Andre and Elena mirrored her parents on the opposite side of the fireplace. Grigore's brothers and the pack mingled in the room. The twins, Darius and Aerian, had their heads together chatting by the fireplace. Geofri, Nandru, and Wadim talked with the security team about new innovations Lupescu Technologies created. Bogdan flirted with the women of the pack, using his devilish charm. Before they arrived, Grigore had informed Kat about his brother's tendency to flirt.

Codrin patted Grigore on the shoulder as he lifted Kat's hand to his lips. His eyes filled with mischief. "Grigore says you are an only child. Welcome to the family. It's a shame you have no sisters, but then they could not compare to your beauty."

"Tis true. The rest of us could use a true-mate as gorgeous and charming as you." Aerian turned from his conversation with his twin.

"I'm sure you'll find the right woman." Kat smiled and snuggled against Grigore's side.

"Maybe we're searching in the wrong area. Who knew he would find his mate in a secluded cabin instead of high-profile charity events?" Florin shook his head, giving them a smile that didn't reach the sadness in his eyes.

Maybe we should take turns staying in that cabin," Nandru laughed. He gazed out the window at the moon.

"We would all love to stay and get to know you better. We cannot leave our territories undefended for long. Perhaps Grigore will bring you for a visit sometime." Geofri kissed the back of Kat's hand, nudging Grigore with his elbow.

Kat covered a yawn with her hand as her eyes grew heavy. She wasn't used to so much excitement in one day. Grigore smiled, pulled her close, and kissed her forehead. "It's time we say good night. Thank you all for being here. The merger of our two companies should appease the press. Hopefully, they will leave us in peace for now."

"We should head to bed. Tomorrow, we depart, and it will be a long day. Congratulations, brother, may you both have a long, happy life together." Wadim raised his champagne glass in salute.

The group and their bodyguards followed Kat and Grigore to the master bedroom, watching him carry his new bride across the threshold. He placed her on the bed and closed the door in their faces. Hearing their laughter from the other side. Geofri smiled. "Be glad we no longer do the bedding ceremony."

Chapter 74

Grigore woke with his body wrapped around Kat's. He splayed his fingers across her stomach, watching her sleep. She looked so angelic. He couldn't believe how lucky he had been to find her. He hoped his brothers were as fortunate in finding their true-mates. Leaning forward, he brushed his lips against her soft forehead. He savored her salty-sweet taste, better than any honey he had tasted. His lips moved downward, devouring the taste of this beautiful woman. He inhaled the citrusy scent that drove him mad with desire. Her eyes fluttered open to gaze at him through a sleepy fog.

"Time to get up, sleepyhead." He kissed her once more. "We must see everyone off. Then we have the place to ourselves."

"Yeah, us and about twenty-five werewolves with superhuman hearing," Kat laughed.

Grigore knew she had a hard time hiding her embarrassment from the others after an amorous night. She would have to get used to it because he couldn't get enough of her. "A drawback of being Alpha is I have no privacy." He brushed her hair from her face.

Kat reached up and caressed his cheek. "I want you to be safe. It is all part of marrying you. I will get used to the fact that they heard everything we said and did. I love you, Grigore."

"I love you too, Kat. I will check into putting a soundproof alarm in our bedroom." Grigore hopped from the bed, dragged her out and pulled her tight. "Hurry, I hear the others in the dining room."

The pair dressed and joined the others for breakfast. Once things settled down, Grigore planned to take her on a world tour to visit his brothers and his parents. Marcus, Kane, and the others pursued any leads for the capture of Moog and his ragtag villainous followers. Until they had some leads, he planned to spend his time with his wife, hopefully without a bunch of lycanthropes surrounding him to hear their every move.

In the dining room they joked and conversed about various topics. Grigore's brother's bodyguards were good, and his brothers were always trying to steal a guard from each other's elite crew. His team were loyal and dependable, if not overzealous sometimes. His pack members were tight among themselves and with many Alts. The entire group was more of a large family than a ruler and his subjects.

When required, Grigore took charge, and they followed his orders. He consulted his father when needed. Since *Tata* was the *Regele Alfa*, Grigore conceded to his wishes for the ultimate ruling. His father reigned in a just and benevolent manner over his kingdom. His brothers seemed to do the same in their territories. One day, Grigore would take his father's place, but that would hopefully come many centuries in the future. He couldn't imagine not having *Tata's* wisdom to rely upon.

After the meal, the group went outside for the departure of the guests. There were several helicopters on the great lawn. The pilots waited for their passengers so they could take them to the airports with their private planes. His brothers and parents loaded into their respective choppers. Elena and her family joined their parents.

Hugs, kisses and well-wishes were given by all before the group went airborne. Grigore's arm tight around Kat held her against his side. They both waved until they could no longer see the group. Grigore gazed into Kat's eyes and wiggled his eyebrows. He gave her a wicked grin. "My love, I had a delightful time seeing my family. Let's resume our honeymoon now. There are still a lot of rooms we haven't tried out yet."

Kat blushed crimson. "What about the others hearing us?"

Sweeping Kat up into his arms, Grigore headed toward the house, calling out to the guards, "Go run outside or patrol away from the house for a while."

A blonde giant with a beard laughed and nudged a red-headed man in the ribs. Both men grinned as the pair disappeared inside.

Be sure not to miss

Nothing's As It Seems

Book 2 of Trish Copeland's
Lupescu Security Series.

Read on for a special preview…

Book 2 of the Lupescu Security Series.

Nothing's As It Seems

Chapter 1

Marcus closed his eyes and squeezed the bridge of his nose, hoping to ease the pain that thundered through his head like a herd of wild horses. He had stared at the computer screen for over twenty-four hours trying to find his nemesis, Moog. The rogue werewolf escaped through a hidden passage during the latest altercation with Moog's renegade pack. Marcus had the job of locating him for capture. Marcus returned from the Lupescu's country estate straight to his office, feeding information into various data banks to no avail.

He would relay his findings in the morning meeting. So far, he remained empty-handed. Another long night lay ahead at this rate. The Versipellis pack counted on him. He couldn't believe that only two nights ago they were involved in a retrieval of Grigore, the Alpha's, kidnapped bride. On the afternoon of the full moon, Moog's gang of degenerates kidnapped her from the estate's garden before her claiming ceremony. A time when a werewolf's instincts to claim a mate releases the primal beast within.

Rubbing his palms over his eyes, Marcus leaned his head back against the malleable leather of his chair. His body still ached from the battle. It seemed like an eternity had passed. A light knock on the door disturbed his brief reprieve. "Enter."

His secretary, Linda, stepped through the door, closing it behind her. "I'm sorry to bother you, sir. There is a woman to see you."

"I'm in the middle of something. Make the woman an appointment with one of the other attorneys in the office." He waved her away, returning his gaze to the computer screen.

"I tried, but she insists she will only speak to you." Linda stood by the door, waiting.

"I'll be glad to see her another time. Not now." Marcus's tone came out harsher than he meant it to. For years, Linda had been dependable and well-organized, always capable of taking care of unexpected problems that arose.

"I'll take care of the matter before I leave. Would you like me to order a meal for you? You should have something soon to keep up your strength." The efficient older woman hovered over him like a mother hen.

"Thanks. I'll grab something later." Marcus waved a hand in dismissal again, typing on the keyboard.

Linda went back to her office to relay the message. Returning to his research, Marcus lost track of time. He tapped away to delve into the deep web databases and almost missed the coded message concerning Moog and his assembled rogue pack. Hitting the back button, he looked again. Pay dirt. He grabbed his pen, making notes. The latest technological devices surrounded him but he trusted the good old-fashioned methods. Scrolling further down, he found Moog using a new code name for his collection of rag-tag Alts, Alpha Ascension. Marcus shook his head. Moog had always preferred to take a grandiose stance. He craved the position of Alpha. No matter how much trouble he created for the pack, his cruelty and violent nature prevented him from ever being Alpha.

Marcus had a new basis for his search. Typing the term into the search engine, he found more entries. Each new post led him to another, keeping him hot on the cybernetic trail. His ability to hide revealed Moog's craftiness. Tomorrow, Marcus would pass on the information at the meeting with the security team. He glanced at his ever-present watch, shocked at the late hour. He gave a grim smile at the fleeting thought of his pack giving him a hard time over the watch. Like all werewolves, his body was attuned to the moon, giving him perfect timing. Maybe it was his way of holding on to humanity he once had.

His first wristwatch had been a gift from Caroline Murat, Queen of Naples and the younger sister of Napoleon Bonapart. She loved jewelry and had fallen in love with the wrist bracelet watch created by Abraham-Louis Breguet. She presented it to him on a whim when he assisted her in the excavations of Pompeii. He kept that one in a showcase at his mansion but had grown fond of wearing a wristwatch. The one he wore now was a technological prototype created by Lupescu industries. It looked similar to an iPhone watch to avoid attracting attention. He took it off on missions when he had to transmute into his wolf form.

Pressing his fingertips to his temples, Marcus took a break. He shoved his phone into his breast pocket and tucked his notes and laptop into his briefcase. He had time to grab something to eat, take a shower and catch a brief nap before his early morning meeting. He secured the building with the latest digital security system created by Lupescu Industries, a company owned and operated by the Alpha's family, the Lupescus. Their technology remained far advanced to any human technology. Some of the more advanced devices they kept for the Alt community, and some they released on the market. Technology was only one of Lupescu's many businesses.

Heading to his BMW, he hit a few numbers and barked into the phone, "Artie, this is Marcus. I'm on my way and want my usual." He clicked his key fob. "Yes, the usual table too." Ending the call, he tossed his briefcase into the backseat, not paying attention to his surroundings. Weariness made his senses lax. He heard footsteps behind him and felt a tap on his shoulder. Whirling around to face his would-be attacker, golden flecks glowed in his hazel eyes, and he prepared to transform into his wolfen form for battle.

Face to face with his perceived foe, he tilted his head down to stare into the emerald green eyes of a redheaded beauty. The sight of her felt like a punch in the gut. She stood a couple of inches shorter than his five foot ten inches, with womanly curves in all the right places. Her eyes opened wide in surprise at his sudden change in demeanor. Sniffing the air, he sensed no threat, only her rose and spice scent tinged with the sharp odor of anxiety. Realizing he faced minimal danger, he relaxed and raised an eyebrow. "Why are you following me?"

"I need to talk to you. Your secretary made me leave. Do you always work this late?" The woman said in a nervous rush of words as she brushed back a tangle of thick red curls that fell loosely onto her heart-shaped face. She inhaled and tugged her green velvet cape tighter.

"I'm sure my assistant informed you that I am occupied with a case that takes up my time. You can make an appointment for later." Marcus said in a flat voice as he slid into the vehicle. He pulled the door to close it. She stuck her arm in the opening, stopping him.

Pulling on the door, her eyes wide, she pleaded, "Please, it's important. It can't wait. My granddad said you were the only one I could talk to. He said not to trust anyone else."

Heaving a put upon sigh, Marcus glanced at his watch. He could either give her some time now, or eat up the limited time he had. "Miss... Who am I addressing?"

"My name is Shannon Ambrose." The redhead tugged on a curl, gazing at him with tear-filled eyes.

Marcus exhaled audibly and pinched the spot between his eyes. "I must be back soon. I'm headed to get something to eat. You're welcome to join me, but that's all the time I can spare."

"If that's the only way I can talk to you." Shannon ran around the car and waited impatiently for him to unlock the door.

Shaking his head in disbelief, he hit the button, hearing the click of the mechanism unlocking. "I thought you might follow in your own vehicle."

Slipping into the passenger seat, she shut the door. "I didn't drive a car. I can get a cab later."

Raising an eyebrow, he glanced at her, started the ignition, hearing the motor purr. He headed to his favorite haunt in the city. "What's so important you cannot wait to set up a conventional appointment?"

"My granddad has disappeared. He told me repeatedly that you're the only one I should trust. That you'd go by the knight's code of honor to achieve the end goal. As if there really is such a thing as chivalry, much less a knight in America. You'll have to do though." The woman looked at the man in the driver's seat.

Marcus mentally processed the information and almost missed his turn into the parking lot. He slammed on his brakes, swerved sharply into the lot and slid to a stop in a spot under a light. Climbing out, he went to open the door for the fiery-red haired beauty. No, he must not think of her in that way. He couldn't afford distractions.

ABOUT THE AUTHOR

Trish Copeland is an avid reader with eclectic tastes. She has a master's degree in psychology. Life and her travels around the world has given her a variety of situational experiences in dealing with many types of characters. Creativity, reading, and animals are her passions. Her clowder of cats walk across the keyboard demanding attention when they think she spends too much time on the computer. She has created stories in her head since she was little. Currently she is writing the ongoing saga of her paranormal fantasy romance/romantasy series.

www.ingramcontent.com/pod-product-compliance
Lightning Source LLC
LaVergne TN
LVHW091123080826
845145LV00008B/2028